TRUTH

The second installment in The Keeper's Trilogy

*Dedicated to all the readers who
have joined us for the ride...*

WRITTEN BY
OLIVIA ALI

INTERLUDE

Letting out a deep breath, I can feel wooden flooring meet my body as I land softly and silently. All around me is quiet, except for the sound of someone whistling and a radiant melody ringing throughout the room. I try to stand, but it is difficult; I cannot even move my fingers as they lie still clasping the medallion. In my head, I can still see that light, still see that seer telling me what I must do. I try to reach him, the man to whom the medallion belonged to. But he would come soon to find entangled in me, his missing memory. The seer had called it a violent oversight; a formless order that in time would begin to rise. Soon, he would remember.

Suddenly there was a bang and the whistling stopped. I lay, waiting for the whistling man to come this way, unable to blink in my motionless form. A scream pierces the space outside the door and I suddenly realise that I know where I am. Five beds are up against the wall behind me and two long bookcases lead to secret doorways either side of the room. Ahead of me was the door, hurrying footsteps vastly approaching it; louder and louder, faster and faster. He would not notice me at first, this would all seem too real to him, too similar; like deja-vu.

I watched as the silver handle on the door began to shake, he was fumbling for the key. This place was sealed off after all; it was no surprise considering what they found here. Finally, the handle shifted and the man ran inside, slamming the door behind him and leaning his head upon the metal rim. He was a man I knew; the man was my foe – a ragged and pale version, veins pulsing all around. He was different from how I remembered him; time had not aged him well. He started to mumble to himself. Slowly, he turned around, slumping back against the door and sinking to the floor. He lay his head in his hands and began to shake violently.

"They're back!" he stammered in whispered sighs. "I can't believe their back. Not again! Not again!"

I heard his voice break and rasp as it left his mouth. He had not noticed me yet, nor the melody that bought peace to me in these unforeseen circumstances. Somehow, I knew the melody, but where from? My enemy stopped shaking now and looked at me straight in my eyes; but it was like he was staring right through me. He rose to his feet, suddenly realising where he was and hurried over to the bookcase on my right. Panicking, he began pulling the books out to see if they opened the other bookcase. If he failed, he replaced the book. Another scream sounded behind the door and I knew it was the Faders. Part of me wanted to tell him that it was the other bookcase – I knew the pain he would face now and if they got to him. I wouldn't wish that pain on anyone, not even him. The words would not form in my mouth. He began to get faster, losing his grip on one of the books and dropping it to the floor. As he turned to pick it up the door blasted open and he dropped to the floor as my eyes blinked once, twice, thrice.

The light faded now, leaving the room in perpetual twilight - a world between that of light and that of shadow. The Keeper was nowhere to be seen and once again, I was all alone. I closed my eyes and began to think of home. How soon would I get there? I had hated this world so much but after three years in it, finally I saw it as beautiful. I opened my eyes again, still unable to move in this void between our worlds. I try to move my fingers, try to take a deeper breath and it works. But even the slightest movement tires me. I don't give in though. This time I try my feet, twisting them in demented circles, trying to re-circulate the blood. Again, I move my fingers, tapping the dusty floor on which I lay. I move my head, thinking that I can almost hear the bones click, like a door with rusty hinges. As each movement becomes easier, the sound of the melody reaches back to me, pulling me towards it, pulling me back to the world of the living. I think of what I will do when I'm back, will you remember me, or will you have moved on. Whatever you'd done, I would know soon. As I clenched my hands into a fist, I felt the medallion pierce my skin, warm hot blood seeping onto the dusty floor. I remembered the cathedral and the light on the hill. Had you really forgotten everything? I blinked; deliberately this time; once, twice, thrice...thinking desperately of you brother and our home.

CHAPTER 1 – ESCAPE!

The brothers entered the Keeper Compound full of laughter having celebrated the announcement of Romeo's engagement. Myrina certainly was a fitting bride and Tristan wondered if his father would approve of this match in the same way he did he and Dagnen's. An eerie silence passed over them as they stepped into the foyer of the compound to be welcomed by a hoard of Keepers with stern faces. Jacques noted their stern faces and shushed his brothers into seriousness. Something was up.

"Alright brothers and sisters," He greeted, noting the solemn look on Isolde's face as her eyes widened in a warning. Charles stepped out from the crowd, a smug look on his face.

"You stand before the Keeper Council accused of the worst sin a Keeper can commit - betrayal." A mutter of whispers echoed the room.

What's going on?"

"The Interpreter is dead! First Keeper Felix was found..." Isolde explained, her voice shaken and broken, like even she couldn't believe what she was saying.

"Former First Keeper you mean!" ordered Charles, rolling his shoulders back and standing tall. "The charge of First Keeper has been pledged to me for the time being." Charles as First Keeper was definitely not a good thing. And the Interpreter dead; Tristan didn't even know she could die. Although it had never been confirmed, she was supposedly at Talus' side when the faction was formed generations ago. Either way, killing her would've been no easy feat.

"The Interpreter...dead?" Jacques questioned, noting the look on the new First Keeper's face. He didn't like it, not one bit.

"Where have you been this evening boys? Did you forget the occasion perhaps?"

"Occasion?"

"This eve represents the Festival of Time." Isolde went on to explain. "The Interpreter was going to make a reading from the Book of Time. But when she never showed in the council-room a Scribe was sent to her Chambers."

"Out of respect for her memory, I suggest you do not recount the sight he saw. It pains me still!" Charles was clearly faking his remorse; it was all too dramatic.

"Me and my brothers were aware of no Reading and are sorry to have missed it." Jacques tried to remain calm, but even for the voice of reason amongst the brothers, he was struggling. He noted Trevor weave his way through the crowd, another warning look within his eyes. He mouthed something to them, but Jac couldn't make it out. Even still he continued to repeat whatever he was warning; 'Get out!'

"One might think your absence on a night like tonight...suspicious..." Charles' nostrils flared, he seemed to be enjoying this torment. Now Jac was worried and he became aware of his brothers backing towards the entrance they had come from. A grip tightened on his arm and he flashed a look towards Acolytes barring the entrance. There was no way out.

"Especially after your involvement in the destruction of the Clocktower." Charles continued.

"Aye, an unfortunate accident. But we did nothing wrong, we aren't responsible for what you accuse us of."

"I wasn't aware I had yet to accuse you of anything."

"Oh pig's shit!" Ramien blurted, he always was the irrational one and it was clear he was now scared and had grown impatient with Jacques' calmness.

Less than a week ago, there was a prophecy reading telling of a Brethren Betrayer among the Keeperhood. The prophecy told of time coming to a halt and the betrayer being pointed to. The brothers had taken it literally and headed to consult the Hammerites about the recently broken clock in the clocktower. The clock had stopped ticking a few days before and try as they may they couldn't restart it. Charles had forbidden them to intervene, it was a matter for the Elders and the Council to deal with. Acolytes and the like were merely present to further their studies. It was not their place to interpret the prophecies.

Upon their visit, the Hammerites had agreed to let the brothers see the clockface to try and deduce what it meant. But there was an accident, an explosion in the lower clockworks. The brothers were lucky to make it out with their lives at the cost of twenty Hammers within the tower.

"I didn't see the rest of you trying to figure out the prophecy."

"You were told as Acolytes to leave the prophecies to the Elders to deal with as is our place." Charles went on with his lecture. "Not only are you all amateurs but you have no idea the repercussions of what you have did. And now, like clockwork I suppose, our Interpreter is dead too."

"You can't..."

"You're lack of respect for orders is what got her killed. Dark magic did this to her and if you insolent fools hadn't meddled in the first place, she would still be alive."

"So that's it?" Tristan piped up after remaining silent for so long. "You're just going to blame us because you have no better explanation? Sounds about right for you."

"What is that supposed to mean?"

"I think you know exactly what I mean. After all, it is you who is the real Brethren Betrayer."

"Tristan!" He heard Romeo cajole.

Tristan was tired of this cat and mouse game - he had to show Charles that he needed to fear the Brotherhood because they were coming for him. If he didn't know they were onto him before, he would know it now. The accusation worked though and Charles' face went pale, the room erupting in whispers.

"How dare you accuse your First Keeper of such atrocities!" Hagen snapped, stepping out of the shadows.

"Charles may be the First Keeper but he will never be my First Keeper. That honour lies with Felix."

"And he too is a traitor!" Charles uttered; the fear still apparent in his quivering tone. "But don't worry you'll soon be joining him in eternal darkness. Especially as you now stand charged of blasphemy as well."

"Blasphemy?" Tristan sniggered as he said it. The accusation itself was hysterical coming from him of all people. "You say that yet the tower points to you for all to see, hands and all."

Silence met his accusation and Tristan spied Trevor again in the shadows who nodded to him with a smile on his face. Although they had spread enough doubt amongst the council so that their innocence was believed, they weren't going to get out of this now. Not when Charles' influence was so high his adversaries feared what might happen if they were to go against him so openly. The whispers began again and Tristan looked to each if his brothers in turn and nodding to them all. They had to get out, now.

"Enough!" Charles yelled, silencing the room once more. "I will have order. Acolytes Jacques, Romeo, Zhaine, Ramien and Tristan stand accused of betrayal, murder and blasphemy of a First Keeper. Your punishment, should the council agree...eternal darkness. I believe the dungeons a fitting place until a trial is held."

The tower went dark and Tristan stared at the faces around them, noting the sudden fear in Isolde's eyes. Porting out was the only way, but something about her look...he gulped. Charles was clearly onto their escape plan. He held up a medallion which blood seemed to drip from as cloaked shadows appeared all around. Many of the Keepers hid their faces out of fear as Enforcers stepped out of the shadows. They bore masks over their faces which red lights gleamed from the eye holes of the wrought iron that seemed to strangle life out of its vessel, like vines climbing a stone wall, roses in the place of eyes. They outstretched their hands, ready to take the brothers to their doom. But they weren't about to surrender, not now not ever - especially when they were innocent.

The Enforcer were a breed of Faders – bound by glyphs just like them but to follow. Their actions could be bent and commanded. They were traitors, bound to commit those of their like to a life of darkness guarded by the Faders.

Springing into life, all five brothers faded from sight, alarming the Enforcers and causing a gasp to escape from all those now watching. Not a moment later though they reappeared behind the line of Enforcers, a confused look shared by each of them as pain began to cripple them. Not stopping to wonder why, they disappeared again, appearing close to the entrance of the compound. What was going on? Pain gripped them but they weren't about to give up. One final time, they closed their eyes and vanished, this time completely from sight, almost cementing their guilt to those wavering in the Keeper Council.

CHAPTER 2 – INTO THE LIGHT

Many people wander which is faster - light or darkness. Most people will tell you light is stronger and therefore more powerful. I will tell you though that darkness is quicker and darkness is stronger. The reason I say this is because by the time the light reaches the darkness, it is already there and they spend an eternity chasing the other around the world endlessly; the other never quite catching up with the one in front. For people, it is much the same. Darkness will overtake a lot quicker than the light. It will corrupt the soul and blacken the heart like a hole opening up in the earth, causing devastation and destruction to all those around it. For someone to accept their darkness and then want to make a change takes courage, takes light. And so the light takes over, but the road is longer and harder. For someone to change...now that is harder. But we must all remember that in all darkness there is light if only we search hard enough to find it and shine it bright.

The blue light that blinded them all began to fade and was replaced by green. So many trees eluded the way forward, but it wasn't forward Tristan was worried about. Taking in his surroundings, he pulled his horse to a halt in front of his comrades as the portal became non-existent, leaving the air to settle around them. Holding Dante steady, Zhaine helped Myrina from her horse as Nielson approached his sons with Merlin in toe.

"My boys?" Nielson choked as he rounded on them.

Ramien pulling his father into a heartfelt hug followed by one for Zhaine as well. He shook Merlin by the hand and Basso too before nodding his head to Myrina. Then he approached Tristan whom he too grasped in a brotherly clinch. So much love filled this reunion now, it was a wonder it didn't shine a beacon for all to see.

"We should make camp somewhere!" Merlin instructed as he and Basso retrieved Dante from the horse. "It would be unwise to travel through the forest under the guise of nightfall.

"I mean I know we're surrounded by trees and everything but are we even anywhere near Landen?" Tristan asked, looking up at the stars above that twinkled through the tall trees.

"I dunno," Ramien replied shrugging his shoulders. "Truth be told I've never been to Az Landen forest."

"So you just imagined trees and hoped for the best?" Somethings never changed and even though he didn't remember everything about his brothers yet, this certainly sounded like something Ramien would risk.

"Pretty much. I've been told a lot about the palace so I just tried to picture it. I know it was a risk but what else was I supposed to do?"

"Surely anywhere is better than being chased by Faders Tristan." Zhaine asked, clutching at his ribs. He was obviously still a little roughed up from his ordeal. Quick healers as they were being Keepers, these things still took time.

"Or we could actually be exactly where Ramien wanted." Basso chirped as they all looked round to see him pointing towards the high spires that glistened above the trees on the horizon.

Supposedly, the spires of Landen palace were made of crystals that sparkled at the touch of light and were so tall they could be seen from the furthest reaches of the forest high above the trees. Some joked that they were even higher than the mountains that surrounded Az Lagní and its provinces but there was no truth to this statement.

"Now aren't you all glad I took that risk?" Ramien winked, a sly smirk upon his face as he watched their angry expressions change to that of relief.

"Why are we here anyway?" Basso asked despondently. "I thought the next stop would be Hasaghar?"

No one answered him immediately, he just looked from one to the other waiting for an answer to meet his ears. Tristan still didn't know how much he knew about his past and he wasn't about to tempt it; not whilst the amount he himself knew was still so little.

"Hasaghar is crawling with the followers of Dharsi," Zhaine answered eventually. "None of us would survive one minute. Here in Az Landen a rebellion is forming against the rising. It's our only chance."

"Didn't realise things were that bad there. Maybe it's best we stop here, take scope, think of a plan."

"My family still reign here in Landen Bass! We will be safe here!" Tristan explained. "They will be able to help Daxon, whatever Hagen did to him." He choked as he almost said Dante, wondering how long it would be before his cover broke.

"Well Merlin is right, we can't very well travel through the night, not in this forest." Nielson said. "I mean I know it well but that's the problem, the moment you think you know your way is the moment you realise you are lost."

The others were silent. Merlin was right, and even so they would never find a clear road in the darkness. Tristan looked up at the sky, the moon just passing below the trees on the horizon. They maybe had a few hours at most before daybreak and then they could find their way.

"We'll wait then," Tristan ordered. "As soon as the sun rises, we set off again so those of you that wish, get some rest. I'll take the first watch."

The others all nodded and started fetching bedrolls from the horses to lay them on the floor. Even if they weren't going to sleep, they might as well have been a little comfier. Tristan helped Nielson lay Dante on a bed roll Merlin had spread, trying to make him as comfortable as possible. He looked awful; his face gaunt and his eyes black and blue. His hair had blood matted through it yet there were no obvious cuts and his clothes were ripped and torn with nasty wounds just visible beneath them. His sleep wasn't easy, his eyes twitched and his head shook as though he were stuck in some nightmare that he could not escape. Tristan sat by his vigil, Nielson perching himself not too far away.

"Why isn't he healing?" Tristan asked dumbfound, his eyes not leaving his brother in arms. Dante had been good to him since he first came to Az Lagní.

"Whatever Hagen did to him he used powerful dark magic." Merlin replied. "Even for a Keeper that's a lot to take on...especially given his existing...condition." He cast eyes over Nielson, choosing his words wisely. "We just have to remain hopeful!"

Myrina began unpacking a pack which was filled with bandages and various salves and tended to some of his more serious looking wounds, removing his ragged clothing as she did so. Tristan watched her as she tended to him, seeing Nielson move over to his sons and they began catching up. *What if he didn't make it through?* He had to stop thinking like that though, if he could survive the Faded Lands for as long as he did then he could come back from this.

The remaining hours of the evening passed quickly and peacefully under Tristan's watchful eye. He had refused to take rest when his brothers offered. He could see how restless Dante was and it troubled him. He couldn't imagine what was going on behind those closed worn eyes. The sunlight began to turn the sky from deep purple to lightened blue with stretches of orange.

"How is he?" Zhaine asked, coming over to sit by Tristan. His ribs had been bandaged by Myrina who had obviously been restless herself during the waking hours. Perhaps it had something to do with what Tristan had told her, she hadn't exactly spoken to him much since her rescue.

"I'm not sure," Tristan answered. "He doesn't seem any better, but at the same time he doesn't seem any worse." He looked away in time to see Ramien and Basso emerging from the trees ahead.

"Hey, I think we found the road that leads to the palace!" Ramien called and the others began packing up their make shift camp in the waking morning.

"Come on, I'll help you get him on a horse." Zhaine offered as he and Tristan rose to their feet.

"Told you I knew where I was taking us!" Ramien joked, trying to lighten everyone's solemn mood, and failing miserably.

The rest just stared, not sharing his sentiment before continuing to get themselves sorted. As per usual, Ramien's jibes fell on a cold crowd who did not appreciate his overly large ego and compulsive need to make a joke of every situation.

Before long they were on the road making their way towards the spires that glinted in the morning sunlight on the horizon. They truly did look as though they were made of crystals. Tristan hadn't been here since he was a kid and truth be told he didn't remember much. He wasn't even sure his uncles would welcome him given the way they had treated his father the last time they had seen him at his mother's funeral. Yes, he was a drunk, but that didn't give them the right to give up on him as they had. It was like they Jensen blamed Theorryn for her death – he would he was her brother by blood. But to turn on his brother by name? Theoden was stuck in the middle of it all just as someone always is.

As they rode, Tristan kept a close eye on Dante, the colour fading from his face even more. He grew worried whether or not they would make it in time for him, let alone how long they would have to travel before even reaching their destination. That question was soon answered by a sign which split the path up ahead in two. To the left it indicated a water well about a league away and the palace to the right, two leagues away. That was at least six miles on foot - could Dante even last that long? Could they even cover all the ground in just one day at their current pace? It seemed impossible right now, and this wasn't just a feeling felt by Tristan, they all shared it.

"We need a plan," Tristan blurted, suddenly fearful. Ramien took in the sign ahead of them, looking up at Dante in deep thought as his head lolled back against Nielson who sat behind him. Tristan couldn't help but think of the irony, perhaps Nielson secretly suspected something anyway.

"No way will he survive if I port us!" Ramien deducted. "It's probably done enough damage that I took us from Dilu."

"Ram is right," Merlin agreed, taking one of Dante's scarred hands within his. "I don't even know what more I can do for him, I know my herbs and healing, but this is out of my depth."

"What if we ride ahead?" Basso suggested, looking to Tristan. "We could race to the Palace, fetch a wagon perhaps along with the healer. It has to be quicker than travelling at our current pace."

"I second that idea!" Tristan agreed, already steadying himself in his saddle. Zhaine set about releasing some of the saddle bags from Tristan and Basso's horses to give them more speed.

"Between the two of us, if we ride fast, we should be able to cover the ground in less than an hour. They know Tristan, they will give us what we need."

"We shall continue at our pace and see how much ground we can cover." Zhaine took the hands of both of them. "Ride true brothers!"

Looking to Tristan, Basso nodded and they ushered their horses forward at full pace, praying they would reach the palace quickly enough to save Dante.

CHAPTER 3 – THE PALACE OF AZ LANDEN

Tristan had lost count of how long they had been riding for as the palace walls came into sight. Basso pulled on his reigns slowing his horse and Tristan followed suit, looking up at the archers in the sentries above. It was odd to find the gates sealed as they were; the Palace of Landen followed suit of most capitals, their gates open in the day as sanctuary to all who entered. Tristan scanned the faces of the guards above, not that much was decipherable from their thimble shaped helmets and emerald green robes beneath the chain mail. His eyes fell on the man in the centre, the only one not bearing a helmet of armour. Deep chestnut hair framed his face resting neatly on his broad shoulders and a neat beard framed his chiselled jawline.

"Tristan?" The man beckoned. Tristan did not recognise him, but from the emblem emblazoned on his chest plate he was the captain of the guard and that title he knew belonged to his uncle Theoden. It had been years, but Theoden clearly recognised him. The captain disappeared from sight and a heavy chain clanged loudly as the gates shook open revealing his uncle in the gap between them. Tristan dismounted his horse to meet his uncle, grasping his hand in a tight handshake, a familiar smile shared by them both.

"What are you doing here?" Theoden asked.

"I'll explain later but for now I need your help." Tristan explained and he nodded as a few of his men came into view behind him. "I have a travel party about two leagues away. One of them is badly hurt. Please will you help?"

"Of course my boy. Jorgen, fetch a carriage quickly now. Harvey, fetch the horses and Jenkins inform the healer that we will require her assistance on our return. You might as well tell the King our nephew is here too." He smiled at the word nephew as he said it and Tristan was humbled.

"It might be better the healer attend." Basso instructed, a wary look encroaching the captain.

"Uncle, this is John Basso." Tristan introduced.

"Well met I am sure." His uncle cast a look up the length of Basso, his eyes untrusting. He didn't even take his hand, the reaction surprised Tristan but he thought nothing of it. "Tell me, how badly hurt is your friend. What happened?"

"We came from Dilu, we were attacked." Tristan explained briefly. "That is all you need to know…"

"Our friend has been injured by dark Keeper magic; the Healer should attend with us." Basso pushed.

"Dark Keeper magic you say? Tristan what have you done?" His look was sceptical, Tristan knew not what his uncle knew about his past, but there wasn't time for this.

"I can't explain right now uncle, but he needs help urgently. Please?"

"Jenkins, cancel that order, instead fetch Isolde. I feel she may be of more use." The name Isolde rang a bell with Tristan but he couldn't think where from.

"Isolde is here?" Basso questioned cheerfully almost.

"Let us get your friend sorted before we rejoice in reunions."

Basso nodded and the men went quickly about their duties and once everything was ready, Tristan lead the speeding party back down the road to try and find his friends. It wasn't long before they caught up; Zhaine and Ramien were either side of the horse supporting Dante and Nielson, holding him steady as they pushed forward. They stopped when they saw Tristan and his uncle. The parties stopped and wasted no time with formalities as they noted the state of Dante. Isolde stepped out from the carriage, muttering a short greeting to Nielson and Merlin, perhaps that was why she was familiar; she was an Elder? Zhaine and Ramien retrieved him from the horse, laying him on the stretcher the guards lay on the floor. Isolde followed them into the carriage to attend to his wounds, Merlin accompanying her for assistance. Nielson steadied himself on his horse alone now and the party followed back to the Palace where the gates lay open for them ready.

Guards met them there and lead the carriage through the city towards the palace steps. The city surrounding the palace was unusually quiet, but Tristan chose not to worry about that right now. Perhaps it had been done deliberately so as not to draw attention to the new guests. The guards stepped towards the carriage and retrieved the stretcher, ushering it into a building to the left of the steps towards the Palace. A healer stood ready to receive them in the doorway and Isolde rounded on the brothers as they dismounted from the horses before trying to follow the party into the infirmary. But Theoden held up a hand to stop them.

"Don't worry boys, he's in good hands here. Now I don't know what has bought you all here at such a time, but I suppose an explanation can wait till tomorrow. Jorgen, take their bags up to the royal apartments and set them up some rooms there. Tristan, there is someone here you will want to see so why don't you all follow Jorgen to your rooms and freshen up, then meet me in the entrance hall."

"If it is alright with you Lord," Merlin stepped forward. "I should like to attend with Isolde. I feel I can be of some use."

"Of course, go ahead. The rest of you will follow Jorgen, now." Nielson looked as though he would retort too but his sons moved to stop him. Tristan could only imagine how hard it must be for them not to reveal themselves as relatives.

Theoden caught eyes with Tristan, and he nodded to his nephew. Jorgen led them up the stairs to the palace and through a darkened entrance hall which stood grand with elaborate purple tapestries bearing the mirkwood tree that was the royal crest. They followed him up the stairs along the right side to a corridor lined with oak doors. At the end of the corridor he turned to them, clearing his throat.

"There's five spare rooms here so divide them as you see fit." Jorgen explained, motioning with his hands to each of the doors. "The two at the top of the corridor house two beds each, the others just the one. If you follow the corridor around you come to Theoden's chambers just in case you need anything. There is also a washroom within each of the rooms here. A guard is always rounding here and they will get you whatever you need."

"Ramien and Zhaine do you mind sharing?" Nielson instructed and they both shrugged their shoulders as though they didn't mind. They were probably used to it. "I will share with Merlin then that leaves the single rooms for you three."

"Is there anything I can get you before I make my leave?"

"I don't mean to...um..." Myrina uttered, wrapping her cloak around herself. "I have no spare clothes."

"That is quite already my lady, forgive for assuming but I imagine the princess and the Queen will have clothes they can spare. I will enquire with their ladies in waiting immediately and have them placed in your room for you."

"Thank you." She nodded to the guard before disappearing through the nearest door and shutting it behind her. It had been quite the ordeal for her. Zhaine and Ramien made their way to the chamber at the end followed by Nielson who took the room next to theirs.

Jorgen remained where he stood as Basso and Tristan made their leave to freshen themselves up and take in the actions of the last two days.

CHAPTER 4 – THE BEGINNING OF A WAR

The sun glistened on the horizon as Tristan watched it from the edge of the balcony where he had found himself. It seemed he had picked the room with a view of the Royal Gardens and parts of the city beyond the wall. He pulled himself away from the wall he leant against, stretching his arms out and clicking his stiff upper back. Easing himself off the banister he stepped back into the grand sized room, wondering if all the royal apartments were this splendid.

A four-poster bed was up against the wall and looked incredibly appealing to Tristan's aches. A chest lay at the foot of it with his pack placed on top. Either side was a bedside table with a candlestick placed in the centre. Next to the door was a dark wood dresser with gold brandishing that gleamed in the sunlight that poured in through the open balcony doors. Atop it was a porcelain bowl with some fresh water in it and a towel folded neatly next to it. The other side of the door was a full-length mirror that matched the dark wood of the rest of the furnishings. The decoration of the room was fairly plain but elaborate; from the purple rug in the centre of the room to the crystal chandeliers above his head. A tapestry showing a queen knighting a young man was raised above the chest of drawers and purple curtains rested on each post of the bed matching that of those around the balcony doors. Another room was joined to this by an archway, adorned in the same curtain, which lead to a wash room. Heavy footsteps sounded outside, and a knock sounded. Tristan opened the door to Jorgen.

"Lord, I presume you fell asleep." He sniggered. *Lord? Asleep?* He looked back into the room and noticed the sun sinking into the horizon. He really had dosed off on the balcony, which would explain his stiffness.

"Lord?" Tristan questioned; his voice croaky. He remembered taking a wash and changing his clothes before taking to the balcony to take in his surroundings. Jorgen sniggered again.

"Come, your companions have gathered in the dining hall for some food."

"I was supposed to meet my uncle though..."

"'tis quite alright Lord. You will see at dinner what my commander was talking about anyway. Come!"

"Is there any news on our companion; Daxon?"

"They have managed to make him comfortable and he is improving albeit slow. But then his injuries are rather extensive. He is the best possible hands I assure you. Now come, you must be starved."

He nodded to Jorgen who inclined his head and proceeded down the stairs they had ascended hours earlier. The dining hall lay through a door directly in front of them and was yet another grand room. It was huge, with long tables that stretched the length of the sides. A platform was at the top of the room with what looked to be the Kings table which everyone seemed to be gathered around. Behind it was the royal sigil upon a large tapestry with portraits of the King and Queen either side. Two other tapestries were there two, one Tristan recognised as bearing the old king – his grandfather. The other he assumed were portraits of his cousins – two girls and a young man.

Smells of roast meats tickled his nose as he spied Ramien and Zhaine sat at the table with Basso. Myrina was sat next to a woman Tristan assumed was his aunt Lucia, a young girl probably no older than five or six at on her lap and on her other side a young lady. Their faces bore resemblances with the portrait above, marking them as the princesses Zelda and Kyra. Zhaine's eyes didn't seem to leave Tristan's elder cousin and she wasn't shy in sharing his gaze. *Zelda and Zhaine did have a nice ring to it.*

Adjacent to the Queen were his uncles, Jenson and Theoden who sat in conversation with Nielson. The only person he hadn't spied yet was Merlin, but perhaps he was still with Dante. There was a man with his back to Tristan too but he merely assumed him a member of his uncle's court perhaps.

"Good evening brother," Ramien perked up winking in Tristan's direction.

"It's still afternoon you buffoon," Zhaine slandered, elbowing him in the side as though he were embarrassing him in front of the Royal family.

"I was only messing Zhaine. Lighten up!" Fresh bandages adorned Zhaine's wounds and he seemed brighter too.

"Yeah Zhaine, lighten up," Tristan sniggered, taking a seat beside them.

"Ah Tristan my boy," Theoden raised a cup in Tristan's direction. "How did you sleep?"

"I don't know if I'd call it sleep to be honest." Tristan replied honestly.

"That's understandable. Here, have some of this - it will perk you up in no time."

He poured Tristan a cup of some brown liquid, topping it with some milk and adding a spoonful of sugar before handing it to Tristan. Nodding in thanks, he took a sip, an aromatic bitterness hitting his taste buds. Despite the acidity of the texture he rather liked it and it was as though his eyes opened wider the moment he swallowed it down his throat. He smiled in appreciation as he greeted the sensation. It had been a while since he had tasted coffee this good.

"Shipped in from Aberson." Theoden praised. "Wicked minds they have to create something to give you more energy. The Salysmans tried with their teas but alas...they were bested." He guzzled down the last of his cup as Tristan began helping himself to food from the platters. A large roasted chicken was in the centre of the table with an assortment of vegetables and gravy. He marvelled at the sight of it as he dug in, feeling as though he hadn't eaten in weeks. He finished his platter in no time at all, burping as he sat back and swallowed some water, causing an eruption of laughter from Ramien and Zhaine. *Childish as ever!* He spied Nielson's eyes glow – he was glad to have his sons back and as good as he remembered them to be.

"Well now that you are fed and watered, perhaps we can all get some answers," Jenson exclaimed, speaking for the first time since Tristan had seen him and clapping his hands together.

As though it were an order, his wife Lucia rose from her seat accompanied by the man to Tristan's left and his nieces and left the room. The door banged shut behind them and Tristan looked to his uncles. Jensen nodded to Tristan and he followed his gaze to the doors to the dining hall.

"Father!" Tristan exclaimed as he rose from his seat and went to greet Theorryn who now stood in the door way where the Queen had left from. It was an awkward welcoming, despite the stiff hug they gave each other. "What are you doing here?"

"That is not important now my son," his father answered. Tristan noted the lack of the smell of alcohol which usually lingered on his father's clothes. It made him proud. Following Theorryn back to the table, they sat once more.

"So," Jensen began. "What brings you to my palace? As far as we were aware," he motioned in Theorryn's direction, "You were in Dilu."

"Aye, we were." Tristan confirmed. "But that's where it gets complicated. You see I had some old...foes there. They made things difficult for us."

Tristan paused. Everything that he had done the past few days seemed to finally be catching up with him. His brutal murder of Boris, not to mention the mutilation he caused to his face in order to send a message to Hagen. And then the mysterious death of Hagen himself at the hands of an invisible man. Felix was dead and Dante wasn't far off. How much could he even tell his uncle of all of this? Not to mention the looks they would give him if only they had known the truth of who Dante really was.

"We heard a rebellion of Keepers was rising here," Zhaine interjected, spying the look in Tristan's eyes. "Those foes made it very difficult for is to stay in Dilu any longer so we thought it best we leave."

"So the murder of the baron and a pawn shop owner had nothing to do with any of you? I also take it the Faders didn't make your journey any easier?" Jenson asked, inclining his head, a sceptical look on his face. The others stared at him in shock. "Let me enlighten you all into how I know all this." He lifted his right palm so every one of them sat at the table could see. It bore the Keeper Port Key, just like most of their own palms. "I'm a Keeper Rune Mage...powerful person really."

"Jenson!" Theorryn warned deeply causing the King to rise his hand and halt his breath. Tristan knew his uncles were Keepers just as his father was.

"Yes, it's true...a Keeper rebellion is rising. Hasaghar is crawling with followers of Dharsi...oh that's right I know about them as well. Not too long ago the King Oruc asked for my help in dealing with them so I sent my best soldiers with what was left of the Light Mages to offer support and eradicate them all. It turns out they were more powerful than we realised, not to mention in bigger numbers than we ever imagined. They didn't stand a chance! It's going to take a lot more than brute force and magic to get rid of this threat so you *boys* best tell me everything."

"Back off Jenson!" Theorryn rose to his feet, his chair sliding out from under him. Theoden took a step forward and placed a hand on Jenson's shoulder, whispering something in his ear.

"We haven't come here to hide away my lord," Nielson began to explain, trying to urge the meeting in a different direction. "We came here to gather our resources. The boys as you called them are very much aware of what they must do," they weren't, Tristan wasn't even sure who was being referred to. "But in case you didn't notice the...things they need are not complete. And you above anyone else should know what is at stake." He said that last word with venom, forcing it upon Jenson with malice. Theoden began whispering in his ear once more, and it was clear to see that whatever was said he didn't like by the way his face dropped and the way he shook his head.

"Very well then!" Jensen sighed at last. "I shall arrange for you all to meet with my Council and we shall see what we can come up with. We are dealing with something much bigger than all of us here and there is a lot at stake. I hope you boys realise just what you've started!"

Jenson rose to his feet and left the room quickly, closely followed by Theorryn who was no doubt now on the warpath.

"Forgive my Kings treatment of you," Theoden begged, placing his hands calmly on the table and addressing all those left seated. "This fight has cost him his son."

"Markus?" Tristan answered, a certain sadness gripping him. Markus was the cousin Tristan remembered most being closest to his own age. Tristan had assumed Markus to be the man that followed his aunt and cousin from the room, but he was mistaken.

"Forgive us both Tristan." He sighed heavily and motioned to his guards to leave the young Keepers and their mentors in the dining hall.

Slamming his fists on the table, Ramien rose to his feet causing a warning to sound from Nielson.

"Don't!" He stormed, raising a hand to his father in insubordination. "I am sick of everyone thinking we knew what we were doing. I am sick of everyone thinking we had a choice in all this. I didn't choose to become who I am...it was forced upon us...we were forced to accept it. And I am so tired of it! I never wanted any of this. We were never given any guidance nor any warning of what had been thrown at us. If I could walk away, I would...and I would never look back."

Tristan looked up at his brother – he was right. They bore a heavy burden and everyone acted like they held it as a banner of pride and not hide it away like the dirty secret it was. The Keeperhood had abandoned the Brotherhood long ago so what right did they have now to be accusing them of starting all this.

Tristan rose from his feet to leave the room, but his father appeared in the doorway once more. He glowered at his son - by the looks of it he had heard everything that had just erupted from the room.

"We both have things we need to explain my son," He consoled, keeping eye contact with him. "So let us please..."

Tristan pulled away from Theorryn's reach and looked into his father's eyes. Could he really tell his father everything and avoid being judged?

"Not now!" Tristan cursed his father, anger suddenly rising in him. Pulling away he took leave from the place and entered the city below, his father calling out in protest behind him.

CHAPTER 5 – PAST ACTIONS

After being denied access to see Dante, Tristan had found himself at a tavern known as the Lucky Penny. There were a few scattered people inside and the proprietor stepped forward as he stood at the bar.

"What'll it be?" he asked plainly. There wasn't anything notable about his appearance, although it had struck Tristan just how regal everyone seemed. Even against those they had seen in Ragnur, Landen was the embodiment of class it seemed.

"Wheat beer please sir." He was still rather riled from what Ramien had said. There was much he didn't understand at present, but it resonated with him and his head weighed heavy on his aching shoulders. The proprietor placed a beer in front of Tristan – he had no coins upon him he suddenly realised. He was about to utter an apology when he was interrupted by a man who rose from a table in the far corner.

"It's on me!" Basso exclaimed and Tristan couldn't remember the last time he had been this happy to see his old teacher. He placed a few coins on the bar and ushered Tristan over. "Pull up a pew boy." He motioned to the empty bench at the table he had occupied in the far corner.

"Thank you Bass, 'tis much appreciated." Tristan applauded, taking a sip of his beer and Basso following suit with his own tankard.

"So, what troubles you?" Basso asked after a while.

"Everything!" Tristan sniggered. "Not only do I not remember my past but my own family eludes me. I mean how is it they all seem to know more than me?"

"Let me...enlighten you perhaps. Tell me your confusion?"

"My uncle is descendent of the Pagan King yet he rules with no inflicted culture...and commands...Keepers?"

"I will assume your father told you not of his own Keeper dealings. Are you aware that your father was born Keeper? He, Jenson and Theoden are all Light Mages. Heck your father and Theoden were orphans raised by Keepers, their own father lost in some nameless war. Jenson on the other hand, supposedly the Queen mother had an affair with a Keeper, scandalous among the royals." The two shared a chuckle. "That is how the three met, as much as Jenson was still known as the prince he was not treated as such. Heck the only reason he got the throne was because Mariah declined it when she met and married your father.

"When you were tried for your involvement in the Interpreter's death, you may or may not remember that the truth about you and the Brotherhood came to light to all the Keeperhood. After the fall of the Compound in Hasaghar many Keepers retreated here in sanctuary and many more when The Faders bought down Dilu. Some of them spoke of your tales to the King and that is how he is aware.

"As for his involvement in this apparent war we have entered...it appears Hasaghar as he said is rife with supporters of Dharsi. Keepers are returning from the shadows in support of them as opposed to the right way due to lack of leadership it seems. Without Felix we are all truly lost! King Oruc appealed to Jenson for aid and he sent his son Markus to heed the aid. Markus was killed and in fact only three men made it back, and even that was only to send a message to Landen that Dharsi had indeed risen.

"As I'm sure you can imagine, your uncle holds a great amount of blame on you boys. Your tale has been told second hand, as it were and therefore, I suppose is open to interpretation. Do not call it ignorance, but grief. The King has lost a great deal since the fall and he is looking for someone to blame. Do not hold it against him!"

"It is just infuriating. We did not choose this Bass!"

"I know that, and soon so will they. Just be patient. I imagine we have no idea of the troubles of the great Pagan king as he were. The whispers in the city tell of war not just in Hasaghar but here to. Something is brewing, and I fear it is only the beginning."

The door to the tavern opened and Tristan's father appeared in the doorway. Perhaps his sober perception of his father had been misled. He spied Tristan and made his way over, avoiding the proprietor's offer of a drink. He smiled slightly; his father had come a long way indeed.

"I'll give you some space, looks like you need it!" Basso nodded to Theorryn and took his beer to sit at the bar.

"Who is your friend?" Theorryn asked as he took a seat.

"That's John Basso. He taught me to master the glyph when I was an Acolyte."

"I see. You've changed a lot my son, I mean I can't even remember the last time you drank a wheat beer let alone had a stubble and unruly hair."

They laughed together for a moment as Theorryn ruffled his son's head. Tristan's father was right, Tristan had changed, but he had no idea by how much.

"You have no idea," Tristan sighed, shaking his head away from his father.

"Can I tell you something Tristan, something perhaps I should've told you both long ago?"

Theorryn held out his right hand and began itching his palm wincing at the slight pain that was caused by a prick of blood that began to appear. The prick turned to a line which formed the Keeper glyph. Tristan gasped, trying not to show that Basso had in fact just told him of his father's past.

"The reason I hated the Keepers was never anything to do with Romeo or you," He explained. "It began a long time ago and you wouldn't believe the lengths I had to go to make sure no one knew. It's why I wasn't surprised when you came home and told me about seeing Felix that day in the alley. You see I was born a Keeper, hence why it is my palm that is marked. I was raised among the books of the Keeper Library right here in this forest. I trained to be a Scribe and spent seven years under the watchful eyes of the Elders interpreting many prophecies. I loved the insight it gave me you see. Me and your uncles craved the knowledge we gained, but in the end, it was our undoing.

"Not long after I met your mother, I scribed a prophecy which spoke of the End of Days and the coming of the Third Dawn. At first, I believed I misread so I asked your uncles and they agreed with my reading. We researched and found all the information we needed to back up our interpretation. However, when we went to show the Elders, the prophecy was no more. It was like it had been unwritten in our absence from the pages. A week later the same prophecy appeared to me again, but every time I showed it to an Elder, they didn't read the passage I had scribed. It was like it wasn't there. I tried to warn people but no one would listen.

"You see it wasn't just me and your uncles. There was also Iolan, a good friend of ours, a blood brother if you like. Because of the Elders ignorance to our plight the Glyphs possessed Iolan, turning him against the brothers he loved and fought alongside. They turned him into a weapon and he bought the entire Compound to its knees. Eventually the Enforcers were unleashed upon him and he descended into the Land of the Faded. If they had just listened to us in the first place and at least tried to do something, what happened to Iolan may never have happened and that is why I have always been against them."

Although Tristan gave his father his dues and respected him for telling him, it was a pretty basic explanation. Perhaps there was more to his tale that he wasn't willing to tell, a part that was even more painful than losing Iolan to corruption by the Glyphs. After all, the Elders had always taught Tristan and his brothers that if the Scribe did not learn to control and master the Glyphs, then the Glyphs would control and manipulate the Scribe to their own gain. Perhaps Iolan was more at fault than anyone knew.

"So why are you back here now?" Tristan asked eventually, fearing that his efforts to change the subject would not succeed.

"For months now I had been receiving letters sealed with the Keeper glyph and for months I had ignored them. But then, a letter came which I could not ignore for it opened the moment I touched it. Part of me wanted to still ignore it, but the words echoed from the page into my ears. Try as I may, I was forced to listen. Your uncle Theoden spoke of a prophecy recalling the coming of the Third Dawn at the hands of the Bleak Unwritten. It spoke of a Brethren Betrayer bringing about the End of Days. They couldn't explain it but the similarities it bore to the prophecy we ourselves had scribed worried them and who could blame them. So, I returned and even though I still don't know what it all means I have to stay and see it through. I owe it to Iolan!"

A moment of silence passed between father and son and Theorryn watched as his son's eyes clouded over. At last Tristan looked up and began his own confession of the last few months. He told of his reunion with Basso and the arrival at Dilu; finding Nielson within the Compound and his confrontation with Boris with every gory detail; the meeting of Myrina and ending with Hagen's last stand. He told his father of all that he had remembered thus far and the story of Unity; highlighting his own role within it. Secrets is what had torn apart their relationship in Az Lagní, they could not afford to keep anymore. Once he had finished, he gulped down the last of his beer, gasping with the final sip as his father stared up at him.

"I would never judge you for all that you have done my son," Theorryn consoled. "Especially when I myself am no better. The sins of the father are always left to the sons to burden but that will not be my legacy." Theorryn sighed heavily. "Tristan if you will accompany me now, there is one last thing I need to tell."

"Accompany you?" Tristan question perplexed.

"You will see."

Tristan nodded, a quizzical look upon his face.

The two rose from their seats, waving goodbye to Basso as they departed the tavern. He followed his father back up towards the palace, up the stairs to the Royal Apartments and to the end of the corridor which led to the Royal Chambers. He knocked lightly on the first of the oak doors before gently pulling down the handle. Inside was a large sized room with a balcony directly opposite. Two archways were either side of the room, each masked by a curtain, probably leading to a bed chamber and wash room Tristan thought. In the centre of the room was sat a little girl Tristan recognised to be his cousin Kyra. Next to her was Zelda who smiled sweetly to them before heading off into the bed chamber without uttering a word. Theorryn remained silent watching as Kyra continued to play with the blocks on the floor, mindlessly building towers and then knocking them down.

"Don't be shy now!" said the voice of his eldest cousin. Tristan looked up to see Zelda standing by the archway again, holding out her hand to something hidden by the curtain.

Tristan gasped as his eyes looked upon the young girl that took hold of her hand and came into view. He knew her; the messy blonde brown hair, the green eyes and the round porcelain face with the rosy cheeks. A single tear fell from his eyes and the girl smiled as she let go of Zelda's hand and walked slowly over to where Theorryn and Tristan stood.

"Evie, you remember all that I told you about your father?" Theorryn asked as he knelt by the child and she nodded in response, taking a step forward to Tristan who sank to his knees, remembering the child he had seen at his mother's grave those few short months ago. "Tristan, meet your daughter."

He gasped again and Evelyn threw herself into his chest as though she had missed him greatly. More tears slipped down his cheeks and eventually he stretched his arms around her tightly, not wanting to let go as she snuggled deep. Theorryn watched with pride upon his face as Zelda too let tears leak from her eyes. When she finally broke away, she smiled sweetly at her father before running over to the blocks to build with Kyra as Tristan watched in wonderment of her. A ripple shattered in the corner of his eye.

"How did you find her?" His voice broke as he asked Theorryn the question.

"I didn't," Theorryn answered truthfully. "She found me about three days ago when I was intending on leaving here and never coming back. I had a rather heated argument with Jenson, both of us said things we didn't mean. When I came to pack my things, I heard Zelda call to me and I came in here to find Evie playing with Kyra. The moment I looked at her, I knew who she was...it was her eyes and that face. It was like I was staring Dagnen in the face. I don't know how she got here but whoever was meant to be taking care of her made no effort to look for her."

"I've seen her before," Tristan gasped, barely giving his father chance to finish. "At the old church in Az Lagní. I assume she was there with Cedric."

"I knew I'd seen him that day in the town square."

"I'd give anything to get my hands on him now."

"The man may have had his reasons, Tristan. Think about it." He paused as Tristan smiled at the way Evie built with the blocks; gently and slowly as though she would build a magnificent structure. "Stay here a while with her, get to know your daughter. She doesn't seem to speak, but it's amazing how much you can learn just from watching. There's no telling what that child has been through."

Theorryn smiled at his son and motioned for Zelda to follow him out of the room. She motioned to her sister who rose and followed them out of the room, glancing back. Theorryn looked back before leaving, smiling humbly as Tristan sat beside his daughter. She handed him blocks to help her build. He smiled; his core warmed at the sight; all the sins he had dealt these last few years redeemed in one sweet reunion.

CHAPTER 6 – OPEN UP YOUR EYES

Upon the third blink I opened my eyes wide and stared out at the scene before me. I could see you brother, sat beside a young girl with strewn blonde brown hair. I couldn't see your faces from my view so I moved to the side a little so that I might marvel at you both. I couldn't believe it. You had found her - your sweet Evie. I knew it the moment I saw those green eyes; the eyes of her mother.

It was then that I looked up and saw Dagnen, her tear-stained face catching the light that shone through her. It must've pained her so to see such a sight and not be able to behold it herself. I winced, feeling a sudden pain strike my hand as warm blood dripped from my palm. Opening it out I saw the medallion which seemed to have followed me back from the Shadow Lands. I found it hard to believe but perhaps it was part of what I had to do. As I looked back up at her, I knew what I had to do. It was like a voice was resonating inside of me, singing words of wisdom and guidance. Strolling over to where she stood, I took hold of her hand causing her to look at me properly for what must have been the first time. She gasped as she did so and I smiled back at her. Oh to feel touched again – it was like it breathed life back into me after all this time.

"Let me help you," I tried to say as I squeezed hard on the medallion once more trying to ignore the pain. I reached out with my other hand, and she took it as though she craved it as much as I.

She nodded to me, and at once the room around us descended into darkness and striking worry into her heart. She tried to pull away, probably thinking this was all some sort of trap - but I held tight on her hand, my grip softening as she stared into my eyes. I wondered how long it had been since she had seen the darkness and what it would show us now that light crept into view bleeding colour into this grey world. A white rose was thrown into view as a headstone stood before them; a rose left to remember. A man stands a few paces away; you brother, stand there, a single tear falling from your scorned face. You are pale on this cold December's day and as snow lands in your hair you whisper goodbye before turning away.

In a moment the vision floats away leaving another to swim into the forefront. A cobblestoned floor upon which her body lands in the arms of her lover, blood forming on the midriff of her yellow dress. I look to my side and see the same stain appear on Dagnen as she grips the place, feeling the pain. I hold her hand tighter, worried as to why she feels pain in our part of the world - but then perhaps that is part of her return, our return?

I look back at the already fading scene of the angels taking her from your arms; the broken face that must've looked up and cursed the earth for taking her from you. For they left you there alone to hold on to yours and her tomorrow. They lay that babe alone in her crib to face the foe that caused you so much pain. We watched silently as fire took you to the ground and as the flames and smoke went up your heart silently sang a bittersweet ballad that told of the relief you felt at joining the eternity but leaving behind your future. The forgetting was not just a curse but a gift in the same – it took away your pain.

Suddenly I feel that her hand is no longer within mine and I am standing in a long winding corridor all alone. I try to call her name, desperation causing my voice to crack as I begin trying all the doors on either side of the corridor, each appearing locked. I imagine her unable to face her own burial, the anger that must've gripped her as she broke away. She would be in one of these rooms I thought and as I heard glass and pots smash, mirrors shatter I knew I was right - the first of many doors finally opening at my touch. Inside, you brother, sank to the floor surrounded by shattered glass as framed pictures lay broken around you. I stand in the door way watching as you cry hysterically and I hear a whimper. Behind the door I find her; broken too and silent with her cracked soul. She breathes heavily and slowly, clutching at the stain on her dress as though she has lost too much blood and was struggling for life. Gripping her hands tightly, I realised that perhaps Dante was right. Even if the legend of the eye of the Storm was right and that it took her soul to the Land of the Faded, perhaps there wasn't a way to save her. Even if I did save her soul, she would still return dead would she not?

I watch as she takes another breath, her eyes slipping shut and not opening again. Was this it, had we really lost her again? I kneel in front of her, taking her hands within my own; bloodied from the medallion that hangs on my wrist. I whisper softly to her, hoping to bring her some peace.

"If you should return my sweet," I say with silent hopefulness for the sake of my brother and the life she shares together with him. "Know that you may open up your eyes and see the world without your sorrow masking it for the first time. No one will have to know the pain you've left behind today and all the peace that you could never find before will be waiting for you. It's waiting to hold you deep and keep you safe. It says welcome to the first day of your new life. All you have to do to behold it is open up your eyes."

Pulling her lifeless body towards me, I cherish her within my arms and rise to my feet carrying her forward. As I take a few steps I see the visions change and you fight your foe for retribution for letting her down and losing her just like you are about to lose yourself. You are struck by some invisible force and I lay her beside where you fall, your arm landing just before her pale face where you can just reach and touch her face. There she lies, finally safe on the other side of me and you, no more tears left to cry.

Then all at once I too feel the pain as a hole opens up in my midriff and I am struck. You, my brother, try to catch my hand as I fall from a tower; just as I had done on that last day of my life. I slip from your grasp and you cry out as the water engulfs me and rips me apart, sending my soul into total and complete darkness.

I think about the darkness now, whether or not it will be there when I open up my eyes. I think about the life I have lived and you as well, her too and you all intertwined with each other. For the first time, we can all open up our eyes, our souls clean of all our pain, our sorrow left behind and peace being all that remains. Welcome to our new world! A world of love and happiness where pain is far away from our hearts, I pray.

CHAPTER 7 – AN OLD FACE

A few hours passed but it seemed like little time at all between them as they built vast structures with the blocks, Evie's radiant smile being the brightest thing in the room. A knock sounded at the door and they were greeted by Myrina whom Tristan had sent for her some time ago, but he wasn't sure how long exactly. He rose to his feet as she entered and smiled sweetly at him.

"Sorry I took so long," she apologised. "Thought I'd make myself useful and lend a hand in the kitchen cleaning up."

"That's alright," Tristan shrugged. "Didn't even notice how much time had passed to be honest with you."

Myrina giggled at the statement, her eyes landing on Evie.

"I take it this is the little Kyra I've heard the kitchen staff complaining about?" She assumed, a twinkle forming in her eyes and her face dropping after, like she suspected her own mistake.

"Actually, this is why I summoned you here. Evie come say hello to Myrina."

She gasped at the name she heard him say, her hands clutching at her chest. Just as her father asked, Evie got to her feet and came to stand beside him, holding her hands behind her back as though she were nervous.

"It's okay!" Tristan reassured her, placing a gentle hand on her shoulder. "She's a friend." In truth, she was Evie's god-mother, but a mute three-year-old was never going to understand that.

Evie smiled slightly and held out her hand towards Myrina as she practically collapsed. Gasping as tears rolled down her cheeks, she reached out a hand to grace her face, her bottom lip quivering.

"By the Gods!" She exclaimed, still in disbelief. "Sweet girl, I've missed your little face."

"Was it cherub you used to call her?" Tristan asked, feeling nostalgic in the memories that seemed to resonate in his head at that moment.

"Yes, because she has the face of an angel." Evie smiled before turning back to attend to the blocks. "Where did she come from...I mean..."

"My father found her in here with Kyra three days ago. But it's strange because no one has seen Cedric, and I'm pretty sure he had her in his charge most recently."

"Well at least he didn't keep it from you I suppose. What the hell is Cedric playing at?"

"I don't know but maybe it's best he stays gone what with how angry I am."

"Ask Evie, maybe he said something to her."

"She doesn't speak."

"Oh poor love. This is so...surreal...I was certain she died in that fire with my father and Cedric...that's what Hagen said..."

"Hagen said a lot of things.

Whatever Myrina was about to say in response was interrupted by a knock at the door. Tristan beckoned and in walked Zhaine and Ramien.

"Hey, your father said we'd find you here," Zhaine announced as they stepped into the room, their eyes landing on Evie.

"It can't be!" Ramien exclaimed, seeing Dagnen through the little girl now staring at them from her blocks. The brothers had grown up with Dagnen and aside from Tristan, they'd know her face better than anyone.

"It is!" Tristan confirmed and Zhaine smiled, clasping a hand on Tristan's shoulder and Ramien beaming from ear to ear. "Anyway, why are you both here?"

"Oh yes, Isolde said you can see Dante now and asked that we find you." Ramien answered.

"Really? Myrina, would you mind watching Evie?" Tristan asked, looking from his brothers to her.

"Of course." Myrina answered, her eyes not leaving the playing angel.

"We'll help!" Ramien snapped, Zhaine smiling mockingly at his brother.

Tristan had forgotten how much the child meant not just to him but them all. She had been a ray of light in so much darkness when she was born; how lucky she was to have so many that loved her. Taking his cue and partly reluctant to leave his daughter so soon, he was gone from the room, begging the air to keep her here this time.

Walking through the door to the infirmary, a powerful aroma of healing herbs and gentle incense tingled his nose. Isolde was pacing the room as though she had been waiting for him and Dante was lying on the bed in the far corner. He didn't look much different from how he had the last time he had seen him, just a little cleaner. The bruises on his face had now developed fully and his eyes twitched as he slept. The healer rounded on Tristan when she heard the door close, a stern look upon her face.

She tutted at him as he entered the room and looked from Dante to his equally ancient healer. She crossed her arms across her smock as she watched him, a speculative look on her face.

"It's a long road to recovery for your *friend*." Her voice was pointed. "Why don't you start by telling me who he really is?"

"Excuse me!" Tristan tried to play dumb however it was obvious it wasn't working because the look on her face didn't change. "He's just a friend from back home!"

"That's what Merlin tried to tell me too, but he should know better than most to lie to me. But then I suppose it isn't his news to tell."

Tristan turned to face Isolde now and stared into her silver eyes. In them he found his memory of her - She was an Elder in every sense of the word, supposedly having been there when the Keeperhood was first formed, which was fitting considering the lectures she had given on the history of the Keepers when the brothers were Scribes. Lying to her about who Dante was would be folly, she probably knew him.

"Whoever beat him beat him so hard that old wounds opened too, wounds I had treated before. They used his past to harm him further. This is dark magic Tristan! Not even Merlin would tell me what he knew. I understand you may be trying to protect him but this...this isn't protecting him." Tristan sighed heavily.

"You already know who he is so what would be the point in me telling you?"

"I need to hear you say it!" Her voice broke then and Tristan sensed a history there. He didn't know the full story behind Dante and his brothers' banishment but perhaps she had been there. He knew many had disagreed with the decision, had she been one of them?

"His name is Dante Ashdown; I assume I do not need to tell you much more."

"You need to tell me who did this to him."

"Hagen!" Tristan hesitated. "I don't know what he did, that is how we found him."

She turned away and looked upon Dante truly for the first time in a long time. Tristan knew not what her association to Dante was and part of him was now fearful there was someone who knew who he was.

"You should not fear Tristan," Isolde assured without turning around. "I knew Dante very well and was rather fond of him as one of my students. I never believed him capable of the things he was led to do, you can be sure that I will not just look after him but protect his identity." She turned to him now. "But you must know I won't be the only one to ask questions and you will need to create a more convincing story then what you have." Tristan nodded. "Does Nielson know?"

"No, I think Dante tried to tell him once but…"

"It will be hard for me to lie to a friend such as he…but I shall…for Dante!"

"What happens now?"

"Well…your friend here is in a very fragile state and far from being out of the woods. But if he is strong then he will pull through. Come and see him again tomorrow, let him rest for now."

"Thank you, for all you have done for him."

Taking one last look at Dante's tormented face, Tristan left the room.

CHAPTER 8 – THE MARK OF SECRETS

"I always thought I'd been so good at watching our actions," Tristan struggled explained as Nielson listened intently.

"I'm not quite sure I understand Tristan; you're going to have to give me some context here." Nielson didn't even know they were Union as far as Tristan was aware, so it was no surprise. Nobody knew. But of all his teachers, Tristan felt as though he could trust him the most. Maybe it was the fact that he had a familial connection to Ramien and Zhaine. Or even the fact he seemed more complacent, more understanding than everyone else.

"Tristan, what's going on?" Nielson had found the boy in the Old Wing, distraught and full of unrest. Managing to get him to his feet, he had taken him to his office where he might find some calm.

"Maybe it's easier if I show you."

Tristan began unravelling the bandage he had strung around his left hand to hide the mark that had appeared. The story was he'd cut his hand but no one seemed to care too much. Anxiously, he looked around Nielson's office; he knew no one else was there but it was like he had to check anyway. Nielson was patient as always, an inquisitive look on his face that didn't budge as Tristan showed the old man his scared Mark of Nobility on the top of his hand and then that traitorous Mark on his palm. His teacher looked up into Tristan's eyes, so filled with guilt and worry.

"You realise it's on the wrong hand," Nielson smirked, trying to lighten the mood.

"What?" Tristan looked confused.

"Your supposed traitorous Mark - that's what you think it means don't you? You think it means you betrayed?"

"It's the same mark though..."

"Might I see?" Tristan held his hand out for Nielson to see. The mark was very similar to that of betrayal but there were a few minor differences to the trained eye. The mark of a traitor always appeared on the right hand to counteract the Keeper port glyph tattooed onto the top and it always appeared with no intention, it would just be there one day. It marked you for all to see, but such a mark is easily hidden. "Do you remember when this appeared?"

"Are you deliberately ignoring the fact that I'm Union therefore I'm a traitor?"

Tristan rose to his feet; angry, but Nielson knew it was out of fear more than anything else.

"Union were not always traitors Tristan, you know that."

"But aren't you angry that I am, aren't you disappointed?"

"Tristan did you know that the fiftieth generation of Union is supposedly the last and final generation? Did you know that you are supposed to break the cycle and save us all?" Tristan shook his head; it must've been a prophecy of some sort. "Now tell me, when did the mark first appear?"

Tristan tried to relax, catching his breath and recounting the events that had taken place two days before.

Raised voices disturbed the peace and Tristan stopped dead in his tracks. He was out after curfew; the Elders would kill him if they found him out again. Since Xavier's death a week ago, a curfew had been enforced but Tristan had spent those days sneaking off to the Shrine for research purposes. The voices seemed to be coming from the gardens below where he was walking. Stealthily, he approached the edge of the balcony and peered over the edge to see two shadowed figures. He had a hunch who they were, the chubby build of the shorter man giving Boris away.

"Their making me a scapegoat brother!" He stammered, anger forcing his voice. "And I won't take the fall for a pawn!"

"You need to keep your voice down brother," the taller skinnier man had a snake like voice, it had to be Hagen. It would also explain the brotherly nature the two shared. "I'm sure the Herasin has a plan..."

"Fuck Herasin! I won't do it!"

"Do what?" Another shadowy figure approached; hands placed behind his back as he walked with an air of importance.

"Herasin?" Boris exclaimed, following his brothers lead as both of them bowed their heads.

"No one is asking you to take the fall Tabacious." The third figure explained calmly, even his voice was arrogant as though he spoke above his station. But Tristan couldn't put a name to the figure. "We are simply asking you not to sway the blame."

"So you are painting me as a scapegoat?"

"Your role is very important Tabacious. For one of our own has come back into the fold."

"Sarisus...he's back?" Hagen questioned. Tristan didn't know who Sarisus was, but it couldn't be a good thing. Whatever syndicate these three were initiating, it didn't sit right with him, something was coming and he had a feeling these three were in the thick of it.

"I will say no more, all of you have your jobs so make sure you carry them out. Your rewards will be claimed in the end I assure you."

The two bowed their heads again and the man walked away. The brothers said nothing more and turned in opposing directions to return to their barracks. But as the silence reproached him Tristan found himself unable to move. A burning sensation ripped at his left palm and the smell of rotting flesh tinged the air. A pain ran up his arm and a blinding light forced his eyes shut. Clamping his mouth shut, he tried desperately not to let the pain he felt be heard, holding his hand close to him as a mark began to etch itself on his palm. The pain faded and he opened his eyes to gaze upon the mark of a traitor. What had he done? He couldn't even think. Surely, he was no traitor, not yet...

Tristan was silent. He decided it best to keep the identities of the figures to himself. After all, he had no proof of it, he only suspected them. He looked up at Nielson, trying to gage his blank expression for a reaction but failing miserably. He was unreadable as usual. He pursed his lips and rose from his seat, casting his hand over the books that littered the shelves behind him. Plucking one from the shelf, he scanned through the pages before placing it in front of Tristan.

"The Bearer of Secrets," he recited as though he knew the words from the passage off by heart. "Tis a legend really. A prophecy proclaimed the coming of a marked saviour, a saviour marked by treachery for the secrets he kept. A Brother of Union should never keep any secrets from his brothers but sometimes, he must and that is when the mark appears. Because by keeping secrets, you have betrayed your brotherhood in short. It also only affects those of the name Nobility as they are said to be the Brotherhood's Betrayer." He paused. "But I wouldn't worry too much, as I said, 'tis just a legend."

"Sorry to be blunt Nielson but this mark is not a legend, I can see it as clear as day, not to mention the pain I felt when it appeared." Tristan was frustrated now; he didn't think Nielson was taking any of this very seriously at all.

"I'm not saying that you are crazy or delusional Tristan. I'm simply saying that you should not worry. Continue to keep the mark hidden by all means but you are no traitor. What you heard does require attention though and I will consult the scriptures before bringing it up at the next council meeting. Rest assured, you are not in any trouble, your secrets are safe with me dear boy. Now go, it's way past your curfew!"

Nielson turned his back on Tristan who grimaced in confusion. This was not the reaction he had been expecting. He rose to his feet and turned to leave, stopping suddenly as Nielson spoke his name.

"Take the book with you. You might find it a good read." Nielson instructed.

Tristan sighed impatiently before closing the book and stomping out of the room. He had expected an unwelcome reaction, but not one with a lack of concern. Nielson had been no help at all. How could he not worry about a mark that any number of Keepers would think him a traitor. Did it mark him for future treachery?

He couldn't think like that though, if Nielson said he was no traitor, then he was no traitor, that much he would take heed from the old man. Perhaps there were more answers in research, the Shrine might have countless books on the Bearer of Secrets. He couldn't just sit back and let himself think it over, he had to know for sure. This mark would not write his fate; he would make sure of it.

CHAPTER 9 – MATTERS OF COURT

The next morning there was a prominent knock at the door, disturbing the peace bought by Tristan's morning coffee. Evie had stirred him early in the morning, she wasn't the most graceful sleeper to share a bed with, but the closeness...well they had a lot of catching up to do. He'd spent most of the morning watching her sleep through, watching her at peace. Rising from his chair by the fire, Tristan answered the door to Theoden, an urgent look on his face.

"Uncle Theoden," he greeted. "Good morning."

"Morning Tristan, how did you sleep?" Theoden asked, clearly just being polite.

"To be honest. I couldn't take my eyes off her."

His uncle poked his head in the door to see Evie watching something through the balcony doors. It was clear she even bought peace to those who didn't know her.

"Tristan I'm sorry to stir you so early, but we have a bit an urgent matter."

"Something so urgent it requires me to miss breakfast?" Tristan joked – in truth he wasn't all that hungry anyway.

"Let's just say, we have some unexpected guests who are rather as you say...impatient." Tristan looked back at Evie in the rising sunlight.

"You're lucky I'm not hungry."

"You mean *they* are."

"Do me a favour and wake Myrina, least then there is someone to watch Evie. Give me a minute."

"I'm going to have to wake them all. Our guest has requested the presence of all Keepers here, your brothers included."

The two shared a look before Theoden turned away, leaving Tristan to sort himself out. He wondered what might be so urgent they weren't even allowed to eat breakfast.

Not too long later, the captain was back waiting to escort Tristan to wherever this meeting was being held. Myrina had already stopped in to watch Evie so he bid them goodbye and followed his uncle down to the entrance foyer where his brothers, Basso and his father were already waiting. Tristan wondered where Merlin and Nielson were, but perhaps they had gone on ahead. Sharing a short good morning to one another, the Keepers followed Theoden through the entrance hall towards the throne room ahead. Three hooded figures stood by the chairs, stopping their chatter to face their apparent brothers.

"Before we go on to the gathering, I think its best we get this out of the way first." Theoden explained, a slight smile on his face as motioned towards the figures who stepped forward; two slightly more tentative than the one in the middle.

The middle figure stepped first, tipping back his hood to reveal dark wavy hair and a scruffy beard. Sea blue eyes and broad shoulders, a smile that would send any damsel's heart racing. Despite the rough look, he had a regal appearance about him, like there was something far grander beneath the seams.

"Jacques!" Ramien exclaimed in joy, approaching his brother and taking him into a heavy clinch. Zhaine followed closely behind along with Tristan, relieved to see his brother well. Now all that was missing was Romeo.

"My brothers!" Jacques exclaimed, shaking hands with Basso and hugging Theorryn too. "It is good to see you all so well. There isn't really time for pleasantries unfortunately, but I assure you all, we shall catch up soon."

"The Tavern better roll out the big guns!"

"Indeed brother. But I fear, your celebration is perhaps short lived."

Without saying anything more, Jacques stepped aside, a stern look on his face as a goading look was given to the figure on the right. The left one revealed his face first though; Hugo, the sight of him caused sighs among the brothers. Tristan formed fists, his eyes falling on the third hood, not even letting it slip before he lunged forward, landing his fist hard on the man square in the face. Theorryn jumped forward to hold back his son, the brothers looking more as though they thought Cedric deserved it. Basso stepped in between the two, helping his adopted son to his feet and observing the damage to his nose.

"If I'm not mistaken Tristan, I'd say you broke it." Basso chuckled slightly, glowering eyes on his son. "I think I'll let it heal naturally, teach him a lesson on priorities." Basso's reaction surprised Tristan, but also satisfied him.

"Can you boys keep this civil?" Theoden roared, trying to gain control over the fallout. "I was lucky I managed to get you boys time to address each other and this is how you show your thanks. Now, if you don't mind, our guests were impatient enough as it was."

Cedric looked to his brother and Tristan nodded, his eyes still locked on him. Hugo shifted past nervously and into the room beyond the thrones, slowly followed by the rest. Theoden kept close to Tristan, slightly fearful his anger would not be contained for long.

The ballroom lay behind the thrones, odd place for a meeting but perhaps the Keeper Compound here was in an even worse state then Dilu. Scattered figures were in the room in small groups; only a few of them Tristan recognised. Some of the other faces pained him, like he should know them. He spotted Nielson and Merlin in the back of the room, both of them nodding to him. They stood with Isolde, making Tristan wonder who was with Dante. Another man stood with them, old and haggard but tall. The brothers strode to stand with them, turning to face the figures in the centre of the room.

Tristan recognised them to be Ivan and Hamish – what were members of the Az Lagní council doing in Landen? He looked to his father for guidance, but his eyes were on the man sat in the chair between the two, a sack over his head, his hands tied behind him.

"I grow impatient with this dawdling," Jenson was stood at the head of a group ahead where Theoden had assumed position. "For the last time tell us why you have gathered us all here. Tell us why Az Lagní seem incapable of dealing with their own problems."

"Patience dear king," Ivan looked around the room, surveying the faces, his eyebrows twitching at a few. He always did have a rather smarmy look on his face. "But alas it seems we are finally all here."

"What is this about Ivan?" Theorryn stepped forward, facing Ivan. "If this is who I think this is then this doesn't even involve Landen, it is for us to decide how to punish him."

"My dear colleague; clearly you aren't in your right mind, tell me there is something different about you…"

"Leave my brother out of this Ivan!" Theoden stepped forward, causing Ivan to round on him, a smirk on his face. He had always taken pleasure in other people's discomfort. "For the benefit of all those you have summoned, I suggest you explain yourself – or perhaps I should look to Hamish."

"Now now brother. As you will all be aware, Az Lagní is presently without a ruler, so I suppose you could say we are here for…guidance. King Rubuen passed a few short months ago…"

"And is your princess not suitable?" Jacques stepped forward, his face pale and his eyes glassy.

"She would be yes," Ivan glanced over at Jacques, looking down on him. "But I have it on good authority that our prince is actually alive and well…here in this palace somewhere in fact…"

"Preposterous!" Ivan turned back and glowered at Theorryn.

"Funny that word should leave your mouth when I heard that he was last under your charge." Theorryn shifted on his feet. Tristan caught the look he flashed at Jacques as Ivan turned back to face the king. Jacques gripped something around his neck, suddenly nervous.

"I still yet to understand why this involves any of us," Jensen was growing impatient now.

"Young Daniel here," Hamish too had grown tired of whatever game Ivan was playing and had stepped forward to unmask Daniel, the late king's advisor as their captive. "Has been accused of treachery to the crown. Not only is it believed that he is the reason the late king thought his son dead, we have reason to believe he is also wanted for treachery to the Keepers."

"If Daniel here is guilty of anything where us Keepers are involved," Isolde spoke now. "It is that he was not quick enough to act. We have no quarrel with Daniel…"

"Then why does he bare the mark?" Ivan piped. Tristan looked to Daniel now, he was curious as to what his story was, part of him felt a connection as they shared eye contact then. It made the mark on his left palm tingle.

"Might I repeat that we have no quarrel with Daniel…" Isolde repeated, a slight break in her words.

Ivan stepped forward, unsheathing a knife to untie the supposed betrayer. Daniel was submissive, yet notably distained. How they'd managed to catch up to him puzzled Theorryn, but then again, fate always finds a way of catching you up in the end. Grabbing hold of his arm he pulled it up, bearing the mark of the betrayer on his palm for all to see. Many gasps escaped the scattered Keepers, a grave look upon Isolde's face. Nielson shared the look too and both Ramien and Zhaine looked to their brother. When Tristan noticed their look, he looked back at the betrayer – the mark was on the left hand.

"Tell me, where is Felix. It is up to him is it not to gather the Council to decide how best to deal with the betrayal?"

Tristan frowned. Was he taunting them now? Mocking their loss perhaps…but then the loss would be his too. A sight like the death of a First Keeper, particularly one like Felix wasn't to be missed – not even by non-Keepers. He remembered that bright blue light filled with glyphs, how it shone from the dungeons of Hagen's estate. It had lured villagers from their slumber to stare into its brilliance as it reached the skies. Not only that, the effect is had on each of their own marks of Keeperhood.

"Felix is dead!" Nielson exclaimed stepping forward into the centre with Ivan, Hamish and Daniel. Ivan's eyes widened, his nostrils flaring as a smirk pinched the end of his lips - he was enjoying this. "As standing Second Keeper, that puts me in charge until such a time the Council can gather to properly anoint me to resume the position. Are there any objections to me assuming the role in this time of precedent?"

No one spoke around them, but Tristan couldn't shake the feeling inside of him. The tingling on his hand had turned to a stabbing pain; someone was trying to tell him something. He looked again to the mark on Daniel's palm and the gloved hand holding it there for everyone to see. They weren't exactly matching with Ivan's robes of grandeur and his sleeves were probably long enough to keep them hidden when not outstretched and it wasn't like it was exactly cold right now. They could've been riding gloves, but then why was he still wearing them?

"Then I guess it is for me to decide how we deal with him. Ivan will you please let go of your so-called prisoner." Ivan threw Daniel's hand, causing him to go off balance and collapse. He stayed there on his knees, not looking up at any of his brothers and sisters from the Keeperhood. Tristan couldn't watch this any longer. Looking to his brothers, he knew it was time they reveal all of their secrets. After all, there once was a time when the Brothers of Union would join the First Keeper in carrying judgement over traitors.

"Nielson wait!" Tristan called, looks casting their gaze all onto him at last, some scorning. He imagined it wasn't just Jensen that blamed the brothers for what was happening right now. But this was a war that had been going on for centuries. "Might I point attention to the fact that Daniel's mark is on the wrong hand." Ivan laughed pitifully. "Am I not right in my thinking that the mark of the betrayer is usually on the right palm drenched in a bloody scab...not some scars on the left as Daniel is marked?"

Many of the Keepers among them nodded and Hamish took his cue to approach Daniel and help him up. He took hold of Daniel's hands in his own and looked over the marks.

 "The mark on his left hand is scared as tough is has been there years," Hamish instructed as he studied the marks. "His right palm is devoid of a mark."

"The boy is correct!" Isolde remarked. "The mark of the betrayer is usually on the right palm."

"I know the mark he bears," Tristan interjected, Nielson casting him a warning look. But now was not the time for secrets. "I bare the same one!" Tristan raised his left hand, removing a fingerless glove. Gasps escaped the onlooking Keepers, Theoden watching for any of them about to make a move. But they were all more afraid, these were strange times. "This mark is not one of betrayal," Tristan continued as Ivan opened his mouth to speak. "It usually affects Brothers of Union, notably Nobility and marks one keeping secrets from the rest."

Whispers erupted around the room, but no one moved.

"Union?" Isolde remarked, glassy eyes upon Daniel...like she didn't understand.

"Either way the man is still a traitor!" Ivan taunted, nervous in his lack of control over the room now.

"Let the boy speak Ivan!" Nielson exclaimed. "You know as well as I do that not all generations of Union were betrayers. I for one would like to hear him explain himself." No one spoke. "Hamish help Daniel onto the chair and for gods-sake somebody fetch him some water!"

Nielson's orders were followed and the inhabitants of the room waited patiently for what would happen next. Many of them cast looks over at the brothers, particularly at Tristan –

fear in their eyes as whispers escaped their lips. Ivan was surprisingly quiet through all this, glowering at Hamish the whole time he supported Daniel. When Daniel seemed refreshed enough, Nielson stepped forward again to address the room.

"Daniel, do you contest the allegations made against you?" He asked calmly.

"Well for starters I didn't kill Rubuen!" Daniel defended. "The royal family of Az Landen meant an awful lot to me. They were my second chance at life." He was silent for a time.

"Daniel, in your own time of course – I want to hear your side of the story...but first I want you to swear that you will tell us the truth."

"Then I need a knife...First Keeper."

Nielson nodded and Hamish offered one from his belt. Ivan made to protest but Nielson cast him a warning look. Daniel took the knife and cut along the Keeper tattoo on the top of his right hand.

"I swear by the glyphs, I will tell the whole truth. If I do not, well the glyphs will skin me here right now." Daniel handed the knife back to Hamish.

"Then in your own time." Nielson instructed, and the room gathered to listen.

CHAPTER 10 – A MISINTERPRETATION

"Some of you will know or at least have heard some version of what happened to my brother Elan," Daniel started. The surrounding Keepers were silent and listened intently. "My brother was a highly skilled Scribe and dreamt of excelling vastly in his field. I on the other hand progressed quickly to Runebound. Around the time I assume he became involved with Union, I returned to find one of them with him…"

"A woman can't be Unity…pogwash!" an unseen Keeper yelled, snorting as though he were mocking the supposed betrayer. He was wrong, as much as one was never elected, women had been chosen as Allies in the past.

"Please do not be so narrow-minded!" Daniel tried to stay calm at the ignorance posed to him. "They were in a deep clinch when I…interrupted. After he left though I demanded my brother tell me what was going on. I'd found myself covering for his whereabouts on many an occasion and risking my own position in doing so, I had a right to know what was going on. It was then he told me he'd got involved with Unity and was in fact their ally. The forty ninth generation had taken my brother.

"He told me it started when he Scribed a certain prophecy that troubled him but every time he tried to show it to an Elder they translated it differently to him." Tristan flashed his father a look but it was not shared. "He wrote it down, he seemed to think there was some form of link between the way he read it and the way they did. It was this prophecy that led him straight to the Brotherhood, Unity of which supposedly read it the same way he did. It was what prompted them to name him their Ally and together their plan was to find the meaning of this prophecy before their time was up."

"Their time?" the question echoed.

"It has long been believed that the Brotherhood was cursed to be evil...cursed to betray. After all, before the sixth generation, they were there to help – keep the balance. Heck Talus himself was Unity hence why he united the Keepers in the first place. The name therefore rather fitting. Dharsi were their long-term enemies, opposed to the original union and although they were all but banished by the third generation, some of them escaped. It is believed that nine in total survived. It is thought that this nine did something that meant that every brotherhood after the fifth betrayed. But I suppose it's never been proven. Supposedly the prophecy proves it.

"The prophecy also spoke of how the fiftieth generation would be the last. They would be the brotherhood to change it all, rewrite everything and end what began all those generations ago. Something called The Bleak Unwritten...that much I do remember."

Tristan turned on his father again. This story sounded a lot like his own reason for hating the Keeperhood and he wondered if it was the same prophecy. Then again, if it was the prophecy he was thinking about, then it was no surprise it had caused so much imbalance over the years.

"From what I understand Dharsi caught wind of their discovery and made their intent clear. The Brothers became fearful for their lives and decided the only way to keep themselves safe was to come clean to the Keeperhood about who they were. Only that didn't go to plan and instead the brothers were arrested and turned over to the Enforcers. I guess they did Dharsi's dirty work for them and Elan felt betrayed. He was enraged, not even I could bring him down. He sealed himself in his room for days...I think you all know the rest of the story – personally I do not wish to relive it."

"To sum up for those of you that do not know," Nielson concluded, choosing his words carefully. "Elan unleashed his rage upon the Compound. He felt betrayed and had lost the thing he held most dear. It's rather tragic if you ask me that we failed one of our own. Surrounded by Enforcers, Elan disappeared. It's not known if they got him or if he simply just vanished."

There was silence for a time. Many looks were shared among the Keepers in the room however Ivan chose to avoid any eye that flashed in his direction. He had gone very quiet, unsuspectedly so while Daniel was giving his account.

"What about the mark Daniel?" Tristan broke the silence, suddenly curious – it was clear Daniel wasn't a part of Unity nor wanted to be so. So why did he share it with himself and Dante? "When did it appear?"

"I was wondering when you would ask that Tristan seeing as you confess to share the same mark." Daniel goaded as though Tristan should now be forced to confess his own sins.

"I'm going to ignore that comment and simply say that I am bound to my secrets. I would rather not divulge anything further to a room filled with people I do not trust."

"Daniel, may I remind you that you are the one on trial here?" Nielson interrupted, a stern look cast at both Tristan and Daniel.

"So be it!" Daniel snapped. "The mark appeared shortly after Elan vanished. I returned to our room after a week or so, I hadn't been able to set foot in it since he went...crazy. What I found was un...unspeakable. It's why I left the Keeperhood behind...because like Nielson said – they failed my brother."

"I have heard enough!" Ivan had grown impatient now. Tristan sensed a touch of panic in his voice but he wasn't sure why – and then he saw it; a certain red glint in those grey eyes of his. 'You see it too!' a voice said near him, but Tristan couldn't tell whom the voice belonged to. It certainly wasn't one of his brothers – in fact it sounded like a woman, but none were near him. "So we've established the Keepers have no quarrel but what about us?"

"For the last time Ivan...I never murdered your King..."

"Our king..."

"Silence!" Tristan looked to Jensen, but the words did not leave his mouth. Instead, it was Jacques who spoke. "I grow tired of your incessant need for control."

"And who gives you the right to silence me. I am the head of the Royal Council devote only to the King of Az Lagní..."

"Precisely that."

All eyes were now on Jacques as whispers echoes around the room. A mocking smile stretched across Ivan's face.

"Do not mock me boy!" Ivan remarked.

"Yet he speaks the truth," Theorryn spoke now. "As you quite rightly said earlier, I took charge of the young Prince after he was cast out by his father. Both I and Daniel tried to convince the King to take the child back but he refused. I mean how could a mere thirteen-year-old be capable of poison? After the statement was released claiming Jacques to be dead, I brought the boy here to be raised by my brother."

"What is this? A drunken delusion or something Theorryn..."

"My brother speaks the truth!" Jensen rose to his feet and stepped forward towards Ivan. "Young Jacques here was in my care from the age of thirteen. When he was eighteen, he was assumed to the Keeperhood as was his destiny."

Ivan looked to Jacques again, a look of disbelief shaking the mockery. Jacques reached deep into his cloak and pulled out a chain from round his neck. The chain had a ring strung onto it which he chucked towards Hamish as he pulled it free. The councilmen bent over to pick it up, his lips parting in shock as he lay eyes on the bronze ring there.

"The Imperial Seal!" he gasped, dropping to his knees and bowing before his king. Jacques' face turned grave and Ivan's aghast. The other members of the Az Lagní court in the room followed suit of Hamish, many of the others bowing their heads in respect to the newfound king. Tristan noted the look on his brother's face – never in his years did he think his life would lead him here, especially after the wrongs his father dealt to him. He didn't even want his birth right in the end.

"Please, it is unnecessary to bow," Jacques' voice was hoarse and croaked. "All of you will rise." His people did as was commanded. "Daniel;" The accused looked up at his king from his knelt position on the floor, his eyes fearful like a rodent being held down by its predator. "I hereby pardon you!"

"What!" Ivan blurted as Hamish stepped forward to help Daniel to his feet, a look of sheer disbelief painted on his face.

"The advisor I remember was more or less shunned every time he offered my father council. My father's decision to cast me out was entirely his own and I'm sure that much has always been clear. You and Isiah just wanted a scapegoat."

"I…"

"I refuse to hear any more of your lies Ivan. Theorryn has very kindly filled me in on that entire meeting after my father died."

"The man was probably too drunk to remember it clearly…"

"Hamish, tell me do you believe that Daniel was the voice behind me being cast out…let alone the claims I had died?"

"No my liege!" Hamish replied, avoiding eye contact with the Head of the Council.

"Other members of my esteemed council; would the Daniel you know be capable of such…manipulation?" His council members shook their heads, an agreement with Hamish on their lips. Ivan had been ruling this council with fear for far too long it seemed. "Then I guess we have our answer, the pardon stands. My Lord, do you have a spare apartment where Daniel might stay for a time?"

"Of course," Jensen motioned for Jorgen. "Set up a room for him Jorgen, it is the least we can do.

"This is preposterous!" Ivan threw his arms into the air in retort.

"I'm not finished with you yet Ivan. Tristan!" All eyes now lay on the Bearer of Secrets as the King of Az Lagní nodded to him. Tristan looked to his brother, knowing what he must do, it was clear his brother saw the glint of red too.

"Part of being a Bearer of Secrets is being able to see traitors for who they are," Tristan explained. "There's a tell-tale red glint in the eyes, something if I am not mistaken, I see in yours Ivan."

"This is…this is crazy…" Ivan laughed to himself, his eyes darting around the room for someone to support him.

"I've seen it too!" Daniel stuttered, not making eye contact with the supposed traitor.

"You're not seriously going to believe *these* two, are you? My king?"

"Then perhaps you will do us the kindness of removing your gloves. If you have nothing to hide, then perhaps you will do us the courtesy?"

Ivan's eyes widened but he didn't move to remove the gloves. His eyes darted around the room, looking for an escape it seemed. It perplexed Tristan as to why he didn't just portal himself – but then if he was marked it meant his glyphs were tarnished. The magic was unpredictable to him, his own balance in jeopardy. Jacques inclined his head, two guards stepping toward Ivan. Almost as though he knew his demise was close, he made a break for the gap in the guards only to run into Theoden who seized him immediately. Jorgen stepped forward and removed Ivan's gloves, revealing that traitorous mark on his right palm.

"Take him to the dungeons!" Jensen ordered as his hands were bound, Ivan's face solemn.

"Wait," Jacques called. "Do you have anything to say for yourself Ivan?" The traitor sniggered.

"Cry Brethren cry, for the Betrayer has cometh!" Keepers all around the room gasped, but it was Daniel who looked the most fearful now. "The coming of the Third Dawn shall be seen upon the land as the opening of the Unwritten Times. The Order of the Glyphs shall be touched by the Ancients and the Wretched, and the words of the Glyphs shall unwind. Our hands will be crippled and we will perish as fools whilst the Wretched One unveils the Bleak Unwritten. Then we will know the face of our Destroyer."

Tristan noted the looks on the faces of the Keepers around the room, some filled with fear and others scared from their own memories of this ancient prophecy.

"This is impossible!" Nielson murmured, his eyes darting between Ivan and Daniel.

"That was the prophecy Elan wrote...the one that haunted him so," A tear slipped down Daniel's pale face. "I am sure of it!"

"Me and my brothers scribed the same prophecy as novices." Theorryn explained, Theoden and Jensen nodding in agreement, a look of confusion shared between them all.

"This cannot be...that prophecy was the last words spoken by the Interpreter before the Faders engulfed us all. What does it mean?" Basso retorted, recalling the fall of the Compound at Dilu.

"Not only that...it was Caduca's final prophecy!" Tristan added, unsure where the words had come from.

"A misinterpretation perhaps!" Merlin spoke now, his voice just as grave as his brothers. "Boys not much is known about what happened to Interpreter Caduca. What do you remember?"

The brothers turned to Tristan, not as an expectation but more a test to see what he remembered. He gulped, not making eye contact with them, instead focused on the ground like he was trying to concentrate.

The room grew smaller and shadowy, a cobble stoned floor enveloping the masonry of the ballroom. The windows became short and darkened by the nights sky overhead in the skylight. The walls of the room were covered in books and even more were piled up around the room. He got the impression not all of them belonged there, like Caduca was researching something. He glanced into the centre of the room where there was a table...encased in stone...just like the haggard woman that sat there over a book.

He took a few steps towards the table, glancing up at the woman to be sure she was stone. What kind of glyph was this...to do such damage? He didn't even know how one might do this.

"It's Caduca...she's turned to stone!" a voice said around him although he didn't see the owner. The only part he could focus on was the table with the woman sat at it. "How would you even do something like this?"

"Is she reading something?"

"Why are you asking me?"

Tristan couldn't tell who the voices belonged to, they sounded so echoey...like the memory was just out of reach.

"You're closest...have a look!"

"Un-bloody-believable!"

The stone woman was now eye level with Tristan, as though he were the unwitting volunteer. He couldn't make out much thanks to the stone, but it was clear she was reading something. Lifting his palm he lit the candle that sat by her, noticing the shadow left on the stone by the indented words.

"Cry brethren cry, for the betrayer hath cometh..."

"To me that sounds like a curse," Merlin deduced. "You remember how we must seek to maintain the balance – it sounds to me like we failed in the misinterpretation of this prophecy."

"But something like that...encased in stone...what if someone did that to her?" Nielson asked. "You will remember when Dharsi first came to power they turned the Scriberium at Telnar to stone as a message to us of their united power."

"Research would be the obvious answer here...but..."

"The Elder's Library!" Tristan uttered. "The books there are untouched by the curse. There has to be something there..."

"How do you boys know..." Hamish started. "Never mind actually! Can we still gain access to it from the compound here?"

"It's worth a try." Nielson instructed. "We also need to figure out Elan's last moments…same for Caduca. Perhaps both of them had their own theories about this prophecy and we need to chase that."

"We also need to locate my brother's diary." Daniel piped up. "It was lost after his disappearance…I never found it but if he knew anything about it, it would be written in there."

"Then it's settled." Nielson instructed, looking to his brethren. "Boys you will consult with Hamish in the library." They nodded. "Then once Daniel has rested, we begin the search for Elan's diary. Does anyone have anything they would like to add before we adjourn?" No one spoke or made to.

"Nessy?" Jensen stood, addressing the handmaiden that was waiting patiently next to Jorgen. "Fetch us all a late breakfast, our search will need nourishment." She bowed her head and disappeared from the room.

CHAPTER 11 – BROTHERS ONCE MORE

Deciding he wasn't hungry; Tristan chose not to join the rest of the room in the dining hall. Instead, he went to see Dante where a healer was changing his bandages while he slept, more peacefully than had previously. A wash of colour had filled his face, and by the looks of it his wounds were healing nicely. The healer quickly finished her work before bowing her head to Tristan and leaving the room. Taking a seat next to Dante, he sighed heavily.

"Man I really wish you could help me out," he spoke to Dante as though he expected an answer. "Keepers are in a right mess. Heck, everything is a mess."

"I thought I'd find you in here."

Jumping up; Tristan turned to see Merlin in the doorway, calming as he realised and sitting back in his chair. Merlin came and sat next to him, perching on the bed behind.

"I noticed you didn't join us for breakfast," Merlin said patiently. "So I came looking for you. When you weren't with Evelyn, it was easy to deduce where to look next." Tristan said nothing. "A problem shared is a problem halved." Tristan still said nothing, he didn't even look at the old man.

The door opened again and Basso walked in with Cedric, his nose still bloodied.

"You know you could just heal it for me." Cedric said, the healer followed them in and sat Cedric down on a bed at the opposite end of the infirmary closest to the door. She began collecting rags and some fresh water.

"But then what would you learn?" Basso replied. It seemed neither of them had noticed Tristan and Merlin sat at the back of the room.

"Are you saying I deserved this?"

"Yes, I am, you should never have kept Evelyn away."

The healer cleared her throat and glanced over towards them, Basso following her line of sight.

"He could've at least been grateful I took care of her…"

Whatever else he was going to say was overtaken by an outcry of pain, making Tristan smirk. Merlin glowered at him, the ends of his mouth curling upwards. He might've agreed with Tristan's rage but not his satisfaction of it. He stood, leaning close to the young Keeper.

"Do me a favour and be the bigger person for once."

Nodding to Basso who followed his lead, they left the room. Tristan looked back through the corner of his eye at the healer as she finished tending to Cedric's broken nose.

"Right, that should do it!" The healer exclaimed, placing bloody cloths into an empty washbowl. "Make sure you take it easy and no strenuous activity."

"So I take it no nose diving off the waterfall anytime soon?" Cedric joked, making Tristan crack a smile. He forgot how they shared the same humour. Unfortunately, the Healer did not share their sentiment.

"Luckily the break isn't major so the bones will heal easily. Just be careful of stretching the skin on your nose…"

"I'll be sure to keep me emotions intact."

The healer sighed heavily, grabbing up the bowl and leaving the room. Tristan looked back down at Dante, his eyelids flickering in his sleep as though he were dreaming.

"Alright I'll do it!" Tristan sighed under his breath to his lifeless friend. Turning, he took a few steps towards his brother. As they caught each other's eyes, neither said anything. They just stared.

"You know all things considered, that was a pretty good punch." Cedric joked in an attempt to break the ice as the silence passed from awkward to uncomfortable.

"Should I take that as a compliment?" Tristan gave in all too easy maybe. But given their past and connection it would've been foolish to not at least give him a chance.

"Oh absolutely!" Cedric was silent for a moment. "You know whilst we're setting the record straight, I honestly am sorry for keeping Evelyn from you for so long. I honestly thought I was doing the right thing by both of you…"

"How?" Tristan couldn't help himself but interrupt, scorning as he slumped onto the cot opposite where his brother was sat.

"I thought I was keeping both of you safe. Someone went through a lot of trouble to make it look like she, Myrina and her father were dead in that fire."

"Wait that wasn't you?"

"No! I think it was Dharsi in an attempt to further get to you. To try and make sure there was no way of you remembering anything. I think Hagen must've decided it wasn't worth it though because he was the one who warned me what they had planned enabling me to get Evie out. He helped me to create the illusion they died anyway."

"Wait, you trusted him?"

"End of the day I had nothing to lose. He came to me in confidence and when I saw him get Myrina out I simply followed suit. It seemed to be a mutual agreement to create the illusion. Unfortunately, I was too late to save Myrina's father as well, otherwise I would have."

"But why three whole years? What happened to make her come to my father?"

"It was an accident, she got away but I got to her after Theorryn. As much as I could've disguised myself and taken her back, something in him knew who she was. I'm not sure how. I figured it was something telling me it was time you know."

"And in Az Lagní...how did she come to be there in that cemetery?"

"That truth requires some more context. Tristan...Dagnen is alive!"

Tristan gasped; he had suspected it ever since he saw her effigy in the cemetery when he first saw Evelyn. But that's all he thought was; the desperate hopes of a man in mourning.

"Well not exactly...but close enough..." Cedric stammered, bringing Tristan's mind back into reality.

"I don't understand..."

"I'm not sure I do either, not fully anyway. You remember when I told you about my powers and how unique they are to me?"

Tristan nodded. Cedric was one of the most incredible Keepers he had ever encountered, or even heard of. Born as a Keeper and abandoned by his own mother at the door of their Compound in Dilu, he was taken under Basso's wing. Without training, Cedric was able to manipulate the most complex of all the glyphs - glyphs that controlled the way the world worked. That was dangerous magic indeed! They soon learnt that his power was that of Unbinding, some of the most unpredictable magic in the books and therefore forbidden for study. Not that they knew at the time that there were Keepers born with the glyphs imbedded into their veins.

"Well it turns out; Hugo actually knows rather a lot about who and what I am." Cedric continued. "When the Keepers faded and we were all that was left I began losing control, losing my grip on the glyphs I possessed." Staring down at his arm, Tristan followed his gaze, watching in awe as the power rippled beneath his skin. "Anyway, to cut a long story short, he found accounts of another Keeper who possessed this kind of power being tortured by the sixth generation of Unity. He was never named but it made me realise how much of an asset someone like me could be to say Dharsi if only they knew. That's why I fled here; it's why I've tried to remain underground as much as possible."

"How did Hugo find out? As far as I was aware it was just us and Trevor that knew?" Tristan asked, not even fully aware of where the question had come from or who Trevor was. Trying to dodge around his own confusion he looked away from Cedric.

"Tristan, you don't have to hide your confusion from me. I'm the very reason you are this way in the first place. That photo I left you;" Tristan looked back at his brother. "I imbued with the glyph of awakening. You see Hugo figured out that whoever bought on your state of mind must possess at least a similar level of power to mine. So, the only way to at least start to undo it was to unbind you."

Noting the look on his brother's face, he took Tristan's left arm in his hand, using his other to trace lines upon his wrist. Beneath the mark of the Bearer of Secrets appeared another Tristan knew to be the glyph of unbinding.

"Whoever vanquished your memory...it was like they bound your memories in your head basically making it impossible for you to access them. It's why no amount of sense memory would help you. I put that glyph onto that picture, so that when you touched it the glyph would transfer itself to you...like a key to a locked box. Dante appearing and showing that glyph already awakened the old Tristan within you but it was struggling to take full control. The glyph on the picture was the final part of the puzzle, but it's like it's still struggling. I think it's because of the person who did this to you. Perhaps he is linked with the magic in some way and therefore it can only fully be broken with his death."

"That Hugo is a useful ally it seems." Tristan pulled his arm back from Cedric.

"How he finds his methods I'll never know but he does make up for not having Trevor around. Anyway, back to Dagnen! It would appear that when you destroyed the Eye of the Storm is took any soul lingering with it to the Land of the Faded. You may or may not remember that the Eye was made as a sentient to bind a person within, thus trapping them. When you united him with his sentient place it was working to release him from his bounds to the diamond, but by destroying it..."

"I sent him to the Land of the Faded…"

"Exactly, and he took Dagnen's spirit with him almost like it was in a half-arsed attempt to stay tethered to this world. The first night we spent in Lakshid I went into Evie's room to check on her to see a spirit watching her. As I opened the door she turned and it was her Tristan. But no sooner had I seen her had she faded again. Wherever she is…was…she was among the Greater Faded meaning I could bring her back…or as I discovered anyway when I later told Hugo what I saw."

"So were you able to? Where is she?"

"Don't get ahead of yourself Tristan she's not here anymore. I don't know where she is now. The last time I saw her, we quarrelled. She was getting impatient with waiting for me to tell her when she could reunite with you. I bought her back to help with Evie, so I wasn't exactly truthful with her as to the extent of your condition. Particularly as I didn't understand completely what had been done to you. She vanished that night with Evelyn in toe and I knew she had to have gone to find you so we came to Az Lagní. My only comprehension of what happened is that perhaps she saw you with Jenni. It's the only thing powerful enough to send her back."

"It was you that day wasn't it…talking to Jenni?"

"When you first went back to Az Lagní I met with her to warn her off. I'm guessing she had other ideas and when I saw they were suddenly falling apart I couldn't resist saying I told you so."

"And Dante?"

"He appeared the same night Dagnen disappeared. As much as I didn't tell him the whole truth either, I knew that potentially he could sway you in the right direction. Particularly as you and he share a lot in common. I told him I thought you were the reason he had been gifted a second chance…and no it wasn't in an effort to manipulate him…I truly believe that was his purpose. It's the only explanation."

The brothers were quiet for a time. There was a lot to sink in after this heart to heart. Dante struggled in his sleep behind them, causing Tristan to look back and check.

"Does Nielson know who he is?" Cedric asked.

"Unfortunately, I had no choice but to deprive Dante of telling him himself when he was imprisoned by Hagen." Tristan explained. "It was the only way I could get Nielson to realise how bad it was if Dharsi had him."

"I'm sure he'll forgive you."

"If he ever wakes up. The thing is I'm not even sure Nielson has been in here much to see him, let alone let himself think about the fact that his brother is back from the shadows."

Cedric clapped his brother on the shoulder as he rose from the cot. Tristan took hold of his free hand, the two reunited as brothers once more.

~~~

Opening my eyes made no difference, the black skies were all around me shielding everything from my sight. Looking around I knew I was back in this home I loathed. I couldn't believe that after everything I had done the fates had punished me by sending me back to a world that craved my light. Something didn't feel right though, not this time - I mean less right than usual anyway. It was like this world of darkness was broken if that was even possible.

Then something flashed - lightning tinting the sky all around. It startled me; I had never seen lightning in these parts. The flashes were bright and fierce and as they got closer to where I stood rooted to the spot, I stared into them. Time was burning within them, my time in this crumbling world was burning. Just then I felt someone watching me; had the Faders found me once more? I looked around through the corner of me eye and a black cloak stood behind me. But it was not a Fader, it was the seer...even in this world, like a startling sign my fate had found me. I was meant to be back but why I did not know - my mission was not yet over. A scream pierced the night and I was deafened by the sound of it, forced to the floor to yell out in unison with it. The scream turned to a shout calling out my name. There was malice in it, a curse willing me to get what I deserved - the lives of those wanting to keep me here, trapped forever in this world of darkness.

Opening my eyes again, I found myself deserted once more. I recognised it to be that Hill where I had first encountered those lightning orbs of my brother's memories. In their places were wooden chests now, the dark wood of which was rotting with age. Curious, I approached the one closest to me and heaved it open, wincing at the creaking it made upon doing so. Unexpectedly so the chest was empty, nothing on the interior save for cobwebs and dust. Feeling curious, he felt compelled to check the others, finding them all empty. Could it be because you had remembered everything - then again if that were so why were so many of us still here?

Something prickled on the back of my neck, drawing my attention away from the chests and to the ash that now fell from the sky like snow. The sight amazed me - never had I seen anything like this here. Could it have been linked to the lightning that still shook the sky?

Was this world breaking before our very eyes? My gaze followed the ash downwards to see the seer standing just feet away from me, his dark eyes fixated upon me. The ground began to shake and cave in between where we were standing and I saw a smile pinch his lips as I was too slow to escape. I couldn't work out though the intention behind the smile. His allegiances were unclear it would seem. Maybe he wasn't even the seer after all.

As I fell, visions passed before me and I saw your memories dear brother. I saw every loss and every lie you ever told. I saw all the truths which the lies the replaced, the truth which you would always deny. I saw each of your regrets and every goodbye you ever said, each one a mistake too great to hide. One last time, that voice found me and it was all I heard, cursing me to get what I deserved. But if anything, it did some good. It proved that I was wrong about the pain I caused to you - in truth you bought it upon yourself by keeping all of those secrets from us; your brothers. That voice washed my memory and my conscious clean, causing floods to fill the distance between my eyes, connecting the space between them as they closed over once more.

Opening them, I stood before a great shattering glass wall. Many stood either side of me, their faces cloaked in darkness but I knew I had nothing to fear from them for they were just like me - faded and past remembering. We all stared at the wall which looked out onto a world of colour, a world of light. This wall formed the new divide between our worlds which was breaking before our very eyes. I was right! The lightning, the ash - this world was dying and that meant that our time here would soon be over. This was bout more than you remembering brother. What was happening to this land was way more than any of us could comprehend.

But I was unafraid! Even as I stood amongst those who would do our world of Light wrong. Soon we would be free to walk the world of light once more, we would walk across this new divide into the world of colour and light and live among you once more. Fate was coming! Light was coming for us all...

CHAPTER 12 – AWAKENING

Everything felt like such an effort - even opening his eyes, Dante found difficult to do. But as he heard a certain voice in the background, he seemed to find it easier; like some form of inner strength had just awakened within him. Flecks of colour began to merge into one forming a wooden ceiling above him and white clad walls to either side of him. There were freshly made beds up against the walls, his seeming to be the only one that was occupied. The bed wasn't overly comfortable but it would do; it certainly beat the floor or those hay laid beds they had in Dilu.

He looked over in the direction of the voices to see Tristan sat next to another man. The next thing he became aware of was his bare scarred torso, a large tarnished white bandage stretched across his midriff where he felt his ribs click as he straightened up. The rustling sound that ensued caused Tristan and the other man to look over, smiles beaming brightly on their faces. The stranger nodded to Tristan as he uttered something and left the room. Dante felt as though he recognised him but couldn't place his face.

"Dante!" Tristan exclaimed as he came to stand by his brother's cot.

"In the flesh," Dante croaked, his bruised jaw creaking as it moved to sound words. "Just a little battered along the way. What have I missed?" Dante hoisted himself into a seated position, wincing at the discomfort his wounds caused him.

"Trust me, that can all wait. How do you feel?"

"A little stiff...okay a lot stiff but I'll get there, I'm sure. How is everyone else?"

"They look a damn sight better than you that's for sure."

"Cheeky git!" The two shared a laugh, it was good to have him awake. "So, where are we? I get the feeling we're not in Dilu anymore."

"We're in Landen Palace. My uncle is the King here."

"Well you kept that one quiet, didn't you?"

"I've not really seen him much since I was a kid. He and my father didn't always see eye to eye." Dante nodded knowingly. "What do you remember? About what happened to you I mean."

Dante looked away from Tristan as though flashes of it were coming back to him now. It would be painful for him to recount not just his torture, but the sight of his dead brother Felix.

"I found my way to the dungeons with Boris' map. I had to see him," a tear slipped from his eyes, staining his taunt skin. "The moment we arrived in Dilu, it was like I could sense him, but every day the sensation got weaker – he got weaker. I had to see him alive! He's my brother…"

Tristan dreaded to think what they did to not just Felix but Dante too, particularly someone of Hagen's standing.

"We gave him a proper burial, one worthy of a great First Keeper. And Hagen is dead, justice is served."

"I'd have been the one to do it if I had the chance. Wait, I thought you told me your brother named him?"

"I never said I killed him."

"I don't understand."

"I don't either. All I know is that when I burst into that room to help Myrina he was already dying. Someone had stabbed him in the back. Like I said, I don't understand it…but I know what I saw."

"Can't imagine what you must be feeling seeing that. Don't make sense to me, let alone you."

"So how is it Hagen got to you?"

"Someone knew I was there, someone had to have tipped them off because I was so careful. I tried to get out the only way I knew how. I haven't used that sort of magic in years but I didn't think that would matter. But I just couldn't, I don't know why. Each time I tried, I would end up a few feet away from where I began…battered and weakened each time…like I couldn't follow the glyph through…"

"It had nothing to do with you or your power Dante. The estate was warded against magic."

"And there was me thinking that was a myth told to young Keepers to stop them using magic before they were ready."

"Well you wouldn't be wrong!" A new voice said and both of them looked around to see Nielson stood a few feet away. How long he had been stood there they did not know, but it couldn't have been long. Dante could feel his fear building up within him, making him freeze, his eyes locked on his long-lost brother. Tristan looked back to Dante; his face full of guilt with a touch of regret in those clear blue eyes.

"Do not be afraid Dante," he said reassuringly as Dante's eyes widened at the mention of his true name in front of a man he did not yet want knowing. "He knows."

"What?" The fear grew. If Nielson knew then who else did? Already too many did and he could not go back to the darkness no matter how great his sins were.

"I had no choice. I had to find you, I had to get you out of the estate. I needed his help and the only way I was going to get it was by telling him the truth. I'm sorry I took that away from you." Dante took a deep breath and Tristan placed a reassuring hand on his shaking shoulder. "I'll give you some time to talk."

Tristan smiled briefly and left the room, Nielson clapping him on the shoulder as he passed. A short silence ensued, one which Dante wished he would not be the first to end. What would he even say to him? It had been centuries since they had spoken as brothers and even that wasn't on the friendliest of terms. His eyes followed his estranged brother as he took the seat Tristan had leant on moments before.

"I don't really know what to say if I'm honest," Nielson finally said speaking truthfully. "I mean it's been centuries...but I guess I'll start with I'm...I'm sorry."

Sorry? If anyone should be saying sorry it was not Nielson.

"Regardless of what you've done," Nielson continued as Dante remained silent. "Regardless of what I may or may not have said to you all those years ago. You are my brother...and I am sorry."

Tears streamed from Nielson's eyes, as did Dante's. He reached forward and clasped a hand on his brother's knee tightly - fearing at any moment that he might disappear. His brother took hold of his hand and held it to his chest. *Please, don't let this be a dream!*

Once the moment had passed, the brothers reminisced on times gone by; choosing not to talk about the last time they had seen each other. Now was a time for remembering the happy times over the bad. All those words that both regretted saying - what was the point in saying them all again.

"Has Merlin told you much about what you left behind?" Nielson asked after the remembering was over.

"I think he told me everything," Dante recounted what Merlin had said that night in Balderick's house, even the part about Tristan being his son-in-law.

"Does Tristan know that part?"

"Well he hasn't heard it from me but I'm sure he does. He knows you're my brother and he remembers that Dagnen is your niece."

"Then I'm assuming you also know about his daughter." Dante nodded. "He found her you know; she was here in this palace."

"What?" Dante exclaimed in disbelief.

"Theorryn found her playing with his niece the other day. He knew the moment he looked at her who she was. Cedric turned up this morning and let's just say he had plenty to say for his actions."

Nielson went on to tell him about the council meeting and everything they had discovered recently. Dante listened intently the whole way through, marvelling about how he was now the brother of a First Keeper. Now he could never be afraid of what might happen if the Keepers found out he was back because his brother would protect him no matter what.

"You have nothing to fear brother," Nielson said after he had finished. "No one will doubt your loyalty to Tristan and that will be considered your redemption. I will make sure of it!"

"Thank you." Were the only words Dante could muster, humbled by his brothers new found loyalty to him. Of course, that loyalty was always there in part but for a while it was just masked by his reaction to the atrocities Dante committed.

The sound of the door shutting echoed through the room and the brother's looked back to see a healer stood in the doorway.

"And so our invalid awakens at last," she said warmly with a smile. "First Keeper if you would permit me some time to check Daxon here over?" *First Keeper*? That was going to take some getting used to, even for Nielson.

"Of course!" Nielson obeyed as he rose, turning to his brother. "I'll come back later okay," he said reluctantly. He'd give anything to talk the night away with his brother. "Maybe I'll bring my boys with me."

"I'd like that." Dante replied, gracious for all he suddenly had in this world.

They smiled to each other and Nielson left the room, looking back before he disappeared out of sight.

CHAPTER 13 – THE CURSE OF THE BLOODROOT

Cambell's Treatise on Curses and Rituals

Contents

I) Pagans

    i.   The Curse of the Bloodroot
    ii.   The Solstice Festivals
    iii. The Tricksters Birth-day
    iv. Shamakra

II) Hammerites

    i.   The Day of St Benedict
    ii.   The Birth of St Edgar
    iii. The Crowning of the Builder

III) Keepers

i.   Initiation
ii.   The Enforcers
iii.   The Faders
iv.   Dharsi
v.   Unity

I.i The Curse of the Bloodroot

The Curse of the Bloodroot has foundations in a Pagan Ritual which is known as the Rise of the Blood Moon. Originally it marked the beginning of the fall when everything begins to die, thus their blood turns the moon red. The ritual was marked by a blood sacrifice of sorts made by a Shaman or Shamaness making an offering of the flesh. Underneath the watchful eye of their Elemental Cocoon, they cut their wrist and let the blood spill. In its place upon the floor would grow a root plant known as the Bloodroot.

In the time of the Pagan King Larkspur the faction became corrupt (see Harper's Treatise on the Pagans) and the festival became more bloody. The fall would begin to mark the death of the blood sacrifice as the new offering to the Bloodroot and magic would be called upon to rise up the spirits from the grave to revel with the 'Manfools'. 'Drinkers me a broth made of Manfools flesh and bes it bring the blood to the moon so we canst takers back what is ours.'

As revellers of Nature, the King based his intent on a hatred for us 'Manfools' for stealing their land and the Hammerites for turning their nature into machine (see Fanhurn's Treatise on the Metal Age). In the end, I believe this is what swayed the Pagans to flock to him and every year the ceremony was performed a spirit would rise who would not sleep again once the moon had gone down. The spirit would reap among us possessing those it liked with nothing to stop it. Tis probably what bought back the return of Olmek himself what with his origin being Pagan (see Raynard's Treatise on Religious and Legendary Figures).

Order was restored under Queen Bess (see Raygar's Treatise on the Restoration of the Pagans) and because of the instability of the ritual, it was outlawed across their nations. However, some of the more reclusive tribes still practised and many rebels took it upon themselves to corrupt the ritual even further. These 'rebels' were usually marked by a symbol on their wrist which was later adopted by Dharsi and were capable of incredibly powerful magic because of their birth as Keeper Light Mage. These individuals have been known to perform the ritual upon their enemies, usually resulting in their unintentional death - the body is supposed to become possessed, an unsuspecting vessel for a spirit to claim. But due to the inexperience of the Pagan Mage, death is what usually occurred to the vessel, that or the spirit's hold over the victim was not as strong as it could be.

~~~

The smell of damp and rotting flesh hung in the air as Tristan and his brothers followed Nielson past the First Keeper's Chambers towards the Council room where Xavier would address them. The brothers did not know why he had summoned them, just that it was a matter of great importance and urgency. The smell unsettled them though, causing Jacques to stop and sniff the air. Tristan stopped too, his left-hand prickling with pain as his mark sunk beneath his skin. He looked towards his brother as the others stopped too, causing Nielson to turn back and usher them along. Jacques looked back towards the door to Xavier's quarters, noticing how rusty the handle seemed to be. Tristan pointed to the floor below it where a red sort of webbing was just visible underneath the doorway.

"Come along boys," Nielson urged. "Xavier won't wait all day."

"Nielson where was Xavier when he asked you to fetch us?" Romeo asked as he too noted the strange appearance of the doorway.

"He was in his chambers. He said he would meet us in the Council chambers so let us be on our way."

"What if he never left his chambers?"

Nielson's expression turned to one of concern as he stepped towards where the brothers surrounded the door and stared at the handle and floor. Reaching forward, Jacques tried the handle, his face squirming as the moistness of the rust met with his skin. It seemed to burn as the damp evaporated immediately leaving behind a sour taste in his mouth.

"Please tell me you have a key for this door?" he asked Nielson who shook his head.

Jacques braced himself and pushed against the door, using whatever strength he could muster to force the door open. Grabbing his shoulder, Ramien urged him to stop and pulled him back. He stood before the door and begun to mutter a glyph over and over again before drawing it in the air and casting it upon the door. No sooner had the glyph touched the wood, the door unhooked from its hinges and fell. The smell grew more powerful now as a red mist seemed to float out across the corridor, fading slowly. The room on the inside was a horrible sight, the red web covered the entire wooden floor and spread up along the walls. Xavier's body lay before the bed in a pool of blood, his face aghast and pale, his mouth still open in shock. His eyes were wide and bloodshot, the pupils small and blown. The sight made the brothers sick and, in the blood, they saw a plant shoot up through the cracks in the wood. It was about knee high with three red petals that opened out with black vines in the centre. They closed in on each other forming an eye like shape.

"Light is a powerful thing," said a voice somewhere in the slowly clearing darkness. "It's not always powerful enough to truly eliminate the darkness though. These are dark times indeed."

They were stood around a funeral pyre, the brothers and the rest of the Keepers. The man who had spoken was Felix and he had been named the new First Keeper in the wake of Xavier's death. Stood beside him were Nielson and Basso. Dagnen whimpered beside Tristan and he put his arm around her shoulders as she rested her head there. He looked around and watched as the men and women raised their heads high and tried desperately to stop their tears from falling. Xavier hadn't been the First Keeper for long but in that time, he had done much for the Keeperhood. For one so promising and young, it was a sad fate to behest.

The crowd cleared to his left as Romeo, Zhaine, Ramien and Jacques walked into the circle carrying Xavier's body on a wooden stretcher. They placed it on the funeral pyre and then came to stand either side of Tristan. Felix held out his hands and addressed the Keepers once more.

"Today, we lay to rest our father Xavier," continued Felix. "He was our First Keeper but more importantly, he was our brother. Now is not the time to talk about how he died...it is time to remember Xavier for the man he was. He was a kind man who could not be flawed in any way. Xavier," his voice grew quieter, but they could still hear his words. "Your final words to me were that we are more corrupt than we could ever imagine, I now understand what you truly meant by that. Xavier, we hardly knew you!"

Basso handed Felix a burning torch and Tristan pulled Dagnen closer towards him as her crying became relentless. He kissed her forehead and stroked her brown locks as Felix lit the pyre before them. Keepers held up their right hands to the sky, Tristan would have joined them if it weren't for the grieving sister needing his comfort. Xavier would have wanted him to protect her no matter what. As his eyes scanned the circle of Keepers all paying their respects to their one superior, he spotted a sneaky smirk upon Charles and Boris' face, Hagen stood behind them looking incredibly uneasy. Their faces unsettled him greatly.

After the wake, he walked Dagnen to her room in the Acolyte quarters. He wasn't supposed to be here but there was no way he was going to let her go on her own. He opened the door and led her over to the bed, lighting some candles as he did so. She sat and stared at the floor, her face pale; like snow. Her green eyes followed the black lines in the wood as her black velvet dress swirled to a stop around her. Tristan knelt in front of her, wiping fresh tears from her face as he did so.

"It will be alright you know," he reassured her. "Xavier is in a better place now. But he will always be with you," he touched her chin and tilted her face up slightly to look at him. "He will always be in your heart, so long as you will live."

He kissed her soft forehead before making his way towards the door. Curfew would be soon, and he was in enough trouble as it was. Out of the corner of his eye, he saw Dagnen rise to her feet.

"Tristan...wait?" her voice was gentle, but it broke briefly as she spoke. "Thank you!"

She hugged him and he pulled her in tightly, making her know he would always be there for her. As she broke away, she kissed him on the cheek and he kissed her delicate hands, leaving the room at once.

Maybe he should've waited to display his brief if not short display of excitement and happiness at her affection as he backed straight into Charles as the door shut. He cleared his throat in an angry manner, asserting control that didn't belong to him. Charles wasn't a tall man; then again, he wasn't a short one either, but his eyes were level with Tristan's yet he still stared down on him.

"And what are you doing down here Scribe?" his voice was assertive where he did not deserve to be so. He was merely just a member of the Keeper Council, nothing important.

"I do have a name you know?" Tristan mocked him. "It's Tristan in case you forgot."

"Don't mock me boy!" his grey eyes turned hard as his eyebrows arched behind his half - moon spectacles.

"Again with the no name thing? What is the matter with you? It is not a sin to say my name..."

"I've had just about enough of you, now answer the question. What are you doing down here, these are not your dorms?"

"I was making sure Dagnen got back to her room safely, which is the least I can say for you."

"I beg your pardon..."

"Don't play stupid with me? I know what you're up to." He leaned in closer so that he could hear him whisper; "I'm onto you...Herasin!"

Charles' face turned solemn as Tristan began to walk away from him. Stopping suddenly, he turned back to face him. His stern face bore a shocked expression, clasping his right hand as though it burnt with a mark of truth. He smirked at him, looking him straight into those callus eyes.

"Oh, and one more thing; I bow down to no-one. You are not my superior...and you never will be!" Tristan's face turned serious again and he walked away, leaving him to stand and watch after him, the shocked expression not leaving his face.

CHAPTER 14 – THE ELDER'S LIBRARY

The following morning, Tristan wondered down to breakfast with his father and Evelyn a few paces ahead with Myrina.

"I wonder if today might be a good time to see if we can find the Elder's Library," Theorryn began saying as they neared the bottom of the grand staircase. "Daniel would have had a decent sleep last night so well rested to help us figure out this mess."

"Perhaps you should handle that," Tristan sighed awkwardly. "You'll be able to handle him better if he's still fragile. He will listen to you with your new council status."

"I still find it hard to believe Jacques elected me head." After breakfast, Jacques had met with his new council and elected Theorryn to take over Ivan's position. He'd asked Hamish to lead as proxy until Jacques could return to Az Lagní. Until then, he was to consult with Iris on every decision to do with the Mountainated City.

"You've come a long way these last few months father." They stopped near the entrance to the doors of the dining hall, Evelyn and Myrina entering ahead. "Mum would be proud of you."

Theorryn smiled to his son, waiting a moment before following Tristan into the dining hall, causing a bubbling from his belly. He recalled the evening in the Lucky Penny last night and how it was filled reminiscing with his brothers for the first time since they were separated three years ago. Heck it was the first time they had met happily in even longer.

Once they had all lined their stomachs with breakfast, Tristan turned to speak with Daniel whom sat opposite him next to his father.

"How did you sleep last night then brother," he addressed warmly.

"It was certainly nice to be back in a bed again," Daniel laughed, beaming.

"We wondered if you might be up for helping us sift through the rubbish in the Keeper Compound so we can try and see what happened to your brother." Theorryn suggested calmly.

"I'm not sure what else I can say if I'm honest."

"That's why I asked for your help. I'm wondering if there will be clues left behind in the wreckage."

"Why? There's nothing left!" Tristan couldn't make out if Daniel was afraid of what they might find or of what they would not.

"No official investigation was ever held into what happened to your brother," Nielson spoke now. "We owe it to him to at least find out what happened to him…not to mention the fact that you deserve the closure after all this time."

Daniel nodded and smiled – comforted. In truth he was grateful for the consideration, he would give anything to gain some closure on what happened to his brother. As much as he was afraid of what they would find, he knew it had to be done.

Later that afternoon at the Compound, Daniel led them through the rubble of the main entrance to the dorms which were mostly intact. The doorway to his own was not easily missed – it had rotted beyond repair and was practically hanging in place. Tristan looked from Daniel to his father.

"These quarters were sealed off in my time here," Theorryn explained. "No one was allowed back here; it was deemed a matter of safety. I suppose they were right; this whole wing was a wreckage even then."

Inside the room were two beds; both of which were broken - the one against the wall covered in a large pool of dried blood on the sheets. How it had survived this long was incredible. The wood below it was also stained in blood and the walls webbed in some dark weed that climbed all around the room. Underneath the bed, just visible, Tristan could make out a dead root of some form. Feeling curious about the similarities between this room and the one now appearing in his mind, he decided to investigate, getting to his knees and reaching for the root. Pulling it out, he stared in wonderment at it as its name rang in his mind. Despite the root being dead, the plant itself was very much alive: the stork a dark raspy feeling green with two red petals that arched around four pollen stems which curved into the shape of an eye.

"What is that?" Daniel asked.

"It's called a Bloodroot," Theorryn explained. "They are symbolic of a curse at play."

"Curse?"

"It was part of a ritual that would bring forth spirits to wreak havoc on our world through possession. It can also be used to draw one's soul from his body and curse them both to be apart. Pagan Shamans used the root to abolish those who sought the power for nefarious needs. Daniel, I'm assuming that was Elan's bed?"

Daniel nodded, lifting his arm and pointing to the left one of two desks against the opposite wall. Both were rotted just like the door. Theorryn nodded and headed in the direction of them. In the centre of the beds was a bookcase, a few books still stacked on the shelves. But they posed nothing useful – the pages all unwritten. Theorryn paced hard up and down the room, having found nothing in either desk, puzzling Tristan and Daniel as they watched.

"What are you doing?" Tristan asked his father eventually.

"Trying to see if there are any lose floorboards. Nothing!" He flapped his arms at his side out of frustration. "You say Elan was a Scribe, right?" Daniel nodded. "Did he have an alcove, like in the Elders Library where he carried out his interpreting?"

"Aye he did and he spent a lot of time there." Daniel spoke now for the first time since they had entered the room. "I will show you."

He led them out of the room and into the lobby. This part of the Compound was derelict but not crumbled like the dorms they had just been in. Adjoining to it was a wide corridor which led to the atrium. On the opposite side of this room was a doorway ascending to some stairs that split in two before joining in one around a circular tower, alighted by a stone Keeper Mage holding a candle. The top most stairs had fallen away towards the observatory, parts of which were scattered among the teaching rooms below. Ahead, the doors hung from their hinges towards the library which Daniel lead them up to. The room was lined with collapsed bookcases and ripped pages scattered across the floor. Desks were scattered around the room – it was a mess.

"Well this makes things difficult!" Daniel exclaimed. "How are we supposed to figure out which is his?"

"That one!" Tristan answered as the others turned to face him.

He was looking at a desk up against the far wall, a glyph scratched into it's top. Not only was it the only upright one in the room, it looked as though it might actually belong where it was. The three of them approached the desk, Tristan's eyes furtively scanning the glyph and the eye it seemed to form…just like the bloodroot's pollen stems.

"I don't understand," Daniel said aghast. "This isn't even Elan's desk…it's in completely the wrong place I am sure…"

Theorryn began pulling out the drawers of the desk, almost panicked as though he were frustrated at their lack of progress. Tristan imagined he too needed answers. He didn't know much about what happened to his father but he knew that prophecy had a lot to answer for in his eyes. Turning up what appeared to be nothing he turned and sighed heavily.

"Whose desk is this?" Tristan asked, something catching his eye. The whole desk was covered in glyphs as though some Scribe had scratched crazy scriptures into its surface. He could make out most of it – it seemed to be a passage repeated over and over;

Cry Brethren cry for the Betrayer hath cometh. A new Age of Darkness is upon us; a Third Dawn under which the Bleak Unwritten will be revealed as the Bearer of Secrets among his Brotherhood of Union. In his wake, the Wretched One will unleash a great Sorrow causing the Son of Unbinding to reveal himself. He will bring about a New Beginning for us all in which Dharsi are no more and in which the Balance we have struck is restored on all sides of the battlefield. For the line between Light and Darkness is getting thinner and only Time will tell which will prevail…then again, perhaps the victory has already been decided…

They all frowned. *Was this the original?* Essentially it was the same prophecy they knew but different…like it was more thorough. The prophecies were never uncertain in themselves though, that is to say unless the Interpreter themself had a clouded vision of the prophecy that was revealing itself, like perhaps the glyph was unclear or the training of the Scribe incomplete. The whole prophecy went against the norm, or was that the warning? Was it always meant to end this way? The darkness…the unknowing – *NO!* The balance had to be restored!

"Daniel whose desk was this?" Tristan asked again, his voice shaky.

"It was Malock's…he was Unity…the man my brother loved…"

Either side of the desk was a bookcase; the left of which had fallen to the ground. The right however was still standing with only one book left upon its shelves. *Curious.* Tristan reached forward for the book, pulling it to the side as though it were a lever. The bookcase moved where it stood, swinging outwards. Theorryn and Daniel looked to Tristan who led the way into The Shrine of Unity.

"What is this place?" Daniel asked bewildered as he starred at the books that encircled the chamber on the other side. Not just the number of books but the fact they had titles marvelled them – they unlike every other book in this entire building, inside every

Compound the Keepers owned were the only ones to still be written. Unity truly was a powerful thing.

Disbanding from the group Tristan began searching the shelves that lined the start of the room, his father watching after him.

"Tristan, what is this place?" Theorryn repeated, a touch of worry in his voice.

"This is the Shrine of Unity." Tristan answered, still searching the books in the shelves. "Around the time of the seventh generation when it became clear that Unity had become traitors, they began recording their actions so as to try and pinpoint when the betrayal happened. It has long been a theory that perhaps their need to betray was in fact a curse that could potentially be stopped, if only they could pinpoint when."

"But wouldn't they be somewhat biased and..."

"That is why Unity did not write them...the ally did." It was almost like Tristan knew what his father was trying to get at. "To this day, they never shared the curse with the Brotherhood and these Annals are bound by Truth, meaning whatever is written within them has to be so. Daniel, I could've sworn you said Elan's was of the ninth generation."

"The forty ninth!" Daniel corrected, his eyes still wondering the room in wonderment.

"That explains why I can't find it here!"

Tristan walked back along the aisle to the centre, making his way to the top shelves where the most recent annals were kept. Theorryn perched himself at one of the desks at the top of the room, his eyes still on his son.

"So I'm assuming not *all* these books are annals?" Theorryn asked.

"No, the ones in this central area are but the rest are books that are better left unstudied. Remnants of the Keepers of Secrets if you like."

"Strange..."

Tristan presumed, pulling out two books and placing them on the desk where Theorryn sat.

"Those books look pretty hefty for a generation that was barely named before they were banished."

"Not only that each is written by someone different. This one by a Fraya."

"Fraya was who died before Elan vanished." Daniel explained. "She stepped forward to try and talk him down. He hesitated but as she took a step towards him, she dropped dead, a knife protruding from her midriff. It was like that action was what enabled Elan to take control again and he faded with her body." They were silent for a time as a sign of respect. "What does her entry say?"

"Well if theory serves me correctly, she may have overseen every generation of Unity except mine. Perhaps these are her observations."

Tristan flicked through towards the end of the book and her final entry.

Today, I did come across a rather interesting reading foretelling the death of one of our own in the wake of an Acolyte's breakdown. Tis not often that any of us read our own deaths but I am fearful of who the prophecies speak of. I am not fearful of who will die for I have lived many a century and to die, for me would be the next great adventure. I am however fearful for a most promising Acolyte who left our ranks due to our own sheer ignorance. I am regretful for the attitudes shown to him and it has made me question my own position here and its effect on the Acolytes who question their place within the Keeperhood. Perhaps if it not mine own death I had read, it is time for me to go; retire from this life I have been leading for so long and take the rest of my years in leisure. I think I would much like that! Yes! It is decided, that is what I shall do. The Glyphs work in mysterious ways and I believe they have shown me what they have to make realise that the end, for me, one way or another is coming...

Tristan gasped solemnly, never had he heard of an Elder who foretold they're own death or the death of one of their own. Heck, never had a prophecy named someone to die. Yes, there had been prophecies telling the deaths of those titled but never personally. It was never clear whom it was aimed at.

Feeling something hard beyond the last page, Tristan pulled a chain of sorts free from the back cover. It was a bronze medallion, the surface of which was stained with blood. Etched into it were a series of lines Tristan recognised as the mark of Saracen; God of Light.

He turned the medallion over in his hands as his fingers passed across something scratched into the back. It looked like it had been made with a fingernail and was almost like a warning to whoever should look upon it next. A shiver shot up his spine as he realised the scratched lines joined together to form a glyph he knew to be Nobility, *why his own mark? Wait a minute! Sondheim was the ally – why would she leave Loyalty's mark on the medallion. Unless the medallion was meant for Nobility and therefore, he be the only one who would know why...but Saracen was Nobility also...did the blood mean something else?*

"What does my brother's book say?" Daniel asked, bringing Tristan back to reality. He reached for the other book, and flicked through the blank pages.

"I'm guessing it has become unwritten in his wake." Tristan presumed. In response, Daniel scrunched up his face and stormed from the Shrine leaving Theorryn and Tristan to stare into the blankness of Elan's pages.

CHAPTER 15 – THROUGH THE EYES OF A TRAITOR

Later that day, Dante's eyes rolled open to see the smiling face of his brother beside him. As he was about to say hello, the door clicked open to reveal Tristan who held a young girl on his hip. He was accompanied by Zhaine and Ramien as well as his father whom Dante had only ever met drunk.

"I would like to formally introduce you to my sons, Ramien and Zhaine." Nielson introduced.

Ramien nodded, shaking hands with his uncle as did Zhaine. The two were definitely feeling rather awkward. It was a lot to take in.

"Dante," Theorryn clapped hands with him, his face filled with appreciation. "Thank you for looking after my son. It is clear he looks up to you and I would have it no other way." Dante nodded to him, his eyes falling on the girl in Tristan's arms.

"Evie," Tristan ushered. "This is your great grandfather." She smiled brightly, waving her hand at him. She may not have spoken but she clearly understood every word her father said.

"Well she certainly gets those locks from my side of the family." Dante joked – they may not have been the right colour but they were close enough. "Those eyes too..."

"Dagnen..." Dante nodded in agreement, thinking of his own Ann Marie.

"So I guess everyone knows who I am then?" Dante said, changing the subject suddenly. In truth, it made him nervous having people know who he really was. He still had a lot to answer for where some people were concerned.

"Actually no!" Nielson spoke. "We think the best course of action for now is to keep it known that you are simply a friend of Tristan's. No one outside of this room...aside from Isolde and Merlin that is knows who you are. At the very least, it will stay that way until you are ready."

Dante nodded silently, thankful. Looking around at everyone stood in the room. For the first time in just under five centuries he was surrounded by his family and that thought bought him peace. He felt a warmth within him as though a new fire was burning, making him want to live for them, want to fight for them no matter the cost. From now onwards, everything he did would be worthwhile so long as they surrounded him.

~~~

Days must've passed and I had finally become tired of this invisible wall that blocked my passage back into your world. I wanted to know what was happening there, I didn't want to be back here. In my fury, I crashed my fists into the invisible barrier, the force leaving cracks in the not so clear surface. I suddenly realised I was staring into the eyes of a man I knew, but it was no welcome face. The face brought me fear and anguish for he was the reason I was here. His treachery had tarnished us all and even after all this time I found myself unable to reveal his identity even to myself. There was something different about him though - an air of mystery surrounding him, making me doubt his true intentions.

I took a few steps back, my heart racing tying to free itself of the fear that gripped it tight. I looked to my brothers but none of them appeared to notice him, like I was the only one seeing him in the cracks. I looked back at me foe, sneering at me as though my demeanour shocked him and suddenly, I was filled with an unquenchable thirst for revenge. He sniggered – could he see me?

Unable to stop myself I ran at him, breaking through the glass and falling into nothingness. His face was all around me as I fell, others forming in the wisps of his mystery; faces of others who had wronged me...my brothers were gone. I closed my eyes and yelled out, wishing them all to stop and as though my prayers were answered I stopped falling. But I didn't land, in fact it was like I wasn't falling at all.

Opening my eyes, I saw nothing around, I was suspended in mid-air. I looked down to see the ground and the sky above turned black as I was turned upright to face a tall tower in the distance. A dark village formed around me, many of the houses charred and damaged. The people that sat in the windows were sad and mournful as though a great tragedy had befallen them all. Turning around to take in my surroundings, a fountain formed at the end of the row of houses, a few flowers scattered around its base. I approached it slowly, picking at a white rose which lay near the top. I felt nothing though as I touched it, after all I was nothing in this world, nothing but a spirit to walk the world of light.

A tear slipped down my cold cheek as a voice crept into existence. The voice called for my name - it was all I heard and yet the voice seemed to be that of my own, but at the same time not quite.

"Why does he always have to be the hero?" The voice sounded exhausted.

I began running towards the source, unable to shake how familiar it sounded. Many of the folk were now peering out the windows and telling the voice to pipe down - not that they were sleeping anyway. But the voice cursed back, they seemed to enrage him further. And then he came into view and I stared at myself. I don't even remember the last time I had seen myself so how I recognised myself I knew not. But I knew it was me...and Cedric.

"Romeo we're never going to find him," He failed to console. "Not if Tristan doesn't want to be found. He's just lost his wife..."

"And we've just lost three brothers to those blasted Faders!" I interrupted.

"Exactly! We are broken so even if we do find him what exactly are we going to do? Burst into the Compound and destroy all of Dharsi. I don't think so somehow."

"I still have to find him Cedric, he's my brother and I swore to my father that I would protect him no matter what."

I had no idea why I was looking for you nor what had happened to the others. It was like I had become so disconnected with myself that like you dear brother, I had forgotten. A shout stung the air and we all looked up to see two figures grappling at the top of Death's Toll.

The tower was so named from days of old when criminals were thrown from the tower into the depths of the sea to meet their maker. Back then, Hasaghar was known as the Sea God's town – they believed the sea was where we came from and therefore there seemed to be the perfect place to return to for judgement to be served.

A shout sounded again and something struck my heart. It was you brother atop that tower, I could feel it and so could the past version of myself. Cedric caught his eye.

"Don't even think about it!" it was a warning. No way the two of them were enough of a match for whatever was ging on up there. They would need backup.

"Romeo!" A woman called my name and my heart felt warmed at the sound of her voice. "What's going on? What's all the noise about?"

And there she was, my beautiful love Myrina. Her presence struck me with a sense of happiness that I hadn't felt in years and still, even now I felt her touch upon my lips. There was a sparkle in her eyes as she looked at the other me with concern.

"Finally, someone who can talk some sense into him!" Cedric exclaimed.

I followed my own gaze; even Myrina's presence wasn't enough to turn my attention. A solemn look overtook and her eyes followed to see the conflict.

"You go!" She ushered, causing Cedric to shake his head in disbelief at what he was hearing. "But promise me one thing? That no matter what, you'll come back to me."

She took his face within her hands and planted a passionate longing kiss on his. I felt it too, and touched my fingers to my lips as though blowing her a kiss back.

"I promise," I watched myself reply half-heartedly as though part of me expected it to end the way it did. It all made sense now, I was watching my own ending.

I guess in a way I had kept my promise to her because I was here now. I wasn't sure how I was or what I was but that didn't matter. No matter what, I would always return to her.

Following my counterpart, we headed for the tower, Cedric choosing to stay behind and comfort Myrina. Now, I stood alone, just me and him; one in the same as we headed towards our combined fate. I let my thoughts take me into a fantasy in which things happened a little differently. We reached the top of the tower with haste and suddenly I was me, we had intertwined and I was reliving my end once again.

That man whose face I had seen before stood over you brother as you lay weakened with grief. Had he wronged you more than physically to render you in such a state? I knew not, but yet you rose to your feet once more only to echo a laugh from our enemy, goading him on further. As he struck his blow, I felt myself jump forward, taking that next blow for you and landing close to the edge of the tower. I rose and he came for me this time, taking me by the collar and throwing me to the other side. As I clambered to my feet, he took aim at you and blasted a beam of light in your direction.

And suddenly everything was in slow motion. I charged towards the bolt of light, taking it for you and toppling over the edge of the tower. Everything stopped as your hand stretched over the edge and grabbed mine tight. You pull me up and together we take down the Betrayer and we face Charles together in the ruined Compound. We return home together to a proud father as he welcomes a healthy granddaughter but sadness still grips at the loss of your love.

But we all know that that's not how things happened. I let myself fall from your grasp and hit the river below, fading into nothingness.

As the water envelopes me now, I think about what it would've been like once more, almost willing it to come true as I felt myself become breathless. I closed my eyes, just wanting the fall to be over as I felt I was falling once again. After a while I became suspended once more and I saw his face again, only clouded in more mystery than before. It was like he was asking me for understanding. He had spent weeks, moths with you now...he was trying for redemption. But after what he had done; how would either of us let that become a reality?

Looking down, I right my posture and countless visions fly past me too fast to figure out their content. Suddenly I feel a burning against my chest and I rip into my tunic to discover the medallion the seer had given me round my neck. Pulling it off, I looked up to see his face watching me, gripping me with fear as I took a few hastened steps backwards. He smirked at me, just as he always did, his eyes focused on the medallion within my hands. The seer was a disguise. What if it belonged to him? I stared at it now, rubbing at the blood that obscured the glyph upon its bronze surface. My eyes stayed focused on him though, my ever-misplaced trust not daring to linger on him. After all, all of this was his fault! If only my fantasy had happened and then he would've been the one to fall from the tower and Charles would not have stood a chance against the both of us. We would've figured out a way to get our brothers back and even her; your love dear brother...we would've done it together...just as we were always meant to. But for now, we remained the broken Brotherhood once more and it was all because of him.

I feel the long-dried blood slip away as I scrubbed and I can gaze upon the glyph, my eyes slipping off of him for one moment. I gasped at the glyph that was there, etched into the surface as though it had been scratched; the eye it seemed to make. Turning it over I noted the mark of Saracen, it's placement here puzzling me.

According to Keeper lore, Saracen was of the First Generation of Unity, alongside our founder Talus himself. In fact he was his brother by blood! He was known as the first ever Prodical and Light Mage, his gifts born unto him. He later became known as a god, bringing light to those in times of darkness. The combining of the mark of the eye with Saracen was curious, misplaced.

I looked up in time to see him jump at me, but not in time to stop him. Instead, I was forced to embrace him as our bodies became one, mine merely a vessel for him to consume. But he wasn't controlling me, and as the blankness before me changed to form a scene I realised he was trying to show me something, and I saw the world through his eyes.

The scene before me changed to a small room and suddenly I had shrunk to the size of a small child. I became aware of a hand touch my shoulder and join to the six other men that stood by a window ahead. A piercing scream struck fear. I looked up at him; I did not know him, but he did bare an uncanny resemblance to the man I had now joined with. He was much older than me, but it could easily have been the current version. Was this his brother?

"This is all Gervais' fault," One of the men by the window skulked forward.

Gervais – I knew that name. He was as much a member of Dharsi as he was the third generation of Unity and he had turned his brothers over to them. But for whatever reason he left out eight names...unknown at the time until what was left of them unveiled themselves some years later.

"Why did he have to rat us out!" I recognised the man to be Boris, and knowing his track record maybe he was the ratter.

"Or maybe it was you!" Apparently, my potential brother shared my thoughts.

"Oh shut Up Murdoch! You know as well as I do his loyalties were always questionable."

"Oh come off it! It could've been any one of us. I mean our very brotherhood is built on betrayal!"

I realised now that what I was looking at were the remains of the brothers of Dharsi. Not too far from Boris stood Hagen and a man I assumed to be the Herasin with a boy at his side, probably no older then fourteen. In the corner were two men with dark skin and eyes as red as blood. Their hair was white and their faces chiselled. I knew one of them was Sarisus and the other Dangur whom we had briefly come into contact with in Hasaghar.

"Besides if it wasn't for Gervais none of us would be here." Murdoch was loyal that much was true.

"We need a plan," Dangur urged. "We need to think of the children." He nodded in my direction and I sensed a connection as he shared his gaze with Murdoch.

"Well they have it easy...the Keepers will take them in thinking nothing of it. I mean his father is the First Keeper for Christ's sake. They don't even have to know we are affiliated." Boris cursed.

"We can use them!" Herasin whispered, Murdoch's eyes on him like a shot. He looked down on me, a worrying look on his face. He probably knew Boris and the Herasin were right but at the same time he wanted to protect him. Stepping towards me, as Dangur knelt in front.

"What do you say my boy, are you loyal to us?" I felt myself nod, a twinkle in the man's red eyes. "That's my boy! All you have to do is go back, with Phillipi. They'll never suspect a thing." I felt myself attempt to retort.

"It won't be forever; we will come back for you when the dust has settled" Murdoch turned me towards him. "We will be together again soon." I looked back to the other man who smiled reassuringly. I couldn't pinpoint how old I was...perhaps about thirteen...maybe the same as the other boy. I was scared yes, but at the same time I didn't want to be treated like a child – I could feel that within myself.

"But what will you do?" I begged.

"Again, they know our faces not, however I cannot say if Gervais will betray us eventually. So perhaps it's best we lay low for now. Once we have an idea of the playing field, we shall regroup."

"What about the Brothers of Union?" Asked Sarisus, his voice full of spite and malice. It was clear he wanted revenge.

"Patience brother," Spoke the Herasin, asserting his control. "I suspect the reason Gervais did not name us goes deeper than brotherhood. He gave over ninety of us...but left eight...us eight." There was something suggestive in his voice and I got the impression perhaps something deeper was at play.

"Speaking of Gervais," Hagen asserted. "What do we do about him?"

"As Sarisus said, we find out the playing field first and then...we make our move."

They looked down at me and once again I felt myself nod. With the plan half decided they took a moments silence to remember their slaughtered brothers and the scene began to slip away from me as the blankness returned. I tried to piece together what I had seen and from what I could gather there was a reason those particular eight brothers were left out by Gervais. Things were a lot more complicated now than I could ever have imagined and I had so many questions. I wondered why he had picked now to show me all this, to bare his scars before us in the hope we would understand. I felt a sense of compassion then for him, like I understood that he was no more than a boy when all this started – he didn't know any better.

I looked up, staring at him again as he looked at me solemnly. He wanted me to understand and I suppose the least I could do was try. Don't ask me why in that moment I chose to let him in...to show him mercy. Just know that sometimes, in order to defeat your enemy – you must first understand them.

CHAPTER 16 – THE PAGAN VILLAGE

The following morning came a knock at the door to Tristan's apartment. It was a rather urgent knock, odd for this time of morning. He opened the door, hoping it was speedily enough to appease the visitor. It wasn't as though he had slept anyway, his dreams were still plagued with patches of his forgotten memories – none of them really very clear at all. He was also worried for Daniel and at a loss for a way to get his dairy to be written once more. Evie on the other hand had slept peacefully beside him the whole night through.

"Morning brother, how goes you?" Zhaine asked, trying to seem casual all of the sudden as the door opened.

"Seriously Zhaine," Tristan sighed confused. "You knocked on my door at this time of the morning to ask me how I was?"

"No actually but I didn't want to blurt it out straight away..."

"Just get to the point. "

"Calm down alright." Tristan shook his head in frustration and Zhaine looked from side to side as though he was checking for people who might be listening in. "Your uncle wants to see us all immediately. He came to me and Ramien personally and said we were only to tell the people he wanted to see."

"Sounds serious. What am I supposed to do with Evie, I can't leave her?"

"I know, that's why I woke Myrina. She'll be along shortly."

"Then I'll be along shortly too."

Zhaine nodded to his brother and departed the corridor back to his own room. Just as his brother had said, Myrina arrived not long after and Tristan bade his goodbyes before heading to the council chambers where his uncle was undoubtedly waiting for them all. Unexpectedly though, Tristan was the first to arrive even before Zhaine. He noted Jensen's grave expression and puzzled over it a while. Not long after, Zhaine, Ramien, Jacques and Cedric entered followed by Theorryn, Merlin, Basso and Nielson. All of them took a seat around the long table in the centre of the room, trying not to sit too far away from where Jenson sat at the head with Théoden at his side.

"Now that we are all here, I have something I would like to tell you." Even Jensen's voice was grave and this worried Tristan as to what he had to say.

"A war has truly begun, and early this morning it claimed its next victims. On the outskirts of my provinces is a Pagan Village. A small number live here, maybe as many as one hundred. About ten Hammerites were there also, helping to restore the settlements that were damaged in the winter. As I am aware, their spring Solstice festival was only a few days away."

"You say that like something has happened to them brother?" Theorryn asked urgently; he could see the distress Jensen was in.

"They are dead, every single one of them."

An echoed gasp filled the room, all of them sharing a fearful look but also as to why this affected any of them.

"I received a report this morning that the village was attacked in the early hours. I do not know who by or the force of which they stood at. I do not even know if any got away as they are still going through the dead."

"This is terrible." Merlin said mournfully, staring down at the gauntlet of coffee in his hands.

"Why are you telling us this?" Tristan blurted, something nagging at his thoughts as though part of him already knew the answer.

"Tristan..." His father warned.

"No father I'm sorry but it needs to be asked, I just don't understand why you're telling us? Unless it involved Union, unless it involves Dharsi."

Theorryn cast his brother-in-law a sceptical look, but that nagging feeling had prompted the question. Something told him there was more to this then some dead Pagans and Hammerites.

"This was left at the village."

Jensen rather viciously pushed a package to Tristan across the table, letting it slide across and fall in his nephew's lap. Silently cursing his uncle's attitude towards him, he unwrapped the cloth sack to reveal a bronze mask with vines engraved all around. The only holes in it were slits made for the eyes above which was a glyph - the sigil of Dharsi. He placed the mask as similar to the like of the Enforcers...but what was it doing with their mark above the eye.

"You know what I would appreciate," Now it was Ramien's turn and his father didn't even try to stop him. He rose to his feet and swept the mask across the table so that it landed with a clang on the floor. "A little less hostility from you." He pointed at Jensen whose demeanour did not change. "I mean I get that these are your people that have been killed and that makes you as their king feel like you've failed them. But we are not in league with Dharsi nor have we personally ever been. We never meant for any of this to happen when the Glyphs chose us. We never wanted the destiny that chose us. So don't presume like we knew what we were doing. Don't think that we are cut from the same cloth as the ones that came before us. Union haven't always betrayed you know!"

"You think your safe from blame then...because you never betrayed?" Jensen spoke with venom. "You started this war against them so you don't think you are in part to blame for all this?"

"Technically, the first generation started the war against them. We got wrapped up in it!"

"Would you like to see what they did? Would you like to see the damage they have caused under your good name?"

"Our name?" Zhaine questioned, looking to Tristan for reassurance. But not even he knew what his uncle was talking about.

Jensen left the room, the Captain of the Guard signalling for them all to follow. Merlin and Theorryn followed, casting the brothers a grave look.

"Uncle," Tristan asked. "Would you mind if we have a moment?"

"Make it quick," Theoden requested. "I can't promise my king will have the same patience."

Tristan nodded to his uncle before turning to Basso and Nielson.

"I can't shake the feeling that I know the relevance the destruction of this village has to us."

"That is because you should know, you all should!" Basso lead, Nielson nodding in accordance. "Ramien, Zhaine and Cedric, you may remember in your learnings on Keeper history a certain curse that befell a village not long after the supposed destruction of Dharsi around the time of the third generation."

"Of course…Vensha!" Cedric blurted, causing a knowing nod from the other two as they too remembered. "The city of Vensha was a home for Keeper families that worked in Hasaghar. After the destruction of Dharsi and the third generation, that village was massacred as the surviving 6 brothers revealed themselves with Gervais back in toe."

"So if this is happening again…" Zhaine began to suspect.

"Then we can assume Dharsi's power is once again rising." Basso finished, looking to Tristan.

"But why our name?" In truth he posed the question to the wrong audience.

"Then I guess we better follow my uncle and see what we can discover." Tristan ordered, the others nodding in agreement as Theoden entered the council room once more to escort them outside the palace.

Two carriages waited outside the palace, the front of which was already full with Theoden taking the last place. The others piled into the second and as the party began to move, silence filled the journey. As they came to a stop about an hour later, the smell of charred flesh and burning wood welcomed them. It made Tristan sick to imagine what they might see, but no matter what he wasn't about to let Jensen blame them for this.

The ground crunched as though a bone had been snapped as the brothers stepped from the carriage, a still smoky sight greeting them. They stood before the Elemental Cocoon of which the Pagans worshipped; three large stones taller than any man, that curved to meet at their points. In the centre of it was a large pyre which had probably only been put out no more than an hour ago. A man was chained to it with vines carved from metal with thorns that cut into his skin. A skull of what looked to be a ram covered his face and his clothes were ragged and worn. Upon the top of his right hand was a fresh cut mark, a glyph Tristan recognised as Union. This man would have led any Pagan ritual taking place. He imagined it was likely whoever had caused this damage set him up like this as an example.

Tristan noted the look his uncle gave his brothers, angering Ramien in particular. He didn't stick around though to see if they retorted as everything suddenly went quiet around him. Out of the corner of his eye, he spied a trail of blood leading off towards the cluster of torn down huts off to the right of the cocoon and decided to follow it. By the raised voices of disagreement that were erupting behind him, he assumed no one had noticed.

As he neared the outermost houses, a fresh smell of charred flesh reached his nose, making him sick to the stomach. Choosing not to look in the houses, he made for the Great Hall in the centre of the encampment where a circle of thick blood surrounded a Hammerite lying dead at the entrance way, his eyes wide open and his chest ripped apart. Whatever had done this was savage and perhaps beyond human. Another Hammerite lay next to him, this one face down with a gold mask gripped in his hand still.

They must've been trying to protect whoever was in the great hall, likely those who could not defend themselves. He gulped, he had to go in for now Tristan felt like he needed more reasons to be angry at Dharsi - a bigger cause than his own selfish endeavours to fight for. Inside were children still standing there, all in the centre of the room, their arms outstretched into the sky and their eyes bloody with tears. Their faces were fearful and their limbs dead but raised all the same. Around the epicentre stood their mother's, chained to the walls of the great hall, their mouths still screaming the names of their beloved as they burnt in the still rotting wood. There is no bravery in any of their still open eyes, fear had chased it away since they have been here. There is only sadness and the knowing that soon they would be with their beloved Trickster goddess.

A tear fell from Tristan's eye as he stood in remorse just staring at the children of all ages who stood there dead with their arms raised as though they were begging their god for mercy. All he wanted was to hold his own child in his arms.

In the midst of them, something caught his eye and from where he was standing, he could see it was a metal mace, blood drenching the point. Curious as to where all the men and young boys were, he passed out of the Great Hall and around it, glancing in the empty huts as he passed them. Up ahead was the graveyard where the Pagans kept their dead, a slightly bigger hut beside it where the Shaman resided. He assumed the shaman to have been the man who had been tied to the Cocoon and his eyes followed the blood trail once more to a series of shallow graves where brothers lay with their faces aghast. They are only young and above them as their headstones were their father's faces tied to wooden crosses their souls and bodies lost without a trace. A glyph had been scarred to their foreheads which matched that of the mark on the priest's arm which was strapped to the Cocoon. This was a message to his generation. As he turned away, he stared out across the huts; burnt beyond repair and the smell of death still lingering in the air.

His eyes wondered back to the Shaman's hut where an old woman knelt, her arms outstretched to the sky as she screamed in despair. The animation of it all told him she probably wasn't really there, just like the screams he had heard in the Great Hall. Upon her head was a headdress, beaded with dark colours. She would have been the town elder, her old haggard body twisted into a kneeling position where she crouched dead.

All of those dead he had seen now seared his mind, fuelling his hatred of Dharsi tenfold. They were a nation now lost in death, hatred for their killers their last impure thought. But still the trail of blood continued down to a cluster of trees with a wooden archway indicating the entrance to the Pagan village. From where he stood, he could see two bodies lying under the archway and he raced for them. Tristan stared in remorse at the corpses that greeted him, the closest to him being a bloodied Pagan boy probably no older than eighteen. But bravery burnt bright in his still open eyes, unlike those of his nation and then Tristan saw why. The body that lay just a few feet away was that of an Enforcer with the same bloodied mace as that had lay in the Circle of children in the great Hall. His mask was missing, and Tristan guessed that had been the mask Jensen had. The face left behind was strained and mangled as though the life was sucked from it. But the open eyes, the were young and so full of woe. Had they not been in control?

"Tristan!" Called a voice from behind him and he turned to see his uncle Theoden approaching him. "I wondered where you'd got to. You shouldn't have wondered off though, not when Dharsi are as large as they are."

"Sorry," Tristan apologised honestly.

"I don't blame you to be honest." Theoden went on. "I wouldn't want to stand around while they argue again anyway. Although your fellow brothers are doing a good job of getting their side across."

"That's Ramien and Zhaine for you."

"For what it's worth, I don't blame you for what's happened. This war didn't start with you, but it will end with you and that is what I have faith in."

"Thank you...I think."

The pair wondered slowly back to the Great Hall, watching the smoke from the charred houses rise to the sky. Pausing there for a moment, the mask that was being grasped by one of the Hammerites caught Tristan's eyes once more and suddenly he became curious of it. Reaching for it, he gazed upon its golden surface, matching that of the one Jensen had thrown at them.

The mask reminded him of those that had littered the memory of his banishment by Charles; the masked hooded figures that had surrounded them as the Enforcers, the same figures that were summoned for Ivan by Nielson, but their masks were different. Surely Dharsi did not have them on their side too. But then the Enforcers were originally traitors anyway, bound to spend an eternity repenting their sins by serving the Keepers. Their minds were easily swayed, and technically they were bound to serve those who called upon them by doing their bidding. That was their curse's flaw, but perhaps it was intentional. The workings of the early Keepers were difficult to gage because so many disagreed with the original Union. There's no telling how many of them may have tried to sabotage its future.

Chapter 17 – The Hammerite Cathedral

By the time Theoden and Tristan returned to the carriages, it seemed that his brothers had grown tired with defending themselves from Jensen. They were simply letting him talk at them about how fated they were to soon betray like their predecessors and occasionally yawning out of boredom. However, this only fuelled him further to the point that his arms were moving in motion with his voice - for added effect most likely. At the sight of Tristan, he stopped and his face was stern; almost as though it were a warning for him not to begin the argument once more. He simply smirked at his uncle and turned to Ramien and Zhaine.

"I'm wondering if it's worth a visit to the Cathedral," Tristan posed to them. "It's clear they were here so perhaps we can get some answers."

"The Cathedral isn't far Lord," Theoden instructed, Jensen casting a look at him. As much as the title was correct, he obviously disagreed with the sentiment. Tristan nodded to his uncle and then turned to his brothers.

"You joining me?"

They all nodded in agreement and they turned to follow Théoden.

"What is your plan boy?" Jenson asked, pulling Tristan by the arm to stop him joining his brothers. Theorryn made to intervene but Nielson stopped him – Tristan and his brothers had to stand their own ground with the King of the forest.

"You wanted us to sort this so let us get on with it" Tristan snapped, his eyes flashing to his father who nodded in approval. It was clear Jensen would not back down the offensive. So it was a case of less words, more action.

Jensen entered his carriage, everyone but the brothers and Theoden following behind. The captain of the guard nodded to the four of them and turned. He explained that the Cathedral was less than a mile away, in fact they could see the steeple just above the trees. Father Federick was the lead there, the name striking a chord with Tristan but his brothers showed no trigger. Perhaps he was mistaken.

Less than half an hour later of walking through trees, they came to a large clearing with the cathedral in the centre, the spires they had seen on the start of their journey now covered by a low cloud. Even at this distance, the smell of charred flesh still lingered in the air but there was something fresh about it that puzzled Tristan. Ramien nudged him where they stood staring at the Cathedral, pointing to several of the stained-glass windows which held cracks and shattered glass within them. His face turned fearful and he looked to Theoden who seemed to have spotted them too, reaching for the sword at his side. He nodded to them and tentatively the four approached the doorway and eased open the oak door slowly to peer at the sight.

"Step no further!" Boomed a voice as the door swung open and ten Hammerites suddenly surrounded them.

Tristan glanced around the room - they had walked straight into the atrium; of which the aisle was bloody with Hammerite bodies littered all about. Some parishioners had been praying near the front but now they knelt dead. Admittedly the massacre wasn't as bad as that of the Pagan Village but it was still a horrible sight to see. The brothers held their hands up as a sign of peace and looked up to the galleries where several others surveying the damage and tending to the wounded. Surprising, it was the number of survivors – had they managed to overpower the might of Dharsi that ripped through the village? Yes, there was a difference in the might of the Hammers and Pagans, but they weren't defenceless.

"Lower your weapons," a voice bought Tristan's attention back to his brothers as a man in red robes approached them. "'Tis Brother Theoden, he shalt not harm us."

The Hammerites lowered their weapons and went back to their duties as Theoden embraced the Hammerite priest. Tristan couldn't help but recognise his face and as he looked to his brothers, he realised they did too. The man's head was bald but he had a beard that stretched the length of his chin before framing his mouth. As the priest stood with his back to them, Tristan noticed the thin ponytail on the back of his head - odd style for a Hammerite priest.

As he noticed it, something flashed in front of Tristan's eyes and his head began to throb, feeling as though it were lead. He dropped to his knees' yelling out as his brothers crowded around him.

The brothers stood before the Hammerite Cathedral in Camto. North of the Mountainated City lay Degstan, a land cloaked in shadow and rot. Long ago, a plague had spread there from a neighbouring land and although Light was returned – parts of the land were forever scarred by shadow. The Cathedral here held what they were looking for; rumour had it the Hammers within were undead – tortured creatures drained of Light and doomed to spend an eternity guarding The Eye of the Storm. The Eye was a crystal the size of a man's fist. It harboured the spirit and magic of one of the most powerful Keepers ever to walk the earth. He and his brother had wrecked devastation on the lands and the third generation had encapsulated them into gemstones having failed to defeat them. The stones themselves were then entrusted to this cathedral and now the brothers stood before it.

The road here had been hard and they were already running out of time. Three full days to get the Eye of the Storm out of this Cathedral and get back to the Compound at Dilu to save all of the Keepers. Because of the shadow still lingering in these lands, they had only been able to port as far as Atventu and Camto was a day's ride there and back, giving them a day theoretically to get the stone before trying to figure out a way to the meeting point Boris had highlighted for them in the mountains on the outside of Dilu. That was the deal they had struck with Sarisus - getting back would be the least of their worries though if they couldn't get the Eye though.

"Any ideas?" Jacques asked his brothers rhetorically.

"I still think we should've disguised ourselves as novices and scoped the place out to give us more of an advantage." Trust Ramien to have answered him in such a manner.

"Would have been a good plan if we had more time maybe but we don't." Zhaine scorned his brother – Tristan couldn't work out if they were being serious or not.

"You do both realise the inside of this cathedral is inhabited by the undead...right?" apparently, neither could Romeo.

"Oh and who's fault is that?" Zhaine answered sarcastically.

"I'm not sure whether you're talking about your lack of knowledge or the fact this place is crawling with the dead."

"I very much doubt he would've given us more time brother." Ramien proceeded the rhetoric. "Tristan says it was a push getting three days out of him. All we have to do is ask to visit the library and from there I'm sure we can sneak around pretty easily."

The pair of them stared at Romeo and Tristan, mocking looks on their faces. Sighing heavily, they turned back to Jacques, but he was already making his way towards the Cathedral doors having spotted two Hammerites standing guard. Realising the lead, he had, they made haste towards the doors with Jacques.

The Cathedral was magnificent, the stained-glass windows giving a riot of colour to the dreary grey world they had entered into since leaving the Compound. The stone work as well marvelled them to the point they wondered how such a building was even built. Then again these were Hammerites and their god was the Builder so build they would. But even still, why should such a pretty house be home to the dead?

"Halt!" One of the Hammerites beckoned as they reached the drawbridge that stretched out towards the Cathedral over a murky moat.

"What business do you have here?" asked the other.

"We simply wish to visit the libraries ..." Ramien posed before Jacques could even say anything. The rest of the brothers rolled their eyes.

The Hammer who called to them took a few paces forward, looking warily to his comrades. He probably thought them a bunch of drunks.

"Be gone with you foolish boys! Take your jokes elsewhere."

A priest in red robes came forward his head bald except for a ponytail at the back. He looked relatively young, no doubt a novice of some sort. But something in his eyes told Tristan he was much older than he looked. He had been stood in between his brothers in arms and the Hammerites nodded to him, signalling their respect. Perhaps he was no novice.

His eyes flashed a look of knowing as he locked eyes with Tristan and he reached for his brothers raised hammers in readiness, forcing them to lower them.

"What is your business here?" he asked calmly, his voice a little shaken.

"We wish to visit the libraries!" Ramien said again, rather pointed causing a look from Jacques. This was more than just a joke.

"Where on earth did you hear that code boy?"

"We are more than boys – we are Keeper Scribes sent here on a mission to retrieve the knowledge which you guard."

"And who spoke of this mission?"

"My brother in arms Pastrocles."

Pastroclus was one of the Elders from the Compound. How could he have known of their mission from Sarisus?

"How do you know that name?" The priest glowered at them; a worrying look cast between the three of them. Trusting Ramien, the others let him proceed with his cryptic words.

"Pastroclus is an Elder within our Compound." Ramien lifted his right hand, bearing the Keeper Port symbol on its front. He did the same with his left, crossing it over and letting his mark of Union shine true, his brothers following suit.

"I shalt not let this happen again..." the Hammer on the left yelled, raising his hammer to strike the brothers down.

"Wait!" The priest braced himself in front of his brother, staring Ramien in the eyes. "That phrase you said, repeat it one last time."

"We simply wish to visit the libraries." This time the five brothers said it in unison, causing white to befall all three faces this time as they realised what it meant.

"Our brother Pastroclus...he is well?"

"Aye and he sends his regards." Ramien continued to speak now. "He sent us on his bequeath...we need the Eye."

"This cathedral was besieged once long ago. The Ruby of Sorrow was taken but we managed to retain The Eye. If you should need it now, then that means...you cannot let him have it!"

"We have no choice." Jacques spoke now, solemnly. "Sarisus has taken the Compound at Dilu. We do not know his plan but he has charged us with retrieving The Eye within three days else he will kill them all."

"Pastroclus knows his plan," Ramien continued. "Before we were taken from the alcoves, he told me the time for darkness had come and that all he could say was to seek the libraries in the land of shadows. I didn't realise what he meant until we came to be here."

There was a moments silence, none of their eyes shifting from each other. The sound of chains dragging across the floor echoed beyond the doors and the sun began to set on the tops of the hills due south. Time was running short already.

"There isn't much time brother." Tristan cautioned. "We must have the Eye."

"You hear it don't you...it speaks to you?" The priest questioned and his brothers looked to Tristan but he said nothing in response. The priest nodded to his brothers and they acted as the five had done moments before, crossing over their fists to show their own marks. But there was something treacherous about them; scars masking their significance as though they had tried to hide their true nature.

"Pastroclus is our brother in more names than one. I trust you realise now who he is and we do indeed stand within the presence of Union. My name is Federick and these are my brothers Jaymes and Merser. We realise now why you wish us forgo our mission, but there are some things you must know first. Come, let us go somewhere he cannot hear us."

Federick's comrades furrowed their brows in confusion as they watched Federick lead the brothers away, Tristan following on slightly behind daring to look back at the doors to the Cathedral where the chains did drag.

"Comes a man to rescue me," the voice in his head echoed. "Comes my kin to reunite with me." He gulped; the voice had been sounding ever since they had arrived in Camto. Did Federick hear it too?

Federick lead them to a quiet grotty bar on the edge of town called The Dark Hallow. Purchasing them a dirty looking wheat beer they sat at a table near the edge of the room trying to be sure no one would hear their conversation. In fairness, there were only a few men here, all of which were sat around the service bar where the barmaids flirted.

"As much as I do not wish to prolong the hour," Jacques started before the priest could even begin to explain himself. "I must ask who you were referring to when you said to come here."

"I'm not sure I'm the right one to tell you that." Taking a sip of his beer, Federick glowered at Tristan. When he said nothing, the priest pursed his lips. "The Eye has been speaking to you, hasn't it?" Tristan looked up at him; fearful. "Curious...the Eye would only speak to its brother...they don't know do they?"

"Tristan, just tell them!" Romeo blurted, a confused look now spreading to the other three. Tristan sighed heavily and placed his left hand on the table palm up. His other he scraped off a scab on his right thumb and tracing the blood that came from it across his palm. Appearing in the centre was the mark of a traitor and at the sight of it, each of his brother's eyes widened but not in a suspicious way. It was more curious, that although they knew it the mark of the traitor, it was strange that it was on the wrong hand.

"Forgive me for perhaps being naïve," Ramien presumed. "It's on the wrong hand so what are you so worried about?"

Tristan let a smile touch his lips, as much as he didn't believe his brothers would jump to conclusions, he had expected a little more hostility from them.

"The mark is symbolic of the Bearer of Secrets. It's not treacherous," Tristan explained. "It does however mean that I kept secrets from you all, the very people I should not."

"The mark actually befalls more than that," Federick interrupted. "The mark means you have seen the face of the Herasin." Now the brothers all looked to Tristan in the look he expected.

"Wait, it's not like that..." Tristan defended. "I would tell you if I could. But just as we are bound to each other not to speak our names...I cannot speak his to you."

"So the Eye speaks to him because he bares this mark?" Romeo asked, less focused on the schematics and more on what it meant for his brother by blood.

"That and he senses nobility, for Storm was Nobility too." They all puzzled at Federick. "The Eye is of his kin; it too is everything you are. Do you boys know the origin story of how the two stones came to be?"

"Wait, there are two Eyes?" Zhaine stammered.

"Apparently not! Consider this a history lesson boys; The Eye of the Storm has a counterpart – The Ruby of Sorrow. Now, a story you boys definitely will not know is that the both of them were Union in their prime. Coincidently, they were the second."

"Wait, I thought the fifth generation were the first to betray..."

"Zhaine how about rather than interrupting, you let the man finish explaining?" Jacques asked, again rhetorically. He truly was the most mature of all his brothers, but then again, he was the eldest.

"As I was saying," Federick continued when the low hum of the bar was all that could be heard. "You boys will know that Saracen was a member of the first ever generation of Union. But I suppose if you really think about what need was there for a second...or a third...or any further generations? I mean the first were supposed to be what bought the Keepers together; their only opposition being Dharsi."

"Wait," They all frowned at Zhaine this time. "How are you able to tell us any of this. I mean I know you too are Union but there should still be bounds...right?"

"That's actually a valid point!" Ramien sided with his brother by blood.

"You see the scarring that covers my marks," Federick showed the brothers his marks once more. "In order to become who we are we stripped ourselves of everything. I am of the fourteenth generation and we enlisted the help of an elite Keeper, one of the most powerful. He was capable of not just removing us of our bounds but, our gifts themselves." Tristan suspected he spoke of someone like Cedric.

"We know such a Keeper, Cedric?" Zhaine hadn't been Cedric's biggest fan back in the day. Cedric had literally found them and made himself their ally and he had always found that suspicious.

"As much as I cannot tell you his name, I can tell you most certainly it wasn't your friend. His name I am bound to keep secret and in all my years I never met another like him. Using his own blood, he stripped us just as I said, removing our name and our magic. We most certainly did not want to be fated to betray...we truly believed we had escaped it. But I fear it is more than just a destiny but a curse. I'll come onto why I believe that in a moment, but you will notice you have only four of my generation. I pray you never meet my fifth brother...another I cannot speak the name of.

"When me and my brothers left the Keeperhood, we came to the Hammerites and chose to recluse ourselves thereafter becoming guardians of relics such as The Eye and the Ruby. You see the Cathedral once housed the both of them.

I don't entirely know where Sorrow and Storm's power came from, or how they came to possess it but they wreaked havoc on all of us. It started with the other factions and the townsfolk, but when they realised their power...they barely left the Keeperhood intact. The Keepers that bound them in stone are those you know to be the Third Generation. You will know the magic as the glyph of Unbinding." Their brows furrowed – what were they teaching young Scribes these days?

"Incredible! The glyph of Unbinding is used to strip a person of their body, unbind the soul from the vessel so that it may be captured into a sentient object. These sentients are linked with places; places of importance to the souls that now inhabit the object. Please tell me you know the rest?" The brothers nodded; they glyph had thrown them but they knew about sentients from a treatise in the Shrine. "Well that's something at least. Now, you say Eye is what Sarisus seeks...that must mean he is in possession of the Ruby."

"Wait, two things!" Ramien stabbed his fingers into the rotting wood table, frustrated. "Number one that was an awful lot of waffling to get us back onto subject...number two you failed to guard the Ruby of Sorrow as is your charge."

"Number one, that wasn't waffling you will understand it all in time. And number two – patience! My fifth brother is the reason we do not have the Ruby. I'm not sure why, but not long after we were charged with our mission there came a troop who wanted the Ruby. You see there is a theory that tells that the brothers were powerful beyond anything we could ever imagine. But their magic is linked, together they are powerful beyond words...and separate...undeterminable. For although they are bound to their objects as you, Tristan, can probably guess – they have a way of manipulating those who seek to possess them. Even now, they have their own agenda. I believe the stones used our brother...and he was all too weak to let them. Like you, he somehow knew the face of the Herasin.

"That is why I bought us here, so that the Eye could not hear why it was required...so that it could not know what was going to happen. You need to keep your mind incredibly guarded dear boy...he cannot know your innermost thoughts. My guess is that Sarisus wishes to use the stones to bring his brothers back from their banishment."

"What makes you say that?" Jacques asked.

"Because they are made of the glyph Unbinding...and to break such a thing you need something of the like. You simply cannot give it to him."

"But we must...he'll kill them all..."

"There must be a way we can fool him though..."

"Surely you should know there is not," Tristan exclaimed at the audacity. "Boris maybe...but there is no way we will be able to fool Sarisus too. And I'm sorry, but I'm not prepared to take the risk if of him not..."

"Tristan is right," Jacques agreed. "There has to be a way...can we destroy the stones?"

Federick began laughing...laughing at them. They didn't seriously think they were capable of such a feat?

"You don't know who we are...do you?" Ramien scoffed. "Not really?"

"You are the same as me; fated to betray…what makes you so different? Why should you be able to do what we could not?"

"Because we are the last ones, the cycle ends with us…"

"You seriously think you are the first to say that? To believe you can break the curse…that you can go against your destiny…"

"It is our destiny…we are the last ones."

"My brother Ramien is right," Jacques explained. "The day we were selected as Union, a book appeared to us. It contained the names of every traitor ever to walk among the Keeperhood…every single last one. At the end of the book was a passage that foretold the treachery would end with the fiftieth generation. Not only would it be the last chance the Keeperhood had to repent its sins, it would be the last hope to strike balance once more. We aren't fated to betray, we are fated to end the cycle. Back then we didn't realise that…not until we realised the first five sets of Annals weren't even written. Could you imagine the things that could've been explained if they'd just started writing it all down from the beginning?"

"Let's get back on topic shall we…we are running out of time!" Tristan ordered, becoming frustrated now. It was about time people stopped underestimating he and his brothers. "Only Union can destroy what Union put there right? We are the last…we have the power…so tell us how to destroy them!"

Federick's eyes flashed as he looked from each of the brothers, his eyes landing on Tristan last. He frowned, like he saw something through his eyes. He nodded – would he help them? It was clear he was thinking about it, but he was torn. There was a lot at stake.

"Alright I'll get you the Eye…but you need to stick together and trust one another. I hope you realise the precipice we stand upon. If prophecy states that our fate lies with you then I must trust it…but I trust you can understand why I am sceptical." The brothers nodded in unison. "Then listen carefully boys!"

CHAPTER 18 – OLD FACES

As Tristan's vision swam back to him, Zhaine's face came into view. His words were echoey as he tried to gage whether or not Tristan was okay. What had felt like hours of returned memories had only in truth been a couple of minutes. And now, having heard everything Federick had said all those years ago, he had more questions than answers. His vision cleared and his senses began to return to him an uneasiness bubbled in his midriff. Looking around, he gained his balance and stood tall.

"I remember you!" Ramien's harsh voice addressed the Hammerite priest. Was there truly any need for such hostility? "You're that priest, from the Cathedral at Camto."

"Well I'll be," Federick replied, staring at them, a smile appearing in gratitude. "You all look very well..." His voice turned solemn.

"This is Cedric, our ally," Jacques explained, noting the confused look on Federick's face as he looked Cedric up and down. He clearly remembered the brothers very well. "Romeo is...no longer among us."

"Well met," Federick bowed his head in Cedric's direction. "I am saddened to hear the latter."

There was silence for a few moments, and Tristan looked around as more faces began to appear in the room. All the men adorned the red robes of Hammer parishioners, silver hammers emblazoned on their toned chests. The robes were hooded, keeping their faces shadowed. Their faces were not recognisable, but something about them struck him – like he was in the presence of brothers.

"What happened here father?" Theoden asked, noting the looks appearing on the brothers' faces as they looked at the Hammers around the room. He too thought it strange so many survived here, they were monks so therefore no mightier than the Pagan force.

"We were attacked, by men without faces and entwining masks." Federick kicked at something by his foot and it span to a stop in front of Tristan who knelt to inspect it. It was the same as the mask he had seen in the hands of the Pagan back at the Village. "A few of our brothers were among the Pagans when they too were attacked by the same foe. We were helping to fortify their dwellings having heard of the threat of Dharsi in Hasaghar. If we know you are here Tristan, they surely do too." Tristan gulped. "One of our brothers did manage to make it back and warn us, but we barely had time to muster our own defence before they were upon us."

"The Pagans are all dead brother Federick, how is it so many of you survived?"

"Have you never wondered why it is your brother always send you here lord? Have you never wondered why he does not come himself?"

Theoden frowned. He didn't understand, but it seemed the penny had dropped for the brothers and a sly smile appeared on Ramien's face.

"Fancy that," he scoffed. "A whole Cathedral filled with not just Hammerites…but Brothers of Union. Now I know why he hates us so!"

"Union?" Theoden was confused that was for sure, but moreover he was stunned that Jensen knew yet he did not.

"You truly are the final generation aren't you," Federick spoke, causing a look of shock to reverberate around the faces of his parishioners. "Apparently out secrets are no longer worth keeping. You've all come a long way since we saw you last."

Tristan looked to his uncle; a look of shock still plastered to his face. He wondered how many more were aware of Union's presence here. Jensen had never been a fan of the Keepers and his hatred of Union was clear but why…were his own people losing faith in him and placing it in Union? Was that why he hated them so? After all, it was the Hammerites helping to fortify the Pagan village, not their King's men.

"How did you come to be here," Tristan asked, curious. "What happened to you after we took the Eye?"

"Well you took away our purpose, there was no need for us there. My Imperial Father did ask me to lead a church here in the forest and I agreed. But your mission inspired me…your hope that you would defy your destinies. It did make me wonder whether there were others like me and my brothers who had sought the sanctuary and unknown the Hammers provided us with. No sooner had I put out the call my brothers did flock here…less than I could have hoped but more than I expected. Confirm for me one thing – it was Dharsi whom did attack us?"

"We believe so yes, or at least their followers." Theoden cleared his throat as he spoke.

"Come, there is something you should all see."

Puzzled, the brothers and Theoden followed Federick as he led them down the aisle towards the head of the cathedral where a podium stood with a pedestal. This is where he would have addressed his brothers and parishioners. As they walked, Tristan looked to his sides, seeing the corpses that had fallen between the stalls. He dreaded to think how they would have been presented had Dharsi finished the massacre. Coupled with the Pagan sanctuary, it would have been a sight that would have scarred him for life; heck it had scarred him - he had never seen such terror still clinging to a dead face.

When they reached the top of the aisle, Federick stopped before a white sheet which seemed to be laid over a body. Kneeling, he pulled it free, revealing a hooded face wearing the mask of the attackers. Pulling free the mask, he backed away as the hood slipped down to unveil a gaunt face which looked beyond human. Its cheeks were sunken, the skin that stretched across the bones almost transparent with harsh black veins drawing lines up from the forehead and across its bald head. Its eyes lay open still, blackness staring up at them as the look remained tortured by those that had possessed him. In those eyes, Tristan saw the face of the one he had seen in the village.

As they stared into the eyes, a pit began to form in Tristan's stomach. Something wasn't quite right here, and as he looked up at his brother's pale faces, he realised they too were unsettled by the face behind the mask.

"You boys sense it too don't you, the presence of a brother. This boy is a Scribe, only…he is no longer…"

"I don't understand…" Tristan said on behalf of his brotherhood.

As he uttered the words a screeching noise struck him and his vision blackened. In the centre of the darkness was a smoking pit and ash fell from the grey clouds above. The dreams he had been having, they were coming back now at the sight of this barely a man before him.

"There is a tear in the wall of the Faded Lands," Federick mumbled. "And spirits are finding it…but they aren't all good and they aren't all intact to a body. There are those who will latch onto those that do so that when they return to our world…they take over. The man you see before you is possessed by an actual brother of Dharsi…the darkness within him is sucking the life out of the Scribe for he was not a strong enough vessel to house such a spirit. It is what twisted his features so. They aren't built for this."

"But how did it open?"

"I think it was me..." Cedric said at last. He had been very quiet since they discovered the body of this Keeper turned Dharsi. "I think I tore the hole when I bought her back."

"For something like this to have happened Cedric there would have to have been a crack there in the first place." Federick went on to explain. "You probably knocked the next domino into place."

"But what could've caused a crack like that?"

"The Faded lands were never designed to hold actual people. It was made to hold spirits; those exiled and in need of containment. The person who cursed Tristan in the first place – that's who I think caused this."

"And how do we stop it?" Tristan asked.

"I don't think we can. I think it was always inevitable. The Faded Land were a manmade world that was barely understood when it was put there...and just like everything manmade, it destroys itself eventually."

There was silence a while. Tristan reached forward and closed the eyes of the Scribe before him. He wondered if it was painful; the possession...if they even knew it was happening or if it just felt like nothing – like you were dead. Perching on the pew behind him, he looked up at the faces still on him, their eyes and how warm they felt. It puzzled him, and he looked to those closer noting that same feeling. It made him think of the words Federick had pondered all those years ago, that Union were cursed.

"So what's the deal with all of Union here now?" Ramien asked, almost like he shared the thought of his brother. "I mean I remember you saying how it felt to want to betray your brothers before, that you couldn't control the impulses you felt and that's why you chose the reclusive life of a Hammer." Federick nodded, his face puzzled and sceptical as to where he was heading with this thought. "Are you all just fighting your impulses together?"

"Funny you should ask that," A hammer behind Ramien scorned. "I've not felt anything for at least three years. It's almost like the urges stopped all of the sudden and I knew who I was again. It's why I came here...why all of us came here."

The Hammer stepped forward and pulled up the sleeve of his left arm to reveal the mark of Nobility. Others showed their palms too, all igniting with the same mark. Tristan rose to his feet, stunned at what he was seeing

"Nobility, you're all Nobility..." Tristan's eyes locking with Federick who nodded. The Hammerite priest looked up and around the room and they all nodded, but by the furrowing of his brow.

"Don't look so confused, you know Storm was Nobility. It is only natural he would speak to those who share his glyph."

The other Hammers in the room began to depart the scene and gathering their dead. As the bodies were placed by a door at the front of the cathedral potentially leading to a courtyard, Tristan counted six dead, not including the parishioners still kneeling in the stalls.

"Is there anything we can do to help brother Federick?" Theoden asked.

"When they realised we were Keepers they backed off. The Pagans however…"

"Aye, I will rally some soldiers and volunteers to help lay them to rest. Boys, we should head back to the Palace."

The brothers nodded to Theoden, Tristan reaching forward for the mask and staring at the inside of it. Glyphs entwined within the gold surface, glyphs of control and manipulation. Between the eyes though, a glyph struck a chord and he called for Cedric to look too. On the other side of their own uniting glyph was unbinding. Both the brothers shared a puzzled look at the unity of the glyphs. If they didn't have questions before they certainly had them now.

CHAPTER 19 – THE FIRST GENERATIONS OF UNION

Back at the palace, Tristan sought out Dante in the infirmary. As he entered the room, he realised Isolde was tending to his wounds and waited in the doorway. As she bandaged, she said he must keep it clean else infection would strike, but as far as she was concerned, he was good to go about some normal activities and get his own room. Once she had finished, Tristan helped him to his room and asked for some beer to be bought to them to celebrate.

"So, where have you been all day?" Dante asked, taking a sip from his beer.

Tristan told him about the meeting with his uncle that morning and how he had taken them to the Pagan village. He told him of the trail of blood and the Hammerites and Enforcers he had found there too. He finished with telling him of Federick and the sanctuary for Nobility, not leaving out a single detail. After he had finished, Dante took one final sip of his beer before getting to his feet and pacing towards the window. Tristan's findings today had given him a lot to think about.

"You're sure," he said after a while. "That Daniel bares the same mark as we, he isn't even Union?"

"I think it has something to do with his brother..."

"But he was only an ally..."

"An ally who had a personal relationship with one of the brotherhoods. Not to mention the fact that Federick said the mark also befalls those who have seen the face of the Herasin."

"Fair point. We have no way of finding out though. And this business with them coming to that Cathedral three years ago…what does that mean?"

"Three years ago I destroyed the Eye of the Storm. I think whatever makes us betray is linked to the manipulations of the Eye. I mean me personally; I have never felt it…but you…what did it feel like…"

At that moment there was a knock at the door and Tristan crossed to answer it. A guard stood in place of the door as it opened and he bowed his head before stepping aside to reveal Balderick. His face lit up at the sight of his brother as Dante, realising he was standing there, stepped forward with haste to embrace his brother. Tristan smiled and the guard nodded to him, smiling before closing the door and leaving. A while later the brothers released each other and Balderick took Tristan's hand.

"It is good to see you both well," Balderick remarked, taking in their features and the injuries still apparent on Dante. "Especially after I heard what happened!"

"How did you hear?" Tristan asked. His arrival here in Landen had come quite quickly considering they themselves had only been here about a fortnight and Hamish and the others had probably only arrived back in Az Lagní yesterday. Balderick couldn't use Keeper magic anymore thanks to his betrayal, but either way Tristan was happy to see the man.

"I saw the light from Felix's funeral…heck I felt him die…he was my brother…" Balderick was respectively silent for a moment. "When I saw the light, I embarked straight for Dilu to pay my respects. When I found the Compound empty, I asked the villagers what happened and they told me the Barron had been killed in the night. I returned to Az Lagní in the hope I could get some answers from Theorryn but he had gone…I don't know where and when Hamish returned…he filled me in. I had to see you Dante, I had to see that you were okay – I couldn't lose another brother." A tear escaped Balderick's eye and Dante reached up to touch his brother's face comfortingly. "I am glad you are okay!"

"And I am glad you are here brother!" Dante turned and grabbed a spare tankard from the table where the servants had placed their flagons of beer from earlier, and poured one for Balderick. Topping his and Tristan's up, they toasted to their reunion.

As they drank, Tristan filled Balderick in on all that had happened since he had left Az Lagní for Dilu. He even told him everything surrounding the Keepers that had come to light since coming to Az Landen. His face puzzled at the accusations against Saracen caused by a simple medallion – it was a confusing assumption. Saracen in his time had been known as the King of Light, descendant himself from the City of Light within northern Salysma to the East of Halsgar. He had stood with Talus to join together the Keepers of Time and Secrets into one

Faction, stood with him when the balance was struck with the Hammerites and Pagans. To call him the original, perhaps ultimate betrayer was farfetched.

"You know there's only one way to find out if what you assume is true," Balderick said as Tristan finished. "Felix's keys work twice fold. Not only can they tell you if a person is alive or faded and so on, in the right hands they could also tell you if someone was a betrayer."

"What do you mean the right hands?" Tristan asked.

"Felix's keys weren't just created by him," Dante continued. "We all helped him. At first it was a way of keeping track of each other. We had heard rumours that a curse had begun...a curse to force Union to betray. When you said Federick had the same theory...I do now believe it to be true."

"What do you know about it?"

"I know that part of Dharsi was discovered in the Maw of Chaos. Six of them were found to be conjuring the glyphs and they had in their possession the Eye of the Storm and the Ruby of Sorrow. According to legend, the sprits within them belonged to unspeakable traitors who caused devastation to the Keeperhood about half a century after the union of the two were struck. Supposedly, there is a way of linking the manipulations of the Eye in particular to the consciousness of Unity...since that is what he was."

"I don't understand..."

"As much as all the brothers betrayed...it seemed to always stem from the Nobility brother himself. The rest were all too easily swayed. The Ruby is said to be able to stabilise and harness the power of the Eye else it is unpredictable and uncontrollable. Only the Eye made it back into the protection of the Hammers."

"Hold on, you said the Eye was the key to the traitorous thoughts within the minds of the Keepers?" Dante nodded. "The Hammers with Federick said they came to be there when I destroyed it three years ago. The impulses to betray stopped then...so with its destruction so must the curse."

"It would make sense."

"How did you learn all of this?"

"There is a book in the upper levels of the Shrine. I believe it is a treatise of the First Generations of Union. It's all we have on their legacy."

"Then I guess we're making a visit to the Shrine this night." Balderick and Dante nodded in approval of Tristan's plan.

Later, as the sun was setting, the three arrived at the collapsed Shrine. They had sent word for Tristan's brothers to join them, as much as they weren't needed to achieve their mission – it was critical they saw wherever their discoveries lead them. The brothers looked tired, Zhaine and Ramien clearly annoyed. It had been a long day.

"Why have you dragged us all out here at this time Tristan?" Ramien churned as Tristan, Balderick and Dante came to join them at the entrance to the Compound.

"That's how long it takes Dante to hobble here maybe?" Zhaine perused, a cheeky smile on his face. Cedric snorted in response, Jacques simply rolling his eyes.

"Cheeky git!" Dante scorned but Tristan could tell a smile was tugging at those serious lips.

"Your presence is required because you need to see what we may be about to discover…"

"And you are?" Ramien patronised.

"Brothers this is Balderick," Tristan explained. "He is Dante's brother by cause."

"So he is Union?"

"Aye!" Dante confirmed and Ramien nodded, standing aside so Balderick could lead the way.

He led them through the main foyer where they had passed a few days ago and into the libraries. He turned to Cedric nodding. Assuming he needed access to the Shrine, Cedric held out his right hand, letting the glyph that named him ally shine through and appear ahead of him. Almost immediately, a bookcase to their left shifted, swinging open to reveal a pathway. The beauty of the Scribe passages; they appeared whenever you needed one.

Balderick smiled, these boys were young but skilled. Their powers had given them experience far beyond their years. Taking the lead down the pathway, the rest followed him through the illuminated darkness. Through the aisles of the Annals of Union they strode, taking the left corridor at the top of the room. The room at the end was plain aside from cobwebs in the corners and again, Balderick turned to Cedric.

"I need you to call upon Felix's keys!" he ordered. Cedric stared at him confused, and then he looked to his brothers, Tristan nodding for him to comply.

Again, Cedric called forth his glyph and the keys appeared to them just as they had when they sought out Romeo's key. Oddly enough, that was the line of keys that appeared – he and his brothers; Romeo's key still shining bright with the shadowy patches. Something about it was different now though, it was like it was less shadowed.

"I need you to call fourth the keys of the First Generation of Union." Balderick asked.

"Can I even do that?" Cedric questioned, frowning. He didn't even know all of their names to summon the right people.

"You should be able to with my help," Tristan offered. "I'm the Bearer of Secrets so perhaps that adds to it." Balderick nodded; he knew enough about the keys to know this should work. Taking a deep breath, Cedric nodded to his brother and Tristan placed a hand on his shoulder, holding his left palm up so his glyph too shone through.

"I call upon the power of Union to aid me in my quest of knowledge," Cedric chanted, a certain assertion to his voice as he commanded the power of the glyphs. "We summon the keys of the First Generation of Union. Show them in their true lights!"

As fast as lightning, the keys in front of them changed. Shifting for the right combination, eventually six keys appeared, all but two of them darkened. Cedric and Tristan both frowned, and as they looked to their brothers, even they seemed confused.

According to the keys; the keys named Talus, Sondheim, Greygor, Isolde, Saracen and Samson. As suspected, all but two of the keys were dull showing their passing. As much as they knew Isolde was alive, they had no idea Saracen was too.

"Wait, so Saracen lives?" Ramien questioned; perhaps that was Dharsi's power source...how they had gathered their following together so quickly.

"Command the keys to show their true form...their true nature!" Dante suggested.

"Keys, show me the true nature of these people...show me their true form!" Cedric said. The other keys stayed darkened, glyphs forming over their keys to signify which virtue they possessed. Saracen's key turned red, signifying his betrayal. The medallion spoke the truth – the King of Light himself had betrayed their kind.

Tristan clenched his fist, not only was Saracen a traitor; he was Nobility. Was that why there was this war between the Herasin and Nobility? Unless the Herasin was Nobility...unless the Herasin was Saracen all along.

Tristan's eyes widened.

"Saracen is Herasin!" Tristan ventured, all eyes on him now. "It's the only thing that makes sense surely."

"But Charles..." Ramien started.

"Is one form of Herasin. One name; he wouldn't be able to walk the land as Saracen for eternity, especially if there were those that knew he betrayed."

"Tristan has a point," Dante agreed. "As farfetched as it sounds, it does make sense."

"But why become a Brother of Union if he didn't agree with Talus." Zhaine questioned remorsefully. It seemed everything they thought they knew about the Keepers and their foundations was a lie. Perhaps the balance had been uneven the whole time and one of them even knew how deep this all went.

"Perhaps he did at first but something changed…" Tristan guessed.

"Either way there's only one person who can tell us if this is all true – Isolde!" Dante was right. Isolde was Sondheim's sister by blood, the first Ally of Union according to the keys, and the only one still alive today that would know all that happened back then.

"How can we be sure though that she will trust us enough to tell the truth…that she even knows it all in the first place?" Zhaine was full of questions. He had idolised the Keepers; placed them on pedistools all his life, he and his brothers. Perhaps they weren't deserved of any of their fame or glory. They were just as corrupt as the rest of them!

"Well perhaps we can educate ourselves in the meantime!"

Dante nodded to them all before turning on his heel out of the room and back into the main part of the Shrine. They followed him up the spiral staircase at the head of the room into the forbidden scriptures, otherwise known as the Scribe's Library.

"You're looking for a treatise on the First Generations," Dante explained. "I can't remember who wrote it, only that it exists."

Everyone nodded and began scouring the shelves that encircled the veranda they stood on above the Shrine of Unity. Tristan had to check every title twice else risk him missing it. Surely there was a way they could use the glyphs to summon the book, but then they'd probably need the whole title. The glyphs were presumptuous like that.

A niggling tickled the back of his neck as though someone had touched the sensitive skin there and he looked up. An image flashed through his mind – he had read the book before, or at least seen it.

"Guys," Cedric's voice was shaken. "I think I've found it…Charles' Treatise on the First Generations of Union."

CHAPTER 20 - THE CURSE OF UNION

Again, I was in a small room with Murdoch now standing before me. This time, we were at eye level with each other and although he had changed a lot since the vision before, I knew it was him – or perhaps it wasn't me that did but my enemy whose spirit was still united with mine. It looked like a dorm room of some form, a bed and a bookcase up against the far wall with a chest of drawers and a washbasin to his left. A large wardrobe was at the end of the bed and a desk angled in the far corner. It was fairly plain in terms of decoration and I couldn't make out the titles on any of the books, but then it wasn't the external detail I was supposed to be focusing on anyway.

"What took you so long?" I heard myself ask in a serious yet jokey way.

"I came back didn't I...and that's all that matters." Murdoch replied with a doting smile upon his face.

"Two generations have been chosen since you left, the second of which is parading around like they are heroes because they helped Jason Orion in his quest to destroy Gallow." Somehow, we had come forward at least a century to the time of the fifth generation. I had no idea he was this old!

"That is precisely why I have left it so long. That and the fact that we had to find something that would work for every generation to come...not just one."

"I don't understand!"

"Most of the magic we explored would only corrupt people and we need to corrupt a movement...the very magic they rely on is what we need to taint. You see Unity are bound by a powerful magic - you take away those bonds and the Glyphs have control. Most of the ones that are chosen are young and naive, easily lead and they are our targets. All we have to do is paint them as traitors for a couple of generations and everyone will automatically believe that is the way they are."

"So what's the plan?"

"Ever heard the tale of Sorren and Storm?" I shook my head, to be honest it sounded rather ominous so it was no surprise. "It involves two Keepers more commonly known as Storm and Sorrow. Each wanted more power than they were being taught, not to mention could learn from the resources around them. So they each constructed stones; a ruby and a diamond which they laced with the Glyphs they wished to control. From these they would be able to command the magic they wanted using the stone as the vessel as opposed to themselves. But their strive for power was never satiated and together they bought devastation to the Keeper faction. Their lust for power and for each other was more powerful than any Keeper could think to face. In those gaps of pleasure, the glyphs festered on their own, their nature warped and unpredictable.

"The Keepers eventually realised the key was to bind them within their stones and sealed them away in separate so they couldn't hope to unite again. Although they have been separated for generations, theory suggests that once they are united by a Brotherhood joined by Unity, the wielder will be capable of corrupting an entire generation. The Glyphs have the power to overtake the Scribe. Their bonds as a Brotherhood will be broken. The theory of course relies on the Brotherhood calling it.

"We have to perform the ritual from inside the Maw of Chaos." I could feel my eyes widen at the mention of its name. That place struck fear into my own heart let alone how I came to realise how it made my enemy feel.

"That old Pagan place? Murdoch did you hear what it did to those Pagans? It was like their own god turned against them...strangled the life out of them. What if the ruins turn on you? Then what happens?"

"I have heard what happened and I have heard the rumours but we have Dangur and Sarisus...Foresaken are the people that erected the Maw in the first place before they were banished to Degstan...before even the Pagans took control of it."

"We will be fine brother - But I need your help! Our father wears a ring which is the key to many secret passageways around the First Keepers quarters. Hidden in one of them passageways has to be the key to the Maw, I need you to find it. You're trusted by him, by all of them, it will be easier for you to slip through than one of us."

"What do I do once I have the key?"

"You summon me...simple enough for you?"

"Maybe a little too simple."

"Feel free to complicate it as much as you like dear brother." He pointed to his wrist and winked at me as though hinting at a hidden mark maybe.

"I may have to. Have you sorted Gervais?"

"Don't worry, he will comply...after all he doesn't have a choice. At the end of the day he chose us over the Keepers a long time ago. He made his bed and now he must lie in it."

There was a moment of silence between them. I wondered what it might be that was concealed beneath my leather sleeve - I mean it had to be a mark of some sort. And Gervais, how was it he didn't have a choice but to follow them? My gaze landed on Murdoch's hand of which the palm was slightly facing towards me and I was able to pick out a glyph in the lines of his hand making a mark...my own mark. *What? No way?* I didn't understand what I was looking at.

I had been so busy theorising that I hadn't noticed the blankness return and again clear to reveal yet another room. This one was a lot larger than either of the two I had seen before with a grand four poster bed at the head. Either side was a table with books and a candle stick. A chest lay at the end of the bed. To his left was a bookcase and to his right a desk. Again, the decoration was minimal but I did pick out the key embroidered onto the purple cloth that draped over the posters of the bed. These were the quarters that belonged to the First Keeper, speaking of whom was snoring in the bed that I now stood beside.

I could feel myself smirking at him loathingly. My enemy was not a fan of his father but from what I knew of his character he was a harsh man who had a hefty shadow to live under. Perhaps like my own father, he had been too hard on his youngest son, hard enough to turn him against his father in support of his traitorous sibling who of course showed him every ounce of support his father did not. In truth he was easily led but then I could understand why he would choose his brother over his father in this situation. However, that still did not condone his actions! Perhaps however, the consequence of his actions was unjust. A man of consequence was my enemy – was I to believe he could've been different?

On the bedside table that stood before me was a ring; a gold band with a single blue stone that stuck out in a hexagonal casting. I picked it up and stared at it, muttering a word which seemed to duplicate it in my other hand. As I did so, I noticed the end of a scar pushing free of my leather sleeve which seemed to glow green as the ring was cloned and the double placed on the table where the original had lay.

Smiling to myself at the same time as sneering at the sleeping man, I left the room, took a left turn into the First Keepers Library and placed myself by the idol of Talus in between two bookcases. Just behind the bookcase on the right was a niche in the wall shaped so that the ring would fit point first. Checking the coast was clear I placed the ring in the niche and the wall seemed to disappear as though it were no more than an illusion. Stepping through we were welcomed by a passageway which led down to yet another library. There were a lot less books here though and desks scattered about. I could even pick out a blackboard behind some boxes in the corner of the room. Perhaps it was some form of classroom rather than a library.

Now where will this key be? I heard myself think; I don't even know what it looks like. Just think that if my father wanted to hide something where would he put it? Nothing happened and I remained silent, probably trying to think where the key might be. The room was pretty bare and I couldn't see why anything would be hiding in this room. In my own eyes it would've been worth it to explore the passageways that continued into darkness on either side of the room. I felt myself grow impatient but I wasn't my sort of impatience, it was an angry sort, the sort that would cause brutal action...potentially.

"Fuck it!" I heard his voice curse as he pulled his wrist free and I laid eyes on the mark I had been waiting to see all this time – surely not, I knew that mark! "Might as well embrace what I am!"

Stretching out he placed his hand on the wall next to him, digging in his fingernails. I felt my eyes slip back into my head and the body of which was my vessel fill with power which churned through my fingers in a green vine like texture. It crept across the bricks like creeper vines growing at an accelerated rate - whatever this magic was it was definitely Pagan in origin. The vines stretched around the arch we had entered through and disappeared down the corridor on the left. I felt that smile slip back and we followed the vines quickly as they began to retract behind us. Eventually the vines came to an end in a small room with nothing but an old dark wood chest in the centre of the room. The vines disappeared and we knelt in front of it, easing open the lid. Something about this seemed too easy but it didn't seem to bother my vessel, and if it did, he didn't make it known.

The chest seemed empty but it was shallower than either of us expected. A niche hid in the top corner and I pulled on it, opening a small hatch containing a purple velvet bag. Emptying it out, a bronze key slipped into my hand, its touch burning slightly but recognising its master. A green vine wrapped itself around the key - this was definitely what we were looking for. Holding my hands side by side, one containing the key, I heard him mutter the same word he had in the First Keepers chambers and the key duplicated. It didn't feel the same but it would suffice as an illusion for now. As we replaced the key and pocketed the original, I became aware of a presence watching us. I was unsure of how long it had been there or what its intentions were but my enemy had not noticed until he stood to leave.

"What do you think you are doing?" The presence asked as we came to face him. I recognised him, and my enemy certainly felt an anger towards him. But it wasn't full anger, part of it was compassion - perhaps once they had been friends. But something about the man bothered me, it sensed something in him that was the same as me and those eyes, those cool grey eyes...

"Balderick!" I heard my own voice say - now I saw him, even with his dreadlocked blonde hair and shaved sides. With his scared face and hands and his strong stature. In truth, he hadn't changed much...except the hair anyway. "I should've known one of you would be lurking around."

"You are the one who is lurking boy!" He truly did not know my vessel's real age. "And besides this is the Shrine, our sanctuary so you tell me what you are doing here."

"If I were you Balderick I'd leave well alone. Trust me when I say it's for your own good." Now the compassion showed. Whatever hatred my enemy had for him was washed away momentarily with a warning that probably would not be heeded. Some dispute had rocked their relationship, and part of we wondered what happened.

"You don't belong here boy...you still haven't answered my question." I followed Balderick's eyes as they wondered quickly to the chest and then back up at me. "He's back, isn't he? You're doing this for him aren't you?"

"So what if I am? What's it to you? He's the only one who's ever been there for me!" I marvelled at how I didn't even attempt to deny it. He obviously wasn't worried about what might happen if their plan didn't work...but then perhaps he had other ideas for Balderick's fate.

"So you're just going to betray us all are you? For a bunch of traitors?"

"How do you know there are more?"

"Come off it boy! We're not as stupid as we look you know. You cannot do this!"

"I have no choice!"

I felt a tear on my cheek and I saw the look in Balderick's face and in his eyes as he looked woefully at a boy he seemed to adore. There really was more to my enemy's story, again it did not condone what he had done but if he didn't have a choice did that mean he wasn't in control of his actions? Or had he just got himself in so deep that he couldn't get out again? Perhaps the ends of these visions would provide me with the answers I surely needed; for part of me truly did want to understand what drew my enemy to do what he did, the other part wanted him to rot for an eternity.

"I'm sorry Balderick," I heard myself gasp mournfully as though he already regretted what he was about to do. "I truly am!" The last thing I saw before the darkness enveloped us once again was Balderick's eyes rolling into the back of his head showing only the whites.

CHAPTER 21 – ANSWERS

As expected, Isolde was in the infirmary setting straight the empty beds as though she were expecting an influx of casualties. She turned to face them as soon as they walked in. Balderick and Dante taking the lead with Tristan slightly behind. The rest of the brothers took the back seat of the troop, none of them really knowing what to expect from what they may or may not be about to discover. The way she looked at them though was as though she expected this in the end.

"What can I do for you men this evening then?" she asked calmly, her far southern accent coming through. She was clearly trying to retain her innocence but her eyes said all they needed to know.

"We're here for answers Isolde," Dante instructed as he perched on one of the beds, crinkling the sheets. Isolde's nose wrinkled at this but she remained silent. "It's time the Elders stopped keeping secrets supposedly for our own good."

Isolde's eyes passed over each of them, her face unchanged.

"I'm assuming this involves my past with the generations of Union?" she remarked, not meeting their gaze but staring forward as the others began making themselves comfortable on the freshly made beds.

"We've made some discoveries of late…well assumptions to be more precise. We need answers."

"Very well…"

Just as she agreed, the infirmary door opened again and in walked Linford. Noting the presence of the boys as he entered the room, he stopped dead in his tracks almost suspiciously.

"I'll come back…" He made to leave again, like he was nervous.

"Actually Linford," Isolde called. "It is time they knew the truth!" Her voice was pointed and assertive, causing him to stop, the lump in his throat moving the length of his neck. He sighed heavily before shutting the door and pacing to stand by Isolde's side. "Where would you like us to start?"

"We'd be here all night if we did it this way Isolde…" Linford cut in, aggression tainting his words.

"They have a right to know everything…they all did Linford. It is time!"

Dante frowned, so Balderick decided to take the lead.

"How about you fill in the blanks and correct us where we're wrong?" He suggested.

"Alright…fire away." Linford instructed; his voice shaky.

"Saracen was of the first Generation of Unity alongside Talus himself…right?"

"Yes, Saracen is brother by blood to Talus." Isolde explained. "He was part of the original generation and known as the King of Light for heading the army that bought Light back to our world in the time of Darkness. It is what began the Union of the Keepers of Time and Secrets; thus they being known as the first generation."

"And Dharsi, when did they come about?"

"It is a common misconception that Dharsi have always been there. However the third generation was bought in to deal with the threat of them. There was always opposition to the union yes, mostly from the Keepers of Secrets and even to this day it is thought to be them that formed Dharsi."

"So if the third generation was who fought off Dharsi, and there was no opposition before then why was there need for the second generation?" Cedric asked patiently.

His question was met with silence at first. Isolde looked to Linford out of the corner of her eye as though for support, but he remained silent. She pursed her lips as though she was trying to find the words.

"He was a traitor wasn't he," Tristan pulled out the medallion he found in Elan's things, throwing it into Isolde's already outstretched hands. Her eyes went glassy as she held it tight.

"She loved him! Sondheim loved the bones off him. But he was messed up…constantly living in the shadow of his brother. He couldn't stand that it was him they looked to and not the five as a collective. Eventually it was too much for him to take and that's when he met Sorren and Strom…you will know them as Sorrow and Storm. They were two Keepers of Secrets who confided in him that they felt he was over looked for the part he played in the Union. They said they had a power in them that would get him the dedication he deserved…that he could share that power with them. He confided in Sondheim and she begged him against joining them…but I guess it was too much." Isolde's voice broke.

"It is long thought that Sorrow and Storm held the power of the Unbinding – the very essence of the power of Union," Linford took over. "They promised Saracen a chunk of that power and together they wreaked havoc on the Keeperhood. Fifty years later the Third

Generation was erected to stop them. But as you know, eight brothers survived the banishment alongside Gervais. It is thought there was a reason why those eight walked away. You see...Gervais too as jealous of a highly notable brother and he assumed his identity...assumed his power..."

"It is thought that in revenge for what they did to Dharsi...other members assumed the Generation."

The brothers weren't really sure what Linford meant, not at first. From what the treatise had detailed about the Third Generation, they were discovered massacred within the Shrine still standing above their glyphs on the Inner Circle. As much as it was always thought to be a message that members of Dharsi had survived...there had never been a deeper assumption.

Tristan's eyebrows rose then as though something were whispered in his ear that surprised him. But he had clicked and Linford clocked that in his eyes.

"Wait...so you mean to tell me that surviving members of Dharsi were Union?" Tristan blurted, ashamed for a moment that he killed one of his own brothers by creed in such a brutal manner.

"It is thought so yes. They are what we consider the fourth generation...a rumour mostly yes...we don't have proof of this theory." Noting the looks on their faces, Linford proceeded his explanation. "Yes, I am the fourth generation truly. The glyphs chose me and my brothers so that there might be redemption...so that the balance could be restored. We dispatched Storm and Sorrow, concealing the magic they possessed into The Eye and the Ruby. Unfortunately, these stones fell out of our hands thanks to Gervais sometime later."

"So like Saracen; he was a member of two different generations?" Zhaine questioned.

"Yes! We recovered the stones after we encountered the fifth generation and what was left of Dharsi in the Maw of Chaos many years later. It isn't known what they were doing with them, but many believe they were trying to corrupt the whole of Union for future generations to come after a prophecy was read naming them the Keepers of the balance. It is thought they succeeded!"

"Well not like it would've been that hard considering our very foundations were traitors!" Ramien scoffed.

"Even yourselves came from good beginnings," Linford gestured to Balderick and Dante. "But I'm sure you both have different versions of what you saw and experienced in the Maw. Not to mention you Dante being Nobility himself of whom seem to be the pinnacle of the betrayals within Unity."

Dante looked to Balderick for guidance. In truth, neither of them had ever spoken out about what happened, not even to each other.

"I think our experiences differ," Dante began, his eyes on Balderick who had looked away before he spoke. "With me there was always a nag...a higher impulse I just couldn't ignore. Like I knew morally what was right...but...

"I never experienced urges as such, but I know I developed a dependency on brandy." Balderick intervened, his eyes on the floor. "When I came back, I couldn't seem to get through a day without it! It was the only thing that made me forget the shadows. Even after I met Marcine and had my kids, it was my crutch.

"These days I'm sworn off it, I wasn't a nice man heck Marcine almost left several times. God bless that woman for staying as long as she has. Having said that, there is a period in my memory that is patchy, like I only remember snippets. It's like I wasn't in control, just watching myself do things that I wouldn't have been party to. I always put it down to the brandy – it affected me giving me memory loss. But there's more to it! I was forced to start the betrayal by letting them into that Maw. They didn't need to curse us...I started this..."

"No! I was the one who incited it all," Dante took over. "I started to hear voices, like a chanting in my head. There was a lot of pressure on me and my brothers to be patrons of balance as it were...saints if you like. Especially after all we helped Jason Orion to achieve. Sometimes I didn't think I was worthy...like I wasn't a part of my creed. It was in these periods of isolation that I began hearing these voices."

"What did it say to you?" Tristan asked, his face ashen like something in his head was telling him he knew the feeling.

"I don't remember everything...I do remember how it would start though. Kin of my creed, brother but not by blood here my call. It always used the word we...we could do great things together. Just me and you! The world meant for us to be together."

Silence passed. Tristan's heart began to thump hard. He knew those words, and in that moment, they echoed in his mind once more. He looked up and his eyes met Cedric whose face was as ashen as his.

"Dante, you remember I told you about the Hammers at the Cathedral," Tristan panted. Nielson and Isolde both frowned. "How all of them were Nobility? I heard those same words in our dealings with the Eye of the Storm. It only spoke to me...what if it spoke to us all..."

"There are indeed rumours that before Storm claimed the power of the other glyphs that he began as Nobility." Isolde explained. "Storm was always considered the more dangerous, his counterpart Sorrow was more level headed. Equally treacherous but had more morals shall we say. For him everything had to have a reason, Storm just needed the initial thought. If you believe it to be Storm that corrupted you all then perhaps that's what Dharsi was doing. Perhaps they were tapping into his power to link it to you all...isolating the weak from the strong."

"You really think us weak..." Dante started.

"I'm not sure that's quite what she means Dante." Balderick cautioned. "Storm's link to you would've provided an immediate weakness...it wasn't your fault...it wasn't any of our faults."

"Balderick is right," Linford proceeded. "We see that now. We were fools to believe ourselves righteous enough to cast you all under the same cloth. And for that...I am deeply sorry."

"You spoke of the Hammers at the Cathedral?" Isolde asked, her eyes on Tristan. "Are these those under Federick?" Tristan nodded. "And you say they are Nobility?"

"About three years ago they all had a calling to come out of hiding and join Federick there. The voices in their heads stopped, and they came together. I think it stems back to when we destroyed the Eye."

"They might be the key you know...to destroying Dharsi once and for all. There aren't many left...without the Herasin they would simply submit to whomever gave them the better offer. Without him...they are nothing.

"You boys named a fair few back in the day...do you remember who?" Linford asked. "There were nine in total who escaped justice.; one of those was Gervais."

"Boris...Hagen...they're both dead..." Zhaine continued. "Dangur as well."

"Sarisus is also dead," Ramien proceeded. "That leaves four,"

"I killed one when we found Dharsi in the Maw," Dante explained. "Murdoch, turned out he was the eldest son to First Keeper Avus."

"So that leaves three including the Herasin whom we know to be Charles..."

"Charles...Saracen is the Herasin, surely you boys realise that after all I have said?" Isolde said coldly, all eyes now glowering at her. She hadn't been in the Compound at Hasaghar when the boys unmasked Charles as the Herasin. But for her to name Saracen as the Herasin...perhaps Tristan's theory was right.

"So Charles is who he came back into the fold as," Cedric stuttered. "We unmasked him three years ago. Why did he come back as Charles? Why did Charles have the standing he did among you all?"

"There was a third brother," Linford went on. "Talus, Saracen and Charles. He was much younger than the other two...and he, like me I suppose and Nielson did many great things for the Keeperhood. And just as they all infiltrated themselves into the Keeperhood...so did Saracen as his own brother...and we were so blind not to see it." Linford looked to Isolde, her face pale. For two Elders such as themselves to admit their shortcomings and failures just now must've been a lot to take.

"If you boys don't mind, I should like to get some rest now..." Isolde croaked. "It is very late."

Linford reached for Isolde's hand but she snatched it away, disappearing into the backroom. Linford nodded to them all before bowing his head, almost in shame. They took that as their cue and left the infirmary behind with plenty to reflect upon and put together among themselves.

CHAPTER 22 – THE DIARY OF ELAN

Their leave from the Infirmary had them all back at the Shrine, sat at the desks in silence. Tristan was reading through the treatise they had found, all the words ringing true with everything Isolde had said. It was a lot to take in – Saracen the king of Light himself splitting off and taking on the Keepers with Sorren and Storm; Dharsi being the real third generation…so much corruption inside a faction that were supposed to be the keepers of balance. Sighing heavily, he shut the book and pushed it aside, knocking a larger book at the edge of the desk onto the floor. The bang it made echoed around the room, dust flying up from where it landed.

The book had fallen near Cedric's foot, so he rose to pick it up, glancing at the cover. It was Elan's annals, every page still blank. Tristan watched as his brother frowned at the blank pages. But as his thumb touched the parchment, Tristan noticed a smudge begin to appear - like ink bleeding across the edges of the pages. He rose from his seat and took the book from Cedric, his eyes widening as the ink stretched to the length of the pages like it was trying to escape.

"What is this?" Cedric asked.

"One of the Annals from the forty ninth generation…an unwritten volume…" Tristan murmured as he watched the ink bleed across the edges of the pages.

"My glyph of unbinding…"

Cedric pulled up his sleeve to reveal the glyph of unbinding on his wrist. It was a mark he was born with, something bestowed upon very few Keepers and only belonging to a certain bloodline. The mark meant that he could unbind any magic or curse – a curse-breaker essentially just like the Nyms.

"Tristan, take the book," Cedric commanded, his brother complying.

The other brothers gathered around Cedric and Tristan who opened the book out for the ally to examine. Each page seemed to have faded writing upon it, so fine it was indecipherable. Pursing his lips, Cedric let his fingers grace the pages, releasing the magic he had at his disposal. The glyph of unbinding appeared across the open book; the writings beginning to become clearer. But before Cedric was even able to read it, a bright light shone from it.

A scene began to play out as colours bled into the light, the lure of it dragging the seven of them in as though the book itself wanted to show them something. The brothers were not reluctant though, they simply let the light take them where it wanted.

"We can't be seen like this Elan," Malock cursed as Elan leant in close where they stood against the wall awaiting the approval of their tutor to enter the classroom.

"There's nothing untoward about me standing close to a brother now is there?" Elan glanced sidewardly at his brother by creed cheekily, winking as he did so. Malock's smile in response was electric, the man sent a fire up his spine.

The door ahead of them opened and they were let into the classroom, Linford glowering at the two as they entered the room a little after everyone else.

After class the boys headed to the Shrine for what little privacy they could muster. From the moment they had met, Malock and Elan were inseparable. Their personalities seemed to combine with one another when together, like they were two sides of the same coin. One without the other never happened, and if it did one felt lost without the other. Many deemed them more than a friendship of course but none spoke of it. Most did not understand, as much as it was something seen upon the land it wasn't something often spoke about. Afterall, how does one politely ask of the fact?

Their privacy was short-lived though as their brothers came storming through the Shrine. A look of anger was smeared across Lewisham's face. Elan wiped a hand across his face at the look, casting a look to the other half of his soul. Lewisham was like the ringleader of their band. Only newly selected, he held the title of Unity. George, Malock's brother by blood held Loyalty. Truth and Freedom belonged to Xander and Harold, leaving Nobility for Malock. Elan took heed as their ally. As much as he had a bond with Malock above all of them, he had been close with all five of them ever since he had met them – like something had drawn them all to one another the moment they walked through the doors as mere Novices a few months ago. No sooner had they walked through the doors, the Shrine had found them. And as much as they had tried to resist, the magic followed them around like a dank smell, constantly reminding them they had no choice in the matter. Destiny was coming for them!

"That's codswalloping swine!" Lewisham cursed as he strode through the aisles, knocking down the ornamental pillars as he went – the vases atop them smashing on the floor.

"You need to calm down brother," Xander called to him as he came to halt by the desks, his brothers behind him all casting looks of embarrassment at how dramatic he was being. "I'm sure he meant nothing by it..."

"When have you ever known me to fail an assignment Xander? Linford failed me deliberately...he knows who we are..."

"Then why didn't he fail the rest of us too?" Malock asked from where he perched on the desks more or less in front of Elan who sat with his front to the back of the chair a little distance away.

"Oh come off it. Don't tell me I'm the only one who wrote our history truthfully?"

The assignment had been to sum up all they had learnt on the Brotherhood of Union over the past week or so. Their histories were written differently to what was often told to the young Scribes – why should they know more than what was necessary.

"We're supposed to be laying low brother," Elan said quietly. "Writing like that will only draw unwanted attention. How could you have been so foolish?"

"Perhaps it's time they saw that Destiny does not control us though," Lewisham scorned solemnly. "We are no traitors and nor do we deserve to be tarnished so before our time!"

"That may be right brother but you know as well as we that we are scorned still. They would not understand!"

"If they come for us now, I swear to god..." Malock tore towards Lewisham. How could he have been so foolish.

"That's enough!" Elan grabbed ahold of his lover by the arm, pulling him back into a tight hold. "We can't tear at each other like this. We are a brotherhood and we must stand together...else they will tear us apart."

The others nodded in agreement and Lewisham looked at his brother sheepishly.

Later that evening, Elan escorted Malock back to his room and the two shared a momentary peace offering. As they broke away, a voice called towards them, making Elan relieved his back was towards their onlooker.

"Elan!" called the voice. "What in god's name are you doing down here?"

Elan turned to see his brother Daniel standing a distance behind them, a burning torch in hand. He and his brother were born into the Keeperhood and had dormitories much further up in the Compound. What with Elan being a Mage, he was not permitted down here as late as it was.

"Dear brother," Elan answered mockingly as he met eyes with his brother. He and his older brother had never seen eye to eye; he always thought Daniel a bit of a kiss arse. Like he was a slave to the Keepers and their corruption. "I was simply escorting my friend here safely back to his dorm."

"I can assure you brother that was not necessary unless Master Malock here is afraid of the dark." Elan glowered at his brother. "Hasten back to your dorms before you get yourself into trouble. I can assure you the other guards will not be so forgiving." He spat those last words. Elan often wondered if the reason his brother held such contempt for him was because he knew what he was...if he knew the way his attractions lusted. Did he judge him for it? Or was it simply his lack of understanding? His fear that others would harm him for it.

Shaking his head, Daniel turned on his heel to finish his patrol. Elan turned back to his lover and bid him goodbye before making back for his own dormitory which he shared with his brother by blood.

He paced slowly back, walking through the Compound in the near darkness bought him solace. As he neared the levels of the Acolytes where his own chambers lay, shouting reached his ears from the courtyard below the balcony he passed. The voices were harsh but fearful. Curious, Elan approached the edge and crouched down low, making out four shadows cast along the grass in the meek lighting below.

"The time is now brothers," one of them cast. "We must strike...we know who they are..."

"We know one of them!" It was clear they were talking about the Brotherhood of Union.

"The rest are pretty easy to assume..."

"An assumption is not enough; we need to be sure."

"We know enough that we can sow the soil..."

"There is a reason we cursed them so. We should just let destiny take its path."

"How can we ensure it's even still working. None have betrayed in centuries...none have even come out of the shadows..."

"Why should we even tempt them...that Lewisham is a ticking timebomb. He will be the end of them!"

"Silence my dear brothers!" A new voice came into ear shot now and Elan laid eyes on Charles. Surely it couldn't be.

"My lord Herasin," Surely not! "Forgive us our outspokenness."

Daring to rise to his feet in the shadows, Elan stood and set eyes upon the darkened figures that were his teachers and mentors. The face that was Charles had changed now to a much older man with silver hair and stark red eyes. It was then he noted the medallion around his neck and its significance. It was the mark of Saracen...were he and Charles were one in the same? It was the only explanation for the sudden change in his appearance.

Elan felt the breath in his lungs become short as it caught in his throat and a burning sensation ripped open his left palm. Staring down at it, he watched in torment as the mark of the betrayer bled through. Everything went silent and numb, his hands tingling. He ran, breaking straight through the wall and into the Shrine where his cries were silent to others.

But it wasn't silent to everyone, and it wasn't long until Malock came rushing to his lovers' side, holding him as he wept. He didn't understand, nor did he know why but he would hold him still until the end of time.

Silence ensued and he rested his head peacefully in Malock's lap who stroked his golden locks.

"What happened Elan," his brother's voice was filled with compassion.

"You wouldn't believe me even if I told you..." Elan's reply came in harsh gasps and he let his left hand slip out of the fist he had it clasped as. Malock set eyes upon the mark and frowned.

"I've read about this," He took Elan's left palm within his and studied the mark. "It isn't what you think." He rose from Malock's lap and stared him in the eye, his whole body shaking.

"I don't understand...I am a traitor surely..."

"My love what have you done? How could one such as you ever betray anyone. Your heart is too kind."

"But that mark..."

"Is on the wrong hand."

Malock unwound the bandage he wore on his own left hand. He claimed he had cut it on his own blade days ago and Elan had thought nothing of it. He wasn't the best swordsmith in the world after all, rather clumsy actually. When the bandage was removed, Elan stared upon a mark the very same as his, his eyes widening as he looked up at his lover.

"The mark appeared on my hand almost as soon as we were selected," Malock recalled. "The night of that banquet that was held after our initiation as Scribes...I did witness a conversation between...a group of Elders. I thought I saw one of them change face – like he was two people in the same body. It freaked me, and before I know it the mark appeared. I wasn't even sure what I saw, I'm still not."

Elan replied by telling him about the conversation he had overheard in the courtyard between the Elders and how he had seen Charles' face change.

"So the mark means we have seen him then?" Elan questioned.

"Aye, I sought out the council of Elder Isolde when the mark appeared and she told me it marks those who have seen the face of the Herasin. She asked what I had seen and I told her I was not sure. She said that it was a common trait among Nobility to share this mark yet none of them seemed to know why or how it appeared."

A few moments silence passed.

"We should tell her what we saw," Elan murmured. "The truth of it...Charles is a traitor and she above all others should know that."

"Aye...but we must first come clean to our brothers. We all need to come clean to her else we will fall prey to Dharsi."

They both nodded. That morning they gathered their brothers and told them of their marks, told them what they had individually seen to get them and that they believed Charles not only to be the Herasin but also Saracen. And later that day they shared their secrets with Isolde. She didn't seem surprised when they told her what they believed...like others had told it too in the past but it had never been proven. It was then that Elan realised they would need something more solid than their word, and what she said next more or less confirmed that.

"You boys are not the first generation to come to me with this belief," Isolde revealed. "But Charles is an upstanding Keeper Elder, as are those you condemn to share his views. If I am to take this to the council then I am going to need more than your word. They will not be as trusting as I."

"The proof is in his medallion Elder," Malock ordered. "Remove that and his disguise is gone. His guise is tethered to that medallion."

Isolde sighed heavily.

The days passed with no notion of their plea being heard. Having said that, the brothers had not come across Charles or anyone else in his nefarious circle since they had been unmasked *so to speak. Perhaps some form of investigation was pending? A new Elder had stepped in to fulfil the teaching of Charles class in Keeper Glyphs by the name of Jon Basso. It was this that had prompted their realisation at the absence of the supposed members of Dharsi.*

On the fifth day there was a knock at Elan's dormitory door and he opened it to find Isolde on the other side. Her face was grave and tears still lingered in her glassy grey eyes.

"I'm sorry Elan…" were the only words she could muster before he was grabbed by shadows circling around him, their hooded red eyes blinding him. Whatever happened next was out of his control, that much was clear the way his vision clouded…like he couldn't even see himself repel the shadows with a bright light, the way even Isolde shielded her face as he stormed past.

The scene faded; whatever insight Elan's diary provided next was clearly not of his hand. As much as the Annals were written by the Allies, they were like an account so they wrote as the Ally saw. That's where they fell short though, because if the Ally was unaware of something then so was the account.

Cedric looked around at the pale faces of his brothers. From what Daniel had told them, the forty ninth generation were arrested and exiled after the council over ruled the decision to instead observe their interactions. At the discovery of this and the attempted arrest of Elan something had happened to him like he wasn't in control of himself anymore and something within him just exploded. What they had just seen more or less confirmed that. Daniel had described it as though his brother was ripped apart by invisible sources.

It was clear now more than anything else that the dealings of Union were now a Faction concern. If they were going to defeat Dharsi once and for all, the whole Keeperhood would need to be a part of that which meant unmasking all their secrets. But then perhaps that was what Union were meant to be from the beginning. Maybe the secrecy surrounding them was never meant to come to pass. Perhaps this was the way Talus intended it from the very beginning.

CHAPTER 23 – THE UNION OF THE KEEPERHOOD

The morning met the brothers in their chambers, all still awake and unable to sleep. As much as they had suspected everything they had learnt, hearing it landed differently. It was common knowledge now that Charles was a traitor, to know that one of the patrons himself was a traitor – it sickened the soul.

Staring at Evelyn's face gave Tristan peace as he lay on the bed in the sunlight coming through the window. As it touched the face of his daughter, he thought of Dagnen and how despite the blonde curls, she resembled her mother. He smiled at the thought, looking up at the prism the light cast on the mirror and how for a moment he thought he saw her face in its reflection.

Moving suddenly, he wiped the night dust from his eyes and stretched as he rose from the bed. A lot rested on his shoulders over what they must do today. In the late hour of the night before, they had called for Nielson and on his instruction a meeting had been arranged for the morning in all due haste. Tristan hadn't known how it had been received, nor if the reason why was stated.

A fresh bowl lay in wait of him in the washroom and he washed his face and let the water trickle down his bare back. He pulled on his tunic from the hook, letting it hang loose as he changed his trousers. As he reached for some socks and his boots, he heard Evie stir at a knock at the door, but he was not quick enough to stop her from answering. Luckily, it was only Myrina who as usual was overjoyed to see her goddaughter. As she rocked Evie in her arms, her eyes glowered at Tristan.

"Oh my," she joked. "I hope you don't intend on addressing the council quite so...casually."

"Not quite, I will be wearing an overcoat too." Tristan assured but he had a feeling she would see even that as not good enough.

"Well at least tuck your shirt in."

You'd never guess she was no more than a barmaid when they met, then again, her time with Baron Hagen had probably educated her on a lot of formalities of late.

Tristan met with his brothers in the corridor a short while later and they headed down to the dining hall where an early breakfast had been prepared for those meeting as part of the newly formed Keeper Council. His uncle Jensen snarled in his direction as they entered the room, his eyes not leaving them as they grabbed some fried bread from a tray near the edge of the banquet table. Nielson and Basso sat at a table too with Theorryn and Merlin. To Basso's left sat a young man Tristan was sure he recognised but he couldn't place a name. There were other faces he was unsure of too, like the few that spoke among Dante, Balderick, Linford and Isolde at the other end.

His eyes wondered back to the man next to Basso and his familiar face. He watched as Cedric went over and greeted him pleasantly, grasping him in a brotherly hug. It puzzled him, clearly he had to have known who he was. The man's eyes fell on Tristan and as they shared contact, he swore he saw something glint there.

"And there was me hoping the Faded Lands would wipe that bastard from our sight once and for all!" Ramien cursed, causing Tristan to turn to his brother.

"Who is he?" Tristan asked quietly.

"You lucky bastard!"

"That there is Percy," Zhaine prompted. "A sly kiss arse of a Scribe he was. Used to share dorms with Trevor and Cedric. We were never very fond of him though, nor he of us...that is aside from Cedric but I suppose they did grow up alongside each other."

Percy looked back over at Tristan again, a certain smirk across his face. A name lingered on his lips, as though he knew him by a different one.

A few moments later, Jensen invited them all into his meeting room upstairs in the tower. It was where he discussed the affairs of his state with his own, much smaller council although the room was more than accommodating for them. Two men were already in the room, one of them Federick, the other again Tristan recognised but he was not sure how. There was a certain dank smell about him, like he lived in a hollow wood or something. His attire was ragged, compromising of a robe made up of many patches in different shades of green. Tristan knew this was symbolic of a Shaman, the patches significant of the clans within his tribe. However, there were surprisingly more patches than Tristan had ever seen on a Shaman, at least forty different stitchings to be precise. He frowned, noting his uncle's expression as he greeted the Shaman both with shock and joy. He imagined words were exchanged regarding the Pagan village but whatever they were, they were unheard.

The few chairs in the room soon became occupied and Nielson took his place at the head of the room with those that weren't seated leaning against a wall or planting their feet firmly. They could be here a while. Silence followed shortly and Nielson addressed the room.

"Welcome friends," he began, opening out his arms in receipt of them. "Before I handover to the reason we are here today I would like to introduce Federick and Leafser."

*Leafser...*Tristan knew that name! He was a visiting Shaman in Hasaghar when he was an Acolyte. He was the one that had told them how to destroy The Final Glyph. A long-lived Pagan, he was also a highly spoke of ally of the Keepers...he being the reason the two factions were at peace.

"Now, with the formalities over...I hand over to Linford who has kindly agreed to speak on our combined behalf."

"Good morning fellow Elders," Linford started...how very formal of him. "Your majesty!" he paused, as though he was working out how to phrase the rest. He shortly decided it wasn't worth it and pressed on. "It has become very clear that Dharsi are once again becoming a growing problem. Federick and Leafser have both confirmed the slaughter of the Pagan village to have been their work. Not to mention the continued notion of our young returning Scribes becoming possessed by Dharsi spirits set free into this world by a crack in the seam between our world and the Faded Lands. As we are all aware the fiftieth generation of Union has come into the frame now and the prophecies have spoken. They are the last to come, our final chance to restore the balance. The prophecies are clear they are our only hope."

Tristan made a sideward glance to his uncle as he rolled his eyes; he probably thought Linford dramatic. Whatever his quarrel with the Brothers, it was getting old now.

"Now a discovery from the past has potentially given us a way to defeat them once and for all. As we all know, nine survived the culling of Dharsi and it is thought they were the primary wall if you like, the Elders of the following. The reason they survived we know to be Gervais; however it has long been believed that there was more to the story as to why those eight others survived over the rest. Alas, we as Keepers have some confessions to make and that is why I have called a gathering of more than what is in this room."

Jensen frowned but Tristan and his brothers suspected there to be a bigger audience then what was there. They followed Linford back down the tower and into the ballroom where hordes of people gathered. Tristan picked out Hamish and in the crowd and the others he mostly recognised from when Ivan was condemned. Also in the room were a few Hammers and Pagans and as much as Tristan understood them being there and needing to know, he couldn't help but wonder if it was something more. Particularly as the Hammers were those under Federick.

"Keeper Linford is this really necessary?" Tristan heard his uncle exclaim as he faced the crowd.

"Everyone has a right to the knowledge we are about to disclose." Linford instructed – it was about time someone stood up to him. "A wise man once said many heads were better than a few." Jensen was silent and the room stopped in motion to face Linford. "It is time we Keepers stopped keeping secrets."

Jensen backed away and all eyes now rested on Linford.

"Boys, if you will please step forward!"

He motioned towards the brothers, Jacques taking the lead.

"I introduce to you our final line of defence, our final chance to restore the balance. I present to you the fiftieth generation of Union!" mumbles erupted throughout the room but they silenced quickly enough. "As I'm sure you are all aware Dharsi are once again becoming a problem, not to mention a force to be reckoned with and I don't know about you but I'm not quite ready to hand our fate over to six boys who are part of a brotherhood known for their own betrayals. Not to mention those that ran from their responsibility to at least try.

"It is high time we stopped leaving them in the dark to fight alone and joined with them. Did Talus not head the First Generation in a plight to join the Keepers together under one head? Did Talus not envisage us to come together as one to keep the balance between light and dark intact? How disappointed he would be to see how far from grace we have fallen."

Linford paused for effect, his eyes glancing over the room. Tristan rolled his eyes; did he really have to be so dramatic?

"This being the case, it is time we came forward with a few confessions."

Linford stepped back and Federick and Leafser took the floor. Frowns were shared with the brothers and Dante and Balderick. Did this all go deeper still?

"We Keepers have kept a great many secrets over the years," Leafser began. He had a squeaky kind of voice, nothing like the voice Tristan expected him to have. "Some would argue that a great injustice that we have kept ourselves…separate." Tristan noticed then the mark on the top of his right hand – Leafser was a Light Mage. "But that is the way of the Keepers – to observe. In the beginning we were as overseers, 'tis where the phrase a Keeper can only be seen by those he wants to be seen by came from. But Talus believed we should be more present in society, exert our specialties in order to help society's progress. Many of you may remember when our patron Saracen bought light back to the world after the darkness struck. But he was probably the most fallen of us all...lost even to us. He was perhaps our biggest oversight."

"You may be wondering why these confessions however are coming from a Hammerite and a Pagan of all people," Federick continued. "Those of you that are forget that the First Generation of Union was made up of the separate factions who came together to preserve society in the wake of darkness. Talus headed, alongside his brothers by blood Saracen and Charles. A Hammerite and a Pagan were also among them with a Keeper named Sondheim taking the head as Ally. The Pagan," Federick motioned to Leafser, "and the Hammerite!" and then to himself. "They were our ancestors and to us, they passed on their secrets."

Tristan scorned, even he had not been completely honest with them. And he of all people should have known not to be so.

"But Pastroclus..."

"Pastroclus was my brother, but not in the way I lead you boys to believe. It's complicated! I'm sorry I was not completely honest with you boys," As though he read their minds, Federick turned to the brothers. "But perhaps you can understand that whilst we knew you boys were our only hope, we could only give you so much rope to tug. We had to see for ourselves that you were the ones the prophecies spoke of, especially after everything the Keeperhood had been through."

"You above anyone else should've known we deserved more..." Ramien scorned, unable to hold his tongue amid the cations of his brother by blood.

"You will remember that I helped you none the less. Despite all my conceptions, I helped you when Destiny begged me not to. Surely you owe me some respect for that at least!"

"Now, back to our history lesson," Linford took the lead once more. "After the union of the Keepers of Secrets and Time...and our introduction into the modern world there was a revolt. It is unclear who headed this revolt but it resulted in the beginnings of Dharsi. Saracen already envied the respect his brother got for being the patron of the Keepers. Simply being the King of Light was not enough for him. As much as I never expected what we have recently discovered to be the case...a part of me wonders why we never saw it coming. He and Charles had always been so close...why would he do that to his own brother by blood..."

"So…and sorry to interrupt," Jensen intervened, a look of impatience shared on the faces of everyone in the room. If he had put two and two together then so had everyone else. The Keeper Elders, particularly the ones as old as Linford seemed to love waffling – dancing around the point and never really getting to the point. "Are we to assume that the Leader of Dharsi is in fact Saracen disguised and assuming his brother's name."

Linford was silent, his eyes wide. Tristan wasn't sure if he was insulted or surprised. The silence though erupted an onslaught from the crowd as some began shouting in anger and others moaning in remorse. One of their greatest patrons; a traitor from the start. For some it all suddenly made sense, for others the shock was hysterical. Even Jensen did not know where to look. So Nielson made the effort to quell the rabble.

"Silence!" the room was silent, all eyes falling on Nielson. "Now more than ever we need to come together…"

"How do we defeat an evil almost as old as time itself!" one shouted.

"He's the King of Light – how do we defeat Light?"

"Why should we even trust you Keepers if you kept such secrets."

"I understand your worry," Nielson regained control of the room once more. "It is why I have decided to come to you with both the confession and a plan."

Nielson stepped back and Federick took the floor again, detailing the story he had previously told the brothers about his band of Nobility. How three years ago, men started to congregate in his chapel of solidarity here at Landen Forest, claiming the traitorous voices in their heads had stopped. Federick then paved the way for Jacques to explain how they believed that perhaps in destroying The Eye of the Storm, some connection between he and Nobility was broken. They had freedom to their own minds once more, his traitorous voice no longer filling their heads with darkness. Jacques then looked back to Nielson who explained the key to getting back ahead of Dharsi was Gervais. The wall between the Faded Lands and the Land of Light was breaking and spirits were slipping through, possessing the weak minds of the young misguided Scribes. Gervais would help them, if only they could find him – perhaps he could give them the bit pf the puzzle they were missing. He proposed that a new stand was needed, a Union between not just the faction but the civilians too. One common cause uniting them all. Dharsi had bought forth the war and it was time they all united together to destroy them once and for all.

There was silence for a time, many an exchanged look among the non-Keepers. Tristan watched his uncle closely as his eyes danced over the faces in the room. Fear was painted on his face, tormenting his leadership. But there was a cunning streak, like he too had a plan.

"You have the force of Az Landen behind you!" he called out, every eye in the room now upon him. The statement had come as a shock to many of those faces in the room who looked to him now, but none of them disputed him. "But as you can understand I have my reservations."

"Of course my Lord," Nielson nodded his head in respect, motioning towards Linford who stepped out from the crowd.

"We know the identities of all but two of the surviving eight brothers of Dharsi." Linford confessed, a low murmur of suspicion reverberating around the room. Four of those are already dead and we believe Charles...or Saracen however you want to call him both to be in Hasaghar surrounded by a new band of misguided followers and protected by Dangur. The other two are a mystery to us."

"What do we know about these other two?" Percy stepped forward, the question puzzling Tristan. He watched as Basso put out a hand to stop his ascend as though he was warning him. *What was his interest in all this?*

"It is thought they are two children!" Tristan picked his words carefully, his eyes not leaving Percy. He wasn't really sure where this knowledge he held came from, but his brothers didn't seem perturbed by it so they clearly knew it too. There was something in the way their brother stood, his posture that stood tall as though he were insulted by the words spoken. The way Basso held him back too was cautious, like perhaps he shouldn't have reacted at all. "

"Or should we say were children." Linford took over now. "It is thought that there was a familial link between the nine survivors hence why their names were left out when Gervais confessed. Not to mention the fact that when we went through the wreckage left by the Enforcers a few child's things were found although there were no bodies to speak of. Had we known there were a pair of children they would've been welcomed back into the fold...but they are lost to us. Heck...it is all speculation anyway! For all we know, that could've been planted there."

Percy said nothing more, and simply stepped back into the crowd, Linford nodding as he did so. Nielson then turned back to Jensen to address him once more.

"Our efforts will be fully devoted now to finding Gervais lord," he promised. "My acolytes are also working hard to determine any clues that may lead to finding out the identity of the remaining brothers. We shall keep you informed every step of the way; of that you have my word!"

Jensen stepped forward and looked the First Keeper in the eye.

"Then I suppose we have our union!" his voice was stony and cold. Like the union was a means to an end, his last resort. But it was something at least.

CHAPTER 24 – PHILLIPI

The conclusion of the meeting seemed to drive the supposed small council to the tavern in the city. Tristan and his brothers occupied one table with Theorryn, Merlin and Nielson in one corner, and Basso, Cedric and Percy in the next. Both corners were exact opposites; the elder circle solemn and decisive as though they were trying to come up with a way forward. The other was happiness. Cedric hadn't seen Percy in about three years and the joy on his face at the sight of his brother was clear. It was clear on Basso's too – only from a fatherly perspective. The man had raised the two of them from orphans and each other were all they knew as family.

The middle circle of brothers was somewhere in the middle. Catching up and reminiscing old times while quietly aware that the real battle was still to come. Tristan simply flicked his gaze between both groups, watching his father's face get more and more stressed and Nielson become more and more taut. It seemed Merlin was trying to be the voice of reason. He watched Percy too...there was something about his eyes he did not trust. Like something in the back of his head was yelling at him to listen to it as though he knew something he wasn't quite aware of. And every time he looked away or blinked, he saw a face, a pale face with stark green eyes and maple brown hair.

He stretched his arms up, taking a sip of his beer to try and clear his thoughts. But his eyes strayed back to Percy, who in that moment caught eyes with him; changing his look of joy to one of reserved fear. And then something sparkled in those grey eyes sparking them with colour; like blood spattering on the inflicting of a wound. And then it clicked, a name forming on his lips.

Tristan rose from his table and made his way over to the three of them, causing a worried look to spread across the rest of his brothers faces.

"Percy," he addressed, planting a smile on his own face. "Nice to see you brother, how have you been?"

Percy and Tristan were far from brothers – that much he did remember. Over their early years as Scribes, Percy had held a lot of resentment for his associates. He'd been a Keeper his whole life yet the brotherhood excelled where he could not. He may have been a know it all in class, but when it mattered his skill lacked. He was even jealous of the friendship Tristan held with Cedric and Trevor, his two roommates.

"Ah, Tristan," Percy replied sheepishly. "Sorry we've not had chance to catch up. I hope your memory is…improving." He didn't mean that – Tristan was sure of that much.

Tristan didn't say much else, he just locked eyes with him. That red glint was starting to become the only colour he could see in those eyes and his left palm began to tingle where his mark was. The silence began to get awkward and Dante had moved over to the bar to observe, Basso's eyes not leaving Percy. As the red became all Tristan could see, the name on his lips formed again but this time more clearly. *Phillipi!*

"It was you wasn't it," Tristan's face turned hard and he was suddenly unable to control his actions and words. "You let lose the Hound of Lost Souls…you're the reason she's dead."

He hadn't said it particularly loud but the whole tavern had gone quiet and all eyes were on Percy and Tristan.

"Are you okay there Tristan," Percy replied arrogantly, trying to avoid Tristan's gaze. "Sounds like you've had one too many beers. Some things never change…"

"No, you're right…some things never do…Phillipi…"

Percy's eyes widened but his expression didn't change, even as his right hand disappeared under the table. He grimaced, Cedric noticing and rising where he sat so that he stood over his brother. Basso however remained where he sat, as though he was believing his adoptive son innocent until proven guilty.

Dante came now to stand by Tristan, a stern look on his face. Percy didn't look at Tristan's dazed manner, he just stared into nothingness, eyes casting over at Basso who thankfully offered no support. When he saw no one was supporting him, he sighed heavily and rose from his seat.

"You've definitely had too much…"

Grabbing him by the arm, Dante stopped him in his tracks causing a look of pure fear. Basso's eyes were on him now, but he remained where he sat. Dante's eyes on Percy's, he used his other hand to pull down the boys sleeve to reveal a mark on his wrist. Fresh blood was dripping from it as though it seemed it were still etching itself there. It almost resembled a stick man on fire, as though burned for all his treachery.

Tristan had never seen a mark of the like, and it puzzled him. In such a place, he expected Unbinding like Cedric held...not this...whatever this was...

"So it was you?" Dante cursed. "You bewitched us on the battlefield...you are the one who corrupted us? I remember that glyph..."

A smile pinched the ends of Percy's lips and Basso and Cedric's faces were ashen, almost as though they couldn't believe the treachery.

"Dante Ashdown," Percy sneered. "What a pleasure it is to see you again."

In that moment, the red took over his eyes and his skin paled as though he were crazed. Dante threw him to the floor, pulling a dagger from his belt. All eyes were on him, his identity finally revealed for all to see, but it seemed they would all rather let him have his way with the dirty traitor then worry about his past.

It was Basso who jumped to the aid of his adopted son, holding up his hands in mercy as he knelt before Dante.

"Wait!" he called out. Dante held fast; his dagger still raised above his head. "We can use him!"

Percy scorned at his father, Cedric looking half relieved and half confused as to the loyalty shown. Zhaine, Ramien and Jacques were on their feet at Tristan's side, Nielson, Theorryn and Merlin not far behind. Thankfully, aside from the barman who seemed to stay out of the way, no one else was in the tavern to see.

"Use him?" Dante questioned, anger ripping across his face. Justice had to be served surely.

"He is Dharsi...Nielson said himself we have only one left now to discover. Perhaps he can help us win this war?" Basso's voice shook; whether it from fear or something else Tristan did not know.

"I don't care! After everything he has done..."

"Justice will be served...brother!" The address knocked Dante, and his eyes locked with Basso. "But let us first try see if he can be useful."

Basso had a point. They were running out of time with the hole in the Faded lands tearing. They had to at least try. He stepped forward, placing a tentative hand on Dante's shoulder. Shaking with unspent rage, Dante lowered his arm, returning the dagger to his belt. Ramien and Zhaine stepped forward to seize Percy by the arms as he scorned, Theorryn taking the lead to escort him to the dungeons.

Later that night, or what must have been the early hours of the morning, Tristan found himself down in the dungeons seeking out Percy. As he came towards the door to the cells, he collided with Cedric. His brother was a mess, his red face stained from tears of betrayal. Tristan tried to console his brother but he shoved him away. He had always known Percy was the jealous type when it came to the brothers...but to have been lying all along about who he was...it bought his whole life into question. How could he have not known?

He watched after him for a few moments before entering the dungeons and coming face to face with his foe.

"I presume you just ran into my cry baby of a brother!" he goaded as Tristan came to face him. He had a snide look on his face as he leant on the bars, his arms through the gaps as though daring onlookers to step forward. "Do you admire my talent, how I kept the persona going so long baffles even me."

Tristan was silent, but he kept eye contact with Percy. He wouldn't show his fear, nor any emotion for that matter.

"Not so imposing without your brothers are you...never had you pinned as the strong silent type." Tristan continued to ignore him, leaning back against the wall opposite the cell and folding his arms across his chest. "Would you like to know about me? Surely you must be curious? Surely you must have questions?"

"Would you answer them truthfully though?" Tristan decided to humour him, doubting he even would tell him anything useful.

"That depends on what you want to know." Tristan didn't answer, but Percy seemed in a boastful mood so perhaps he would leak something useful. "I was a mere boy when all this started...no older than thirteen would you believe. My lineage may surprise you...Sorren and Storm – they are my parents."

Tristan raised his eyebrows in disbelief. He was mocking him surely...there was no way that was true.

"Oh don't tell me, you assumed Sorrow and Storm to be men...to be brothers?" he laughed menacingly. "Sorren was my mother – Storm my father."

"Many assumed they were brothers – no one really specified."

"I was a babe when they became encased, but my link to them was apparent and they were with me every day. Call it what you like – they spoke to me; my parents were always with me...and then you took them away. First my mother...and then my father...so I took your loves from you." Tristan didn't say anything – he wouldn't rise to the ammunition Percy was throwing. "And I must say the display you put on...how exciting it was."

"How did you do it?" Tristan asked, suddenly unaware of where the question had come from.

"I told you your curiosity would get the better of you. But be careful, your nine lives are running a little short are they not?" He starred down at Tristan's vacant face through the bars. "Then again I suppose you would want to know...your revenge has been taken away from you because I am already named – but you can at least know what I did. Closure!"

Tristan frowned. It was like part of him knew everything Percy had to expose and the other had no clue.

"Come closer brother. Let me show you what I did to him."

"Him?" he questioned. He hadn't meant to say that out loud. He took a step towards the bars.

Percy's smile stretched wider and his eyes shined with glee.

"Well yes...he was my moment of greatness! My parents would have been proud of what I did to him."

"Trevor...you turned him?"

"And the penny drops." He clapped slowly, mockingly. "Come, let me show you!"

Stupidly, Tristan did as he was told – as though he were charmed to do so, and two cold hands slithered onto his cheeks making everything go dark, the sound of the traitor's eerie laugh ringing in his ears.

CHAPTER 25 – THE HOUND OF LOST SOULS

The blackness cleared and everything was tinged with red. Echoes rang in his ears as Tristan tried to take in his surroundings. The room he was in was like a hall of mirrors, smoke rippling from them. They didn't show a reflection though, they seemed to show places and other people – like he was watching people. The room was circular in shape and he was watching what he realised was himself and his brother Romeo. He couldn't hear what they were saying; the voices in his head were too loud. He noticed they were the same voice – a voice he recognised.

"Sees you a man of great weakness," it echoed. "But I think we doubt his cleverness. I think he will be the end of us."

"Not if I have anything to say about it!" his own voice sounded but he realised it was different; like he was now a different person.

"You'll send yourself crazy staring into that thing you know," another voice echoed in the room and he felt himself turn and look towards the middle of the room where a man stood.

The man had skin as black as the night sky with stark white hair and red piercing eyes. He stood at least seven-foot-tall, a tower in comparison to any man and an imposing one at that. His muscular arms rippled out of his armoured vest top that masked a red tunic with a chain mail kilt and heavy black boots. A tattoo of a red spider was on his forearm with tribal markings in white decorating the rest of the skin. An intimidating figure indeed.

"Dangur," his own voice addressed as he realised he knew the man that stood before them. "How long has it been dear Uncle? Nice to see you looking...well!" the voice was mocking and spiteful.

"Have some respect boy!" Dangur roared. "You forget your place Phillipi."

Phillipi? Tristan was seeing through Percy's eyes now. He was showing his own delusions, making him wonder what he might learn.

"So you expect me to just bow down to you after more than a century of you not being on the scene. I have been forced back into the fold of the Keepers, acting like some measly Scribe who doesn't know his runes from his glyphs and you demand respect. Do be serious!"

"I am told you have decided to take matters into your own hands. The Herasin has experienced an extreme level of disruption from you. He has expressed concerns!"

"The powerful Herasin didn't want to come discipline me himself. Decided to exact a more firm hand in the form of my uncle."

"You should let him take care of matters. He has a plan and you need to step in line. Else, you will ruin everything."

"You of all people should understand. They destroyed my mother...your sister..." *Sorren was Dangur's sister?*

"Your parents have been dead a long-time boy...long before those boys came along..."

"But they have always been with me, and now...she is gone. And it's all because of them! I deserve revenge!"

"I'm not saying we don't deserve our revenge..."

"Our...there's no ours about it! You haven't been around to warrant it..."

"You honestly think I've been sitting idly by all this time. You have no idea!"

There was a silence; eerie and cold.

"Whatever your feelings Phillipi, I urge you to have patience. The Herasin has a plan and if you act alone, you risk throwing a spanner in the works."

"I know what I'm doing!"

"Well if you're going to be stubborn at least promise me you won't underestimate those boys."

Phillipi didn't answer him, he simply stared after him as Dangur faded into the blackness.

The scene dispersed and the room changed to a perfect square. Large cogs moved around the room as though it were some form of clocktower. *Hold on!* Back when Tristan was an Acolyte, they had sought out the Hammers to help them with a prophecy that foretold the traitor would be pointed to with the stopping of time. They had been told to stay out of it, the prophecies were not theirs to decipher, but growing tired of the dead ends they took matters into their own hands and instructed the Hammers to stop the clock. But something had gone wrong...*Was he the cause?*

Phillipi held out his hand where a window like void appeared, seeing the brothers speaking with a Hammer priest. The clock sounded loudly at midnight and a cunning smile appearing on those thin lips. The void faded into his outstretched hand and he took a hammer which lay leaning against the wall and wedged it into the cogs, jamming them. The metal began to screech, sparks flying. Shouts could be heard from below and the tower itself began to shake as glyphs ripped up Phillipi's arms. *He was the same as Cedric!*

As the shaking of the tower began to cause cracks in the walls, the room around them evaporated again.

"A cunning plan indeed my boy," came the echoey voice of the Eye. "But you have perhaps just wiped out our greatest pawn to play."

"Trust me father...there was an even bigger one in the midst." Phillipi answered as they appeared outside the clocktower and watched it fall to its knees.

Tristan and his brothers had risked their lives to save a lot of Hammers that night. And as a result when they escaped the Compound a few days later after being detained for meddling in the affairs of the Elders, had hidden them from the Enforcers. Perhaps Percy had planned to kill them in this destruction, or perhaps turning the Keepers against them was his plan all along.

Ironically enough, when the clocktower fell the steeple pointed towards the quarters of the First Keeper who, at the time, was Charles. So either way, the clocktower had done its job.

The next room to form through the red tinge was what looked to be a dormitory with three beds, one being occupied by Percy himself. He was pretending to sleep in the darkness but could just make out the figure in the opposite bed making to leave the room. Suddenly all the candles in the room lit and Percy shot up to block his roommate.

"Where are you sneaking off too Trev," he asked ghostly. "You know it's past curfew."

Tristan remembered Trevor now; a mousy looking man with ginger curly hair and freckles upon his cheeks. He had deep green eyes that seemed forever fearful. But there was courage there too, as though he was some form of underdog everyone rooted for.

"Relax Percy," he reassured his voice quiet but with confidence there. "I'm not getting into any trouble."

"Then where are you going?"

"Just to see some friends…"

"You're going to see the brothers, aren't you? You know you're not supposed to…you'll only get into trouble."

"I've not been caught yet…"

"What do you see in them? They're just trouble makers!" Tristan could tell even Percy was tired of his own persona.

"Their good lads Percy, if only you tried, you'd really like them."

"If I let you go Trev, you have to promise me something? That you won't let them lead you astray and if you need anything you simply only need to think of me."

"Percy, that's a little…"

"I want you to have this," Percy reached into a pocket on his tunic and handed Trevor a medallion. It was then that Tristan realised it resembled the same one they had found in Elan's journals. *Had Trevor been the reason it was there?* "It's very important to me and will act as a direct link to me. That way if you're in trouble I will know!"

Trevor turned the medallion over in his hand, his mind puzzled as to its form.

"The Mark of Saracen?" he noted. *There was more than one mark?*

"Close!" Trevor frowned. "You see Saracen had a brother by the name of Charles and the passing of the mark of Saracen which is their family name is known as Herasin. The mark of brotherhood."

Manipulation! Herasin meant father of treachery – Hera for father and sin for, well, sin.

Trevor's face was cautious, like he knew Percy was potentially being untruthful. But he took the medallion and smiled slightly. Perhaps he was right to keep Percy on his good side and at least play along even if he didn't fully trust the intention.

The scene changed again and they were suddenly in the meeting room of the compound. Hasaghar's city was built around a large circular tower known as Death's Toll. It was this tower that Romeo fell from into the sea below. The compound buildings were somewhat separate from the tower, joined by a beautiful garden which held memorials for many great First Keepers and Elders. The tower itself is where the council met and prophecies were read. The prophecy books themselves were also kept there and it is long thought that beneath the tower was a passageway to an ancient shrine.

The part they were in now was an alcove in the upper levels where they looked down to the base. Many alcoves encircled the room – they were where the Keepers stood when hearing the First Keeper and Interpreter speak.

It was then that he realised they weren't actually a part of the scene before them but watching it as though from a window. Stood in front just in the darkness were he and his brother...and Trevor. He remembered this moment, better than he cared to. Of all his memories, this was one he least wanted to remember.

The voices spoken by his brothers were silent, as though Percy was too busy focusing on someone else to even care what they were discussing. They fell silent and the red tinge came back. After a few moments, he noticed Trevor catch himself on his feet, as though he were about to faint. His brothers looked around and he saw the fear in their eyes. He tried not to look, but Tristan wasn't in control anymore.

The brothers were blasted back suddenly and the council members from the room ahead began to crumble, their screams silent in Percy's concentration. All that was left in their wake was a pile of rubble drenched in blood as though they had been turned to stone and then smashed to pieces. He sensed a feeling of glee in the eyes of his possessor but there also was the fear of Trevor.

That night, he and his brothers had been accused of possessing and manipulating Trevor for their personal gain in order to destroy the Keeperhood. They were arrested and held for trial where they were found guilty alongside Felix himself. They were already in trouble for the clock tower business, let alone this as well. Charles took over as First Keeper until one could be elected in his place; not that his reign lasted very long.

Suddenly he felt fear in Percy as Trevor began ripping apart the Elders in the main part of the tower. Their figures turned to stone at the touch of his hand and with the other he pushed against their head, rubble falling to the ground and their cries echoing through the dark. Some ran, others weren't quick enough. Soon all that was left was Charles who was rooted the spot, a mixture of fear and anger in his eyes. In that moment he felt Percy's control falter as though he underestimated the power of whatever he let possess Trevor.

As Charles' and Trevor's eyes locked, he felt a coldness and the red glare was mirrored in the eyes of the acting First Keeper who frowned, almost commanding him to stop. But in those eyes of his was a familiarity as though he recognised the power that possessed Trevor and was surprised to see it within those once green eyes.

Trevor faded from sight and now they were staring into Charles' cold grey eyes. They were angry and they smouldered as though they knew Percy was watching.

The scene changed for what Tristan hoped would be the last time, especially when he realised where they stood. The fountain of Hasaghar's centre stood to his left and he could see himself hovering in the darkness of a shadowed alley. All around him innocent people fell into rubble as Trevor tore through them; glee plastered upon his face. Whatever was in control of him had banished every sign of Trevor. He was gone! Tristan knew that but a part of him still wanted to try and save his brother.

This foul night had seen them procure the Jackal's hand and the Chalice of the Builder in order to protect the faction sanctuaries. The Hammers and Pagans were each trying to shelter as many people as possible from the wrath of the Hound, but not everyone had been so lucky. And now the brothers stood ready to unite the Eye of the Storm with the fountain on the promise it would bind the glyph that was causing Trevor's onslaught.

Percy hadn't noticed the brothers lurking, he was too busy watching Trevor destroy himself. Even if they could break the possession on him, he would never be able to live with himself; was saving him really what they should be doing.

"Our time is coming my son," spoke the voice of the Eye in his head. "Soon this world will be ours. Their naivety is amusing!"

So the Eye was playing him. It had been all along!

Tristan was now kneeling in front of the fountain and he inserted the Eye into the alcove. It shone brightly, a light shining around Trevor as his power seemed to grow. He felt Percy laugh hauntingly, almost menacingly.

"You promised!" he heard himself yell at the crystal. "You promised he would be released."

"You really believe your brother can be saved," The Eye echoed. "Fool!"

And there she was; Dagnen appearing out from the crowd yelling her husband's name. He didn't need to see what happened next. He saw it enough in his dreams, her dying face every time he closed his eyes. The scene happened timelessly; a blast of Trevor's power ricocheting off a wall and hitting Dagnen. She collapsed into the arms of her lover, her face pale and aghast. Her last breaths were that of love for the life they held and as the fight faded from her eyes; anger and grief overtook Tristan. There was no way Trevor would be able to live with himself now.

Panic hit Percy as he spied Tristan pick up the hammer. But he was not quick enough and the voice of his father was gone. He was alone, for perhaps the first time in his entire life. Everything was so truly quiet as he warped back into the smoky hall of mirrors they had found themselves in at the start. Now Tristan was facing Percy who hunched against a mirror, his face awash with grief and fear.

"I told you to leave well alone," The deep voice of Dangur sauntered into the room. There was a boastfulness there, but it was tinted with concern for the boy. "You had no idea the sort of power you were dealing with."

"He's gone...my father is gone..." Percy's voice was shallow.

"Storm has been gone a long time Phillipi. He was never truly there in the first place."

"I feel so lost Dangur, so truly alone. I've never not heard their voices. Dangur, what do I do?"

Dangur approached Percy and placed a firm hand on his shoulder. The boy collapsed into him and he held him there comfortingly. The scene faded and Tristan was left in darkness.

An echo bought Tristan back. His right cheek had a coldness there and hot breath slithered down the back of his neck. The echo sounded again and he pulled away, his vision focusing on the face in front of him – the face of a traitor. There was a look of glee, neurotic glee! He tried to pull away...

CHAPTER 26 – THE SONS OF UNBINDING

"How have we gone all this time not knowing!" Cedric raged. He had been ranting the same line for at least half an hour. 'How could we not know?' – the eternal question on everyone's lips over a realisation. Basso sighed heavily before deciding he'd had enough of listening to it and rose to his feet to leave the room. "Where are you going?"

"I can't sit here and listen to you any longer!" Basso said quietly. "I need to see him!"

"How can you after what he has done?"

Basso paused by the door to the room without looking back at Cedric. He could feel his adopted son's eyes on him, searching him for any emotion. Opening the door, he left the room. As the door shut, something banged against it making it shudder – probably a book or something.

As he approached the dungeons he frowned. Where were the guards? Maybe Theoden had sanctioned none – that was for sure a mistake, even to Basso. He looked all around, assessing the situation. Perhaps they had been called away? He peered through the bars in the window of the door, spying Tristan close to the bars of a dungeon cell. He frowned as he noticed a hand around the back of Tristan's neck and Percy's own face very close to his. Taking a step forward allowed him to see more of what was going on.

The echo sounded again, and Tristan heard the dungeon door clang open. He pulled himself away from his foe in enough time for a dagger to miss him and plummet into the body of the man who pushed between the two of them – the man he assumed the echo had belonged to.

Basso slumped backwards into Tristan's outstretched arms, Percy erupting with noise as the dagger clanged to the floor. Whatever he said was inaudible; Tristan was too focused on Basso's face as the life began to drain from it and blood poured from his side. Even his eyes seemed to fill with blood.

"Help!" He yelled as Basso's eyes rolled shut. He yelled it again and again until the guards returned to their posts to hear him.

Tristan laced his fingers together and stared into the lines on his palms. He had been waiting outside the infirmary for an update on Basso. Zhaine and Ramien had joined him and Jacques was cajoling the guards for leaving their posts at the same time. He didn't have the right technically but clearly Theoden had more important things he should be doing.

"Percy is distraught," Jacques said now as he came to join them on the bench they were perched on. "And those guards are liabilities. They slipped out for a smoke – their words not mine. I don't even think they know who they are guarding. I mean does Theoden not care…"

Jacques' ranting was interrupted by the infirmary door opening. They all stood to face Isolde who looked up at them with a stern face. Her overalls were covered in blood, it didn't look good.

"Jon Basso is very lucky!" She exclaimed and the brothers sighed with relief. "I managed to stop the bleed and heal the skin. It's going to be a few days, but he will be okay." They nodded with understanding. "You boys should get some rest."

Isolde nodded to them all and walked away, tearing away the bloody overalls from her clothes as she went.

"I take it that means we can't see him…" Zhaine exclaimed, rising to his feet just as Cedric came storming out of the room – a look of pure anger on his face. "We should follow him maybe!" Cedric stormed right past them as though he hadn't even seen them there.

Had Basso woken and said something to him? Or was the sight of him enough to enrage him against his once adopted brother? No doubt that was where he was heading.

The brothers figured it best just to linger by the door to the dungeons. It wasn't like he could get to Percy – the two weren't able to cause each other damage. Tristan hoped they wouldn't want to. As much as Percy was a traitor, they were still brothers. If that was

Romeo…the wish of his death wouldn't even cross his mind. All he would want is an explanation.

The others had their backs turned, only daring to turn around every now and then. Tristan watched tirelessly – it felt wrong to watch but they had to for his own safety. Percy had tried to kill Tristan and now knowing he was Dharsi…there was no telling what he was capable of.

Cedric was pacing up and down the space in front of Percy's cell. The one word he kept yelling was 'why'. From what Tristan was focusing on, it didn't sound like he was getting much back. He stopped then, staring at his brother. His face was twisted into a look of sadness and anger. He was crestfallen.

"Let's go," Tristan said. "We're useless here! I don't think anything is gonna happen."

He turned away and walked off, the look on his brother's face scarring his eyes. There was only one face he wanted to see right now.

There was a knock at the door. Tristan shot himself up from the bed in the early morning glow – he must've fallen asleep. Evelyn was lying next to him, her blonde locks masking her peaceful sleeping face. He pushed it to a side so he could see those small features of hers, thinking perhaps he had imagined the knocking. He looked around his chambers, shadows seeming to linger in the dim light that shone through the gap in the curtain across the balcony doors.

The knocking came again, making him shake his head. It had been a long night. Not wanting the noise to wake his daughter, he strolled over to the door lazily, checking the mirror on his way to make sure he wasn't too scantily dressed. Luckily, he was just lacking in a shirt. He opened the door to Daniel who stood there - pale faced. His eyes said he had been crying…a lot, they were tired and bloodshot. He looked him up and down, noting a book in his hand – Elan's diary.

"Daniel, are you okay?" were the only words he could muster. He could see the look of anguish on his face.

"The Glyph of Unbinding!" he muttered; his voice raspy. "The Scribe must seek to control the Glyphs, lest the Glyphs control the Scribe…for we shall know which is more likely to win."

Those words were the first Tristan remembered of his education with the Keepers. Felix had disclosed them as an introduction to the Keeperhood, a goal…something they all needed to remember for the rest of their lives. He remembered the Glyph of Unbinding was supposedly the hardest to control and many had tried and failed. Many thought there was some kind of secret to it. Either way it was prohibited for young Keepers to even try.

"What about the glyph?" Tristan asked, something in the back of his mind wishing he hadn't.

"You should know! You above all people should know about the Glyph!"

That last word was said with malice and spite as Daniel shoved the diary into Tristan's chest, slumping away back to his room. Tristan watched after him, noticing Balderick and Dante watching from their room, a questioning look on their faces. The look in Balderick's eyes though unsettled Tristan and it dawned on him that only one person could answer his questions and that was the Son of Unbinding itself – Cedric Baldwin.

"What was that all about?" Dante asked as he approached Tristan.

"I'm not entirely sure, but I know someone who might."

A few hours later saw the brothers in the Shrine alongside Dante and Balderick. Tristan told them of his encounter with Daniel and Jacques took it upon himself to explain their past with the Glyph. The Glyph of Unbinding had been unleashed by Sarisus in the first year as Keepers. He had attempted to crumble the Keepers from the inside out, corrupting their very framework using the Ruby of Sorrow and the Eye of the Storm.

Their second encounter with the glyph was through the eyes of Trevor. They had reversed the glyph using the Eye of the Storm in order to try and save him, but the power tore him apart. In truth, he was too far gone in the first place.

He explained how the glyph is strictly prohibited to anyone lower than a Runebound and even then, they are advised to take extreme caution. The glyph is one of the most unpredictable in nature and no Keeper known has ever been able to master it. That is to say except for those who were known as the Sons of Unbinding. These Keepers were born with the glyph upon them as though it were a birthmark. It is thought they were the true masters of it. However, they were rarer perhaps than Lightmages, none even being recording among the Annals. Perhaps it was because they used the glyph for illicit deeds...traitors and corrupted by what ran through their veins.

Cedric was one of these such individuals...although he proved the theory of corruption wrong on all counts. Cedric knew the bounds of his powers and the brothers with their combined powers of Unity helped him to harness it. Without them, he risked losing control completely and probably would end up just like Trevor.

"And so it would seem, Elan lost control just like Trevor," Cedric surmised as Jacques finished his history lesson. "My guess is Daniel thinks you boys are the cause of that what with his connection to Unity."

"You mean us right...mister *ally!*" Ramien jeered, rolling his eyes. Cedric shrugged in response, dropping the diary on the table.

"We need to figure out who this Son of Unbinding is that's corrupting everyone..."

"Well we know now!" Ramien glowered at Cedric.

"If you would let me finish...Percy isn't a Son of Unbinding. Just a misguided Keeper who thought he could control a glyph he had no right to. That's why Trevor took as he did, because Percy was not in control. There's somebody else...we need to figure out the last member of Dharsi."

"Perhaps I can help with that," Balderick muttered as he stepped forward. He looked rather sheepish and everyone apart from Dante looked sceptically in his direction. "I was a victim of the Unbinding glyph too!"

They stared, hardly able to believe their ears.

CHAPTER 27 - DEATH OF A BROTHER

The vision faded from me now and once again I was left in blankness. My feelings towards my enemy were changing, not in the sense that I as forgiving him; but I did have a newfound understanding and sense of compassion for his assumed predicament. It seemed as though he never meant for any of it to happen and perhaps his intentions weren't as clear as they were made out to be. Truly – he did not have a choice to do the things he did, or was this all some farce to manipulate my thoughts towards him in the hope it would cause me to turn a blind eye. Well, that would not work if it was the latter. A lot of me still held hatred for him, after all he killed your love brother, he broke us apart forever, he took me from you and put you where you are today - forgotten and broken. For all those things, I could never forgive him...but I could try to understand at least why he did what he did.

Suddenly he was before me again, his face solemn and full of loss. He bared his wrist showing me the mark; his face pained as though the mark caused it. Power came at a cost; it always did so what was his?

He launched at me and I let myself embrace him; unafraid, and we became one once more. I was eager to learn more of his past, learn what drew him to his breakdown...to his fall from grace. When I opened my eyes again, I stood outside of a mountain; the gateway that led inside guarded by two Keepers. We were waiting, crouched behind a rock so as not to be seen by the guards. Perhaps he was waiting for the remaining Brothers of Dharsi and his theory was soon proved by a spark that shot into the dark sky. The guards didn't appear to notice it, and we moved towards the origin of the spark to be greeted by Murdoch. After embracing my brother, I looked around the faces of his brothers; the Herasin, Hagen, Dangur and Sarisus.

"Where is Gervais?" I heard myself ask - to complete the ritual they needed him.

"Oh don't you worry about him; I have him under control." Murdoch assured slyly and I peered around to see Boris keeping Gervais close. He was crouched behind all the others - pained and broken.

"Do you have the key?" The Herasin asked, a quizzical look on his face

"Of course."

"So how are you going to get us in?"

"I'm not going to," the others gave him a fearful look as though they thought he had betrayed them. "*He* is!"

Suspicious, the brothers peered over the rock as I inclined my head in the direction of the gateway. There stood a man they all recognised and feared. I could feel the Herasin cursing me as though he thought I'd betrayed them all to Unity. I winked in his direction cunningly; these were my brothers too.

"Balderick?" One guard shouted to the hooded stranger that appeared to them suddenly. "That you?" The figure nodded. "What do you want?"

"Please, I beg you," He pleaded with them. "Just stand aside and let me through."

It was then that I realised what was happening and I felt sick to be a part of it. He wasn't in control of himself and now my enemy was going to make him commit an Ultimate Betrayal, I was sure of it. I was forced to look down as he pushed a nail into the mark, drawing fresh blood that struck him with slight pain. I followed his gaze upwards to watch tears fall from Balderick's eyes as he was forced into motion, using great magic to throw the guards out of his way with a simple flick of his arm. Once the act was committed, he sank to the floor, grief-stricken at what he had just done.

It was then that I realised the significance of the mark. It was the Glyph of Unbinding, making him a Son of Unbinding as Cedric was. Wait, did that mean the two were related? Supposedly the bloodline was distinct and rare. Or was it?

"You learnt to control the mark?" Murdoch exclaimed in disbelief.

"Of course I did, I had a great teacher," He winked at his brother who smiled to him, his eye full of worry.

"You mean to tell me that you are controlling a Brother of Union?" The Herasin asked, a look of amazement on his face.

"Yes. The Betrayal and corruption might as well start somewhere and I figured where better. Plus, he got in my way anyway so gave me no choice."

My enemy was sounding as cunning and malicious as I knew he could be and that scared me. He showed a malice capable of even striking his own brother with a little fear as I turned and saw the look on his half smiling face. This wasn't his little brother anymore!

"Then what are we waiting for!" The Herasin rose to his feet alongside his brothers and we headed for the gateway.

I began to think of what it must be like to be standing where Murdoch was. He was torn, between following his Brotherhood and his devotion to his brother. Something in him had changed and he saw that and maybe I had too. The core I felt within him had been the same as when I had looked into his eyes when he had dealt me that final blow and even now it hurt me thinking of his betrayal. Murdoch was indeed proud that his brother had become the man he was but perhaps he was fearful of what it would make him become. Murdoch always seemed to have had a cause from what I had learnt about him in my time; a true rebel with a cause who had only tried to get justice for the wrongs he felt were dealt to him. I couldn't quite remember what those wrongs were now and I was brought out of my thoughts by a change in the scenery. Balderick stood a few steps ahead, a crippled hooded figure slipping from his grip and onto the floor. A bloody dagger was in his hands and he dropped it to the floor, his face paler than a sheet. He was tormented by what he was being made to do, but the more blood that he shed the more contented my enemy was, the more the Herasin urged him onwards, the more apprehensive Murdoch became of his brother's nature.

"Here we are!" Dangur welcomed as we entered the main room of the Maw of Chaos.

It looked exactly as I remembered in my own trip here to stop Sarisus using the Eye and the Ruby to bring back his brothers of Dharsi. Three large tusks stretching up in the centre, their points meeting in the middle. In the centre across the floor was a large engraving of a rune inside a circle. The rune I recognised as the one on my enemy's wrist and others stood at the five points of the rim of the circle. I knew them to be the Glyphs of Union - so did that mean the rune in the centre was somehow a Pagan rune for Unity? Were Unbinding and Union somehow the same? It was farfetched but it made sense considering this sanctuary was of Pagan descent.

"Right then Dangur," the Herasin ordered, his brothers rounding on him. "What's the plan?"

"Step with me, we don't have a lot of time."

Dangur ushered them towards the centre of the Maw where a podium stood. At either side of its base was a hexagonal insert where the stones were intended to go. I looked back and ordered Balderick to stand guard and I too listened in on Dangur's instruction.

"It is almost time my brothers. At precisely midnight, when the moon has positioned itself in the space up above," He pointed to the hole in the top of the mountain where all I could see was the starry night sky; "We must place the stones within their places. The Eye must go here," He pointed to the left insert, "and the Ruby here." He pointed to the right insert. "The spirits of Sorrow and Storm will be united as soon as you start the ritual. At precisely the same time, when the moon is full the wielders must place the stones in place and turn them left, right and the left again to push them deeper still. As quickly as they can, they will then take their places in the Circle of Chaos; it shouldn't be too hard to find your places my brothers. Once you are in your place, and the light from the Maw strikes its path to you, you must cut across your mark in blood, tainting its trueness and purity and corrupting its nature. Sarisus will then command the power and corruption to the whole generation by standing in the centre and wielding it on behalf of us all. It's as simple as that!"

"What do you mean by cut across your mark?" Boris asked, he truly was an idiot and how he was chosen as a brother of Union I would never know - if that was truly how it happened.

"You really are as stupid as you look, aren't you?"

"Dangur!" Hagen cautioned. "Just elaborate, will you?"

"Like I said it's rather simple!" Dangur grabbed ahold of Boris' left hand to reveal his mark of Truth - ironic that, Boris was the biggest liar going, unless that was the whole point. It was then that it struck me how his mark was on the opposite hand to mine and my brothers; they really were our opposites. "Just draw a line with the dagger across your mark. Cut deep, but not too deep can't have you dying on us yet. Once you've cut, hold your hand down so that the blood drips onto the glyph below you, tarnishing its nature. Our aim is to turn the Glyphs to their opposites and the only way to do that is change them, taint them...corrupt them."

"So who wields the stones?" Murdoch asked, his arms folded across his chest, his eyes full of respect.

"I wondered who would be the one to ask that. The Eye must only be wielded by one who has seen time - you in other words my dear boy."

It was clear that Dangur shared that admiration and looked to Murdoch as a son. It warmed me slightly but only very slightly for it reminded me of the love I shared for my own brother. "The Ruby on the other hand can only be wielded by true evil and who better than a Foresaken who is a being of pure evil." Dangur passed a sack to Murdoch obviously containing the Eye. He grimaced as he took it, was the Eye was speaking to him?

"What about me?" I felt myself ask. It was clear my enemy wanted to be involved and of course he should be. He was the reason they had got this far after all.

"You have done well brother and proven your worth," the Herasin addressed, a smile at the ends of his lips. "But your part is over for now, you must leave the rest to us."

"The Herasin is right dear brother!" Murdoch turned to him and placed a hand on his shoulder. "You have done so well and I am so proud of you. But now, you stay hidden...you keep back no matter what happens. Keep Percy safe, promise me?" The Herasin nodded to Percy.

"Murdoch is right," Dangur agreed. "No matter what happens we need you in the fold...you must remain in joint loyalty to the Keepers."

"Bit late for that."

My enemy mumbled making even I wonder what he was insinuating. Something told me he wasn't talking about what he did to Balderick. I had been with him every step of the way so far but was there something I had missed?

"What is that supposed to mean?" The Herasin demanded but I shrugged it off confidently.

"Promise me champ!" I looked to Murdoch seeing the tears in his eyes as he moved his hand up to my face. I felt his warm touch of reassurance, of brotherly love and yet a reluctance to leave. "Promise me that no matter what happens, you stay hidden. I'd never forgive myself if something happened to you."

"But what if something happens to you Murdoch?" He asked his brother, tears forming in his own eyes.

"These brothers of mine have promised to protect you. You are as much a part of this as any of us, the hidden member, the one hundredth brother of Dharsi. No matter what happens to me they will protect you, they will always come back for you. They owe me as much to do this for you." I looked around at the others as they nodded humbly, silently promising to do as Murdoch had asked of them no matter what. Dangur's looked the most sincere.

"I promise!"

Murdoch smiled and placed a longing peck on my forehead before pushing me away where I took shelter behind some rocks near the entrance to the Maw with Percy by my side. I wanted to be hidden yes but in a clear enough view to watch the events take place.

The Brothers took their places around the circle, leaving Sarisus, Dangur and Murdoch to stand in the centre. I watched intently as the wielders nodded to each other before freeing their stones and looking up to watch the moon come into full view. Suddenly, my position had changed. I was no longer at one with my enemy but separate, on the outside of the action watching from the centre beside Murdoch and Dangur. I was close enough now to hear their shared words of encouragement to each other.

"Are you ready my boy?" Dangur asked, a doting look twinkling in his blood red eyes. Murdoch nodded, he was nervous; apprehensive even. "I couldn't be more proud of you; you are everything I imagined you would be...my legacy lies with you."

Murdoch nodded again, smiling slightly to his mentor. They joined their right hands, a brief look of devotion shared between them as they looked up in time to see the moon come into full view above, shedding white light into the Maw. It was time! In unison and hands still joined they united the stones of Sorrow and Storm placing them in the inserts and turning them left, right and left again. I watched as the brothers let go at last and ran to their places in the Circle, pulling their knives free and standing as the mirror image of their brothers. Patiently they waited as moonlight poured down on the stones, turning red as it hit them and sending a stream down each of the five lines that met the brothers of Dharsi. As it struck them, each in turn drew their dagger and dragged it across their palms, damaging their bounds forever and letting the blood drip onto the glyph below. As each drop fell an immense sense of power surged through each of them as Sarisus began to draw the magic from them, commanding it to corrupt an entire legacy of Unity and break them indefinitely. I watched as Sarisus chanted, the louder he got the more pained the brothers faces became as their magic was pulled from them, momentarily borrowed before it was thrown back at them with an immense force.

And then, all at once the light disappeared suddenly and I heard a solemn cry for Murdoch's name. I looked over in time to see pain fill his newly pale face as a sword appeared at the front of his midriff, blood dripping from its point. I looked over to see my foe being held back by Percy, a firm hand over his mouth so as not to give away their position. The man who had dealt the blow I recognised as Dante who pulled his blade free and let Murdoch crumble to the floor. At the sight of the current generation of Union, the others disappeared in fear, Dangur the only remaining. Union did nothing, they simply stood and watched. Had the corruption really been that instant?

The Foresaken approached his fallen brother, tears staining his own dark face. I took a few steps forward so I could hear their parting words as Dangur placed a hand on his cheek and used to other to clutch as Murdoch's shaking and bloodied hand.

"Stay with me Murdoch!" His voice broke in grief. "Please!" As the other members of the fifth generation of Union tried to approach Dangur they were blasted back by his pleading. Part of my heart felt pained, as though it were breaking to see such a loss. Perhaps it was because my own brother had lost me and although I had never seen his remorse, I imagined his feeling was something similar to this now. "Please, please don't leave me!"

"Remember...your...promise..." Murdoch kept saying, over and over again as the life began to leave his face and his hands became limp.

"I will do what I can but I cannot promise..."

"Promise...brother...promise..."

"I will!"

Dangur nodded solemnly and as the last breath left Murdoch's lungs, he closed his eyes for him and disappeared as Union raced to try and finish the deed with him. I could hear Dante trying desperately to console Balderick and bring him out of his crazed state, but my eyes were searching for my enemy and I found him behind that same rock he had been moments before, pushing into the mark on his wrist and drawing blood.

"Balderick you're okay," Dante consoled, grabbing ahold of his brother's shoulders and trying to steady his shaking. "He is dead, Murdoch is dead...you are free!"

"I killed them, I killed them all..." Balderick muttered, grief stricken at what he had done.

"You had no choice, you were being controlled. But he's dead now...they will understand."

"He's dead...but..."

"Murdoch is dead Balderick, he's not controlling you anymore." I wasn't sure why they were so convinced it was Murdoch controlling Balderick – they had to know of his gift. It was right if he shared it with my enemy – they were brothers after all.

"He wasn't..."

For a second there I thought I would hear his name spoken, hear my enemy's betrayal spoken and his status known by Union themselves. But Balderick trailed off deliriously, he didn't remember who and I realised that was what he was doing, making him forget - just like he had done you, perhaps my dear brother. As he did so, I became joined with my enemy once more and I saw Dangur appear behind us and watch him work his magic, a proud smile pinching at his lips.

"You have done well my boy," Dangur whispered as his spell was finished. "Murdoch would be proud!"

"What are you doing here?" He asked; he obviously believed they had left him behind despite the supposed promises they had made to Murdoch. Then again, these brothers of Dharsi were true that their name but obviously not loyal to each other now that their numbers were so scarce. Perhaps they didn't think him worth the risk, but it seemed Dangur thought differently, he was more true to his original mark of loyalty than the others were to theirs.

"I came back for you, just like I promised your brother. Unlike the others...I keep my promises. Now we must go!"

"Wait, just one more minute."

I followed his heartbroken gaze to the bloodied lifeless body of his brother by blood, fresh tears staining his face.

"I don't remember...I don't remember who was controlling me..." Balderick mumbled.

"That doesn't matter now," Dante reassured him, making his brother look at him. "It's over brother."

"They have no idea!" Dangur whispered confidently.

"Did it work?" Basso asked - the ritual had been interrupted.

"Only time will truly tell."

"You know I wouldn't be surprised if they planned this," I recognised Felix kneel beside Murdoch's corpse, turning his face towards him. "I mean first Avus turns up dead and a few hours later his own son betrays. We'll have to keep a close eye on the other one."

"Avus is dead?" Dangur muttered in disbelief, suddenly looking at my enemy a moment later as he realised what it meant. "You...you killed him?"

"Yep, part of my genius plan you see. My father is dead and I'm going to make it look like they did it." He explained, a spark of cunning in his eye as he admired his own plan.

"Plan?"

"Well we had to have a backup plan didn't we, in case this didn't work...and now, it's a good job I initiated it."

"You really are one of us champ, now and forever."

Dangur placed a tentative hand on his shoulder and the three vanished from sight, leaving the blankness to return to me one final time, or at least so I hoped...

CHAPTER 28 – THE ALLIES OF UNION

The brothers listened intently to Balderick's account of what he remembered. It was patchy and loose; painful. He told of how he remembered patrolling the passages of the First Keeper's chambers and came across a figure rummaging in the reliquary but the face was absent; like it had been removed from his memory. He told of how he tore through his fellow brothers easily but with remorse – he could see what he was doing, wish it to stop, but any resistance was futile. Even after, he could not remember the face of his controller, he just remembered the words – unbound, bent and broken – like some form of chant.

"So whoever enchanted you bears the same marks I do," Cedric deduced, showing his mark. "Perhaps I can undo it!"

"And how do you plan on doing that?" Dante quizzed; he was rightly wary of his brother by creed delving back into his own darkness.

"I can use my glyph to potentially unlock the memory…"

"You said potentially!"

"Well I don't know if it will work. In theory if I can access the memory, I can unbind the magic used to cloud the face. But it's just a theory, my powers are unknown even to me."

"It sounds too dangerous, I vote no…"

"You have no say in this Dante," Balderick blurted out, his frustration clear. "It's my choice and I say it's worth a try."

Dante shook his head sparingly but understood. Balderick took a seat next to Cedric who took his hands and lay them out flat, palm up so his bounds were visible. The others gathered round to watch intently as he drew a line across his unbinding mark with his index finger. Closing his eyes, he then placed it upon the Royal Guard's forehead, a light emitting there.

"Think of the last thing you remember before being enchanted and only that." He commanded and the others watched. Both were grimaced but it wasn't clear whether it was working or not.

The Unbinding Glyph appeared in the light that settled on Balderick's forehead, making it grow and emit seemingly around the whole room. Everyone shielded their eyes, the light blinding. The ground began to shake, books falling from the shelves around them. And then, almost as soon as it appeared, the light faded again and everything stilled. Cedric and Balderick looked around, both with a bewildered look on their faces.

"Did it work?" Dante asked, his echo breaking the silence.

"No…I still can't see his face…" Balderick answered, not making eye contact with any of them.

"What a shock!"

Dante rolled his eyes and stormed away towards the exit to the Shrine. But as Tristan looked around their sanctuary again, he realised something was different. The floor around the central foyer where all theirs and their predecessor's names were written seemed to have more. Each segment had an extra name, their own one containing Cedric's.

"Wait!" Nobility called.

Dante turned and the rest of his brothers followed his gaze, making the same realisation.

"Well Cedric you might not have unlocked Balderick's memory but you did broaden our horizons." Ramien clapped his brother on the back, his eyes gliding over the new names. Dante's own eyes went crazy as he realised the change – but not because of the change.

"Hey, did anyone know that Basso was an ally?" he asked as everyone's eyes glared towards the sixth generations' names and John Basso's name at the bottom of the list with the glyph marking him as ally just as Dante had said.

Tristan looked around at his brothers who all slowly shook their heads. Cedric even looked in shock. Dante headed for the shelves of Annals, scouring for the books belonging to them. Finding only one, he opened it but the pages were stained in blood and they smelt foul.

"What the…" he distained as he promptly placed the book back on the shelf. "Well I guess that's rather fitting considering they were the first truly traitorous generation."

"Then maybe that means he had a reason not to tell us." Jacques surmised, looking to Cedric who hadn't said a single word.

"Perhaps the subject is best broached by you Ced?" Ramien suggested.

"Give him some space Ram!" Zhaine scorned.

Barging past his outspoken brother, Cedric made for the way out of the Shrine, his eyes holding back tears. Something else a member of his supposed family had failed to tell him.

The brothers dispersed back to their chambers, all feeling a little awkward over the whole situation. They didn't know how best to help their brother, nor did they really know what to do next. In the morning, perhaps speaking to Nielson would be the best point of call.

As Tristan passed Daniel's door he stopped, taking a deep breath. He sighed, knocking the door and waiting a while. Surprisingly it opened a crack, Daniel's tired and emotional eyes peering out. He was about to close it again when Tristan raised his hand to stop him, pushing Elan's diary through the gap and into Daniel's hands.

"You should know," Tristan muttered, trying not to make eye contact with him. "It wasn't Union that killed him, just his connection to them. You want to blame someone for his death, blame Dharsi, typically those who unbound him in the first place."

He didn't wait for Daniel to reply before continuing down the corridor to his own chambers where Myrina came running out from the door; grief-stricken.

Tripping, she fell into Tristan's arms, her face ashen and pale as guards came rushing towards them. Tristan's eyes flashed to them before reverting his gaze back to his brother's love.

"Myrina," he asked concerned. "What's the matter?"

"It's Evelyn!" she gasped. "She's gone!"

Tristan's eyes widened and his breath caught in his chest as though his heart had stopped. More guards ran past, forcing Theorryn out of the room opposite to see the commotion. He glanced at his son as he grabbed the arm of one of the guards.

"What's all the fuss about?" he asked impatiently as Myrina mumbled the same two words over and over again – 'she's gone'.

"It's the prisoner lord," the guard hastened. "He's gone!"

Theorryn let the guard on his way and looked to Tristan. Percy was gone...and Evelyn too – surely it wasn't a coincidence.

CHAPTER 29 – THE VEIL OF THE FADED

The room around him was echoing with conversations of how to best deal with the situation at hand. The events had found the brothers in the small council room, most of them silent as Theorryn quarrelled with his own brothers about how to catch up to Percy and find Evie. Tristan looked to each of his brothers; Ramien and Zhaine were both watching the conflict with sceptical looks on their faces – probably trying to deny the similarities between the two sets of brothers. Jacques was deep in thought across the table, occasionally glancing a look at Cedric over in the corner who was pale faced. Dante and Balderick were in the other corner with Nielson and Linford, their conversation a lot quieter than the royal cohorts.

The temperature was rising and his breath was shortening. None of this was helping the situation, none of this would find his daughter. He made to rise to his feet but Jacques beat him to it, his chair sliding backwards causing all eyes to fall on him.

"I have an idea," he said, his voice shaky, his own eyes on Cedric still. "But Ced...the decision is yours." The brothers looked around at each other quizzically; Cedric looking fearful. "You can see him, can't you? Percy, I mean...you could see him."

"I could try...but I'm not sure it will work." Cedric replied slowly as he looked to Tristan.

"It is works and finds Evie it will be worth it." Tristan replied, his voice breaking.

Jensen looked like he was going to say something but Theoden gave him a look that said otherwise. So without opposition, Cedric held out his hand for Tristan to take. Turning over his right hand, he traced over the mark on his left forearm, a green light shining there. Both the brothers closed his eyes and silence enveloped the room. After a while Cedric gasped, prompting Jacques to step to his side in support`.

"What do you see Ced?" he asked calmly, attempting to reach out but Nielson batted his hand away – there no telling what might happen if another person broached the contact. Could Cedric even hear them?

The brothers watched helplessly a while longer, Cedric's frown becoming more and more worrying. Ramien made a move to break the contact but again he was stopped by Dante this time. Whatever was going on was potentially working, or at least they hoped.

What felt like forever passed until finally Cedric and Tristan opened their eyes, releasing their grasp and gasping for air.

"What did you see?" Jacques repeated again after it seemed like they had caught their breath.

"It's hard to describe." Ramien swore as Cedric answered, his father dismissing him immediately.

"Just try Ced, tell us as you saw it." Nielson fished, trying to push him to try at least.

"Well it was a room with beds, maybe ten of them. But there was like a ghostly presence about it, like a mist across the whole room and faces here and there. At the head of the room was a podium and that's where Percy was stood."

"Did you see Evelyn?" Tristan asked exasperated.

"No, but there was another figure there too. He wore a hood but from the colour of his skin and his height...it was a Foresaken...

"Dangur!" Balderick interjected but he was ignored as Cedric continued.

"He was angry, kept asking why Percy had to take the child...why the child was necessary. He came back to save Percy not help him kidnap a child. Percy said how Herasin would be proud he had managed to get to Tristan, but all the Foresaken could say was fuck Dharsi. I think he's lost it."

"I think more accurately they've lost him," Zhaine assumed. "That could be helpful to us."

"I was actually talking about Percy – surely he isn't capable of this..."

"Cedric tell me more about the room," Nielson asked, trying to keep him focused. "Were there any windows...identifying features?"

"There were a few windows yes, one which looked directly out at trees...like it was some tall tower." Cedric explained.

"I know where he is. As you will all know, near every Compound there is a tower where the Readings happen. The one here is no different, in fact it's the very tower Dharsi were dispatched from. This is where it gets risky though; the ghostliness you were talking about Ced is because the barrier between our world and Faded realm wares thinnest there. The Faded realm was never meant to contain the power and treachery that it does and some say because of that, Dharsi's presence there weakens it. The very power that was used to put them there is slowly destroying it."

"Why would Percy go there though?" Ramien questioned.

"I don't know…but I have a very bad feeling!"

"We have to get my daughter back!" the others nodded in agreeance with Tristan.

"Well if I can distract Percy, then you guys can get Evelyn out." Cedric suggested.

"Percy is unstable Ced, distracting him may not be enough. You may not be enough!" Nielson said gravely.

"I know." There was a lump in Cedric's throat; the traitor was still his brother after all.

"The Elders and I can form a barrier around the tower. It will prevent him from escaping should he manage to…by magical means or otherwise. My liege would you be able to spare some guards to help us surround the tower? With the barrier being so thin there's no telling what we could be up against."

"Theoden, take the Light Mages. Use any force necessary to get the child back!" Jensen ordered his brother-in-law. Theoden nodded in response, bowing his head and leaving the room.

"In that case I will rally the Elders. Everybody necessary, meet at the tower in half an hour." Nielson ordered and the room obeyed.

The brothers said nothing to one another as they made their journey to the tower of the Compound; knowing the mission at hand. They simply followed Cedric out of the palace and towards the compound to face the traitor who awaited them, marching as though they were reapers of justice.

The tower soared over them as they stood in the courtyard staring up at it. Without a moment to lose they stepped up to the doorway as Nielson and the Elders formed their wall around it alongside Theoden's guards. It was like a large bubble had trapped them all in the vicinity making Cedric wonder if Percy too had seen it appear. Nielson nodded to the boys, Dante opening the door for them as it appeared from nowhere.

The tower had been sealed off not long after Dharsi were banished and now a long stair case opened out before them, seeming to stretch up to the heavens themselves. As soon as the door opened it was like the shadows dared to embrace them – the theory of the barrier being thin here was probably another reason it was sealed off.

"Reminds me of Death's Toll," Jacques gulped, casting a look at his brothers.

"Don't worry, we'll be sure not to go near the edges!" Ramien joked, causing a scowl from Zhaine and a bitter look from Jac. Now was not the time!

"Guys can we take this seriously please!" Tristan asked through gritted teeth as he began to climb the stairs.

Ramien shrugged his shoulders and they all followed behind Tristan. About half way up a bang sounded and they froze where they stood. A child's cry rang through the tower, echoing off the brickwork.

"Evie!" Tristan yelled, sprinting up the stairs as fast as he could.

"Well there goes the element of surprise!" Ramien grunted as he followed up after Tristan with the others.

Tristan didn't care what was coming, he just wanted his daughter back in his arms. A door was vastly approaching him but he didn't slow down. Instead he raised his arms to cover his face and burst through the wood, splinters flying out of the hinges as Tristan came to a stop inches from the doorway, his brothers gathering around behind him to see a room just as Cedric had described aside from the podium. There was another stair case hidden to the left corner of the room – this was clearly the first of several rooms like this. And as they passed each floor, the ghostly white sheets across the beds seemed to wear faces of those that had once occupied them. Some were children, some men and even women. Dharsi had consisted of one hundred members, nine of which had escaped the Enforcers including Gervais. But none of the brothers were aware the membership was so diverse. As they neared the fourth floor of beds, their skin felt cold to touch, the hairs on the back of their necks standing on end. They had ascended half the tower now and couldn't tell if the change in atmosphere was down to where they were or how high they were.

Nearing the staircase to the ninth floor, a voice crept down to them, stopping them in their tracks.

"I won't let you do this Percy!" a deep voice rumbled. It held compassion and sorrow – it clearly upset Dangur to see Percy like this.

"What are you going to do to stop me huh Dangur!" Percy screamed. "Are you going to kill me?"

Tristan made to run up the last flight of stairs but Jacques pulled him back. For all they knew they could hear something useful. Dangur's position in all this could be very useful. Not to mention the fact they needed an advantage here and bursting in on a loose cannon and a Foresaken probably wouldn't be the best idea.

"There's no coming back from this Percy. What did those boys ever do to you?"

"They killed my parents..."

"Sorren and Storm were gone long ago..."

"No! They took them from me..."

"They were just crystals...they were never there..."

"And neither were you!" Percy was distraught now. "You left us..." *Who was us?* Tristan thought.

"On the contrary I was the only one who came back for the both of you. And I checked back as often as I could. I did my best by you both!"

"You left us with the Keepers..."

"Because it was safer for you. You would be away from Dharsi, away from Herasin, away from all the shit that went with it. I tried to do what was best."

"I would rather have been left with them – with the Herasin..."

"If you had any idea just what he did..."

"I don't care! They were the only family I ever knew. I was alone in the Keeperhood, I had no one."

"You had each other...

"And look how that turned out...you had to take him away and then you forgot all about me. I had to find my own way...and that's when they came to me. With their voices...I was never alone."

There was silence.

"I see nothing I say is going to convince you otherwise...but I can't let you hurt the child."

"And what exactly are you going to do about it?"

Tristan wasn't waiting any longer. He wasn't going to risk his daughter getting in the way of whatever was about to occur here. He raced up the stairs before any of his brothers could grab hold of him and burst through the door.

Both Percy's and Dangur's eyes were on him, the traitor's widening with glee and the Foresaken suddenly fearful. With one last look to his once brother, Dangur disappeared in a puff bf black smoke and red lightning, blinding them all momentarily.

"Where is she you bastard!" Tristan lunged forward only to be held back by Zhaine as he wrapped his arms around his midriff and Percy vanished from sight. Evie was nowhere to be seen – he started to panic. A laugh echoed through the room, menacingly.

"You always were a sly cocky little prick!" Ramien yelled into the air.

"And your bark was always worse than your bite!" Percy's voice came casually. "What brings you here brothers?"

"You've finally lost it haven't you?" Cedric sighed heavily and Percy appeared in front of him, crouching to the floor; weak all of sudden. Perhaps he had hit the wall the Elders made. "Something clicked in you didn't it. We were always so close...what happened brother?"

"They happened! Them with their quick wit and special privileges. You know it took me years to get to where they got to in just a few months and even then, the only title I got was the know it all."

"So you were jealous?" Tristan stepped forward now, approaching Percy from the opposite direction as Cedric. "That was it? How petty considering who you really are!"

"You think it's petty, do you? They even took you away from me Ced. Because of them, I am all alone. "

In that moment a child's cry echoed once again, causing Tristan lurched forward at his foe striking him to the ground. They rolled in each other's clutches; punches thrown about as they tried to fight against the others grip for freedom.

Ramien rolled his eyes, it was a pathetic fight really. Percy gained the upper hand though with his grip around Tristan's throat, choking the life out of his foe. A laugh escaped his lips.

"Phillipi!" Cedric yelled out, naming the traitor and crippling his brother and rendering him to the floor in pain. He cried out as Tristan rolled out of his grip and held his neck as though the hand was still there. He rose to his feet slowly and stood over Percy as he held a hand to his face, a sideward glance at his once brother.

"Where is my daughter Percy?"

Percy didn't answer him. His eyes were bloodshot and wide as he looked up silently, moving his hands away from his neck to reveal his own traitorous name etched there as Boris' had back in Dilu across his cheek.

"I used to think we were pretty close you know," Cedric uttered coldly. "Me, you and Trevor were brothers. We did everything together. But all that time...it was a lie!"

Percy's eyes lulled towards his brother and he smiled dryly in a menacing manner. He wasn't repentant in the slightest and Cedric saw that. He rose to his feet, his eyes on Tristan as he took a step forward, a silver glint appearing in his hands. In that same moment, Cedric lunged at him, Percy collapsing into his grasp. He gasped, blood spitting from his mouth onto the stone floor. The ally collapsed to the floor, his brother sprawled in his arms, a knife sticking from his midriff. His brothers stared, compassionately, their hearts bleeding for him – no one should have the grief of killing their family, no matter what they did.

Turning away from his brother, Tristan turned his attention back to finding Evie. Looking around the room, he saw a ghostly figure appear behind the podium Percy had been stood at moments before. It was her, his beautiful Dagnen. He let a gasp escape him, hastening towards where she stood and following her gaze down. There was an etch in the floor as though there were a trap door hidden there.

"Guys, someone give me a hand!" he called to his brothers. Jacques had gone to Cedric's side so Zhaine and Ramien joined Tristan at the podium.

They saw what he was looking at, both of them looking around the room for something they could prize it open with. By now, a couple of Jensen's guards had come up to the room lead by Theoden. They stopped at the sight of Cedric with Percy in his arms, the colour draining from their faces.

"Hey tin heads," Ramien called, casting a look from Tristan. "One of you pass me your sword kindly?"

Theoden sighed heavily but stepped forward to hand him his blade. Prizing it in the crack he wedged open the slot. In its place looked to be an escape hatch, probably the way the original eight survivors got away from the Enforcers. In the small crawl space was crouched a strewn mess of blonde locks, snivelling. Tristan's heart lifted and he called to her, tears escaping him. Her little face looked up, those green eyes that were her mother's lighting up. She reached up and Tristan grabbed her by the waist and lifted her out, pulling her close to his chest. He turned around to face the spirit of Dagnen watching them with a half-smile on her face. He so wished he could reach out to her and embrace her too so they could share in the joy of having their daughter back in the arms of safety. As her form faded, he hugged her tighter in his arms, never wanting to let go again.

CHAPTER 30 – NO ANSWERS

The next few days Tristan spent with Evie by his side constantly. He had been afraid to so much as take his eyes off her, even sleeping had been difficult – his dreams haunted by Percy and the ordeal of the tower of shadows. He had to get some answers about Basso, that much he knew. Maybe that would offer some closure.

For the first time since the kidnap, Tristan opted to leave Evelyn with Myrina while he got the answers he needed, rounding up his brothers after to go speak to Linford. As a member of the third generation, he was probably the best person…maybe even the only other person that would know.

They found Linford in the palace library searching the endless shelves of old looking books. Since the last meeting, many of the Elders had taken to scouring the various libraries they could access. With their own books unwritten, it made research difficult. He looked over at them enter sceptically, probably dreading whatever they had to say. Luckily it seemed Linford was the only one in the library, or at least the only one close, so their chat would be private.

"Hello boys," Linford folded his arms as he turned to them. "To what do I owe the pleasure?" he was his usual arrogant self clearly.

"There's something we've found out," Zhaine began. "And we can't quite work out why no one has told us before."

"Go on!"

"You know the Shrine has the names of all those that have come before us." Linford nodded. "Well…Cedric kind of…Unbound the place and a new column appeared."

"Hold on…you Unbound the Shrine?" Linford looked at Cedric critically. "How even? That glyph is strictly off limits due to its unpredictability…What do you think you were playing at?"

"We were trying to help Balderick remember who controlled him way back when…"

"Besides the point! How do you think Basso would feel if he heard you were putting yourself in such danger?" He looked to Cedric. "Especially since Percy!"

"Speaking of Basso," Tristan spoke, causing Linford's eyes to dart towards him. "Why didn't you ever tell that he was an ally…in fact why didn't anyone tell us?"

"You mean…none of you knew?" Linford waved his hand over the boys, pure surprise painted on his face. "He didn't even tell you Ced?" he asked when the brothers shook their heads.

"Nope, he never said. Even after I told him that I was the ally to them when it came out who we all were…he said nothing." Cedric replied.

"Well to be honest boys, I don't blame him. And asking me why I didn't say or anyone else for that matter – it was not our place!" It was clear Linford was angered by their entitled attitude. "I'm going to assume the power you unleased told you he was ally to the sixth generation?" They all nodded. "And as your teachings should have told you the sixth generation were the first to betray?"

"Why are you patronising us?" Ramien piped up, taking a step forward.

"Humour me! Their book…"

"Had nothing in it. It was just stained to the brim with blood."

"Admittedly I did not know that." Linford paused, choosing his words carefully. "Look when the sixth generation betrayed, they didn't just do so to us…in fact their most heinous crime was to Basso himself. So with that said boys, I trust you will think it wise to *not* confront him with this given everything he has been through. Now if you will excuse me."

Without saying why, he brushed past the brothers and left the library. They all looked to each other, all noting Tristan's sudden paleness but saying nothing. Linford had been utterly useless to them!

"Ah lord," a guard entered the library and faced Cedric. "There you are. I have been searching tirelessly for you. Isolde sent me, the patient John Basso…he has woken up."

"Convenient timing or what." Ramien cheered, causing a scorn from Zhaine.

"Thank you." Cedric gasped as he strolled past the guard, heading for the infirmary. Without waiting for an invitation, the rest of his brothers followed.

Cedric practically crashed into the room, interrupting a conversation between Basso and Isolde. She was perhaps catching him up with all the events that had passed since he took the knife. He looked mournful; he was definitely up to speed. Isolde took a step towards the boys, stopping them in their tracks.

"Be gently," she warned. "He's still groggy. I'll be back soon and then you boys will be going." She nodded to them and left the room.

"Ced!" Basso called to his adopted son. "I am glad you are okay." Cedric went to his father's side. "I am so sorry about Percy. I had no idea he was so off the rails."

"That's not your fault." Cedric consoled.

"Tristan," Tristan looked up at Basso, a sudden coldness creeping down his back and the hairs on the back of his neck stand on end. "I am sorry to you as well. Is Evelyn okay?"

"She's fine..." Tristan trailed off as he focused his eyes on his mentor's. His left hand burned. He tried to hide the discomfort.

 "That's the good thing about kids, they're pretty durable..."

"Is that what you think?" Tristan snapped, suddenly filled with anger. He felt sick. He wasn't sure what was going on with himself – perhaps he was still reeling from his altercation.

"Hey, he didn't mean it like that." Zhaine made a grab for his brother as he took a step forward. "Sorry Bas, he's not been sleeping much."

"Hardly surprising." Basso said it in an undertone as Tristan shrugged his brother off, and heading to the doorway as Isolde came back into the room holding some fresh linen bandages.

"Times up boys!" she exclaimed, pacing the bandages on the bed by the door and folding her arms impatiently.

Tristan didn't need an invitation and he stumbled out the door.

"Cedric, you may stay if you like." Isolde nodded to the ally who stood unwilling to leave by his father's bed. He nodded in acceptance and the other brothers gave their goodbyes before leaving the infirmary as well. They watched, bemused as Tristan dazedly strolled in the direction of their apartments. The tiredness was clearly kicking in now. They hoped he would be okay.

As Tristan turned the corner towards the royal apartments, he practically fell through an open doorway. He stopped himself before interrupting Dante as he tried to calm Balderick down.

"He was just a boy!" He kept saying, over and over again.

Dante seemed to be trying to get something else other than that phrase out of him. They seemed not to notice Tristan there, or even that the door was open. He preferred to keep it that way and backed out of the room, pulling the door to as quietly as he could. Shaking his head, he made for his room. Fetching Evie from Myrina probably wasn't the best idea right now, considering the dizziness was starting to be coupled with visions, shadows seeming to be littered everywhere. Finding his own room, he crashed onto the bed, everything turning dark and the only thing he could feel was his hand where his secrecy mark lay burning.

CHAPTER 31 – THE END OF SHADOW

Those visions that had so often haunted his dreams came back to him now as the pain in his hand became unbearable. He shut his eyes, and just as always - the shadowed figures were all he saw, coming back all at once in a scrambled mess. Usually he would ignore them, feign sleep and open his eyes immediately. The shadows haunted him; their darkness terrorising. But he could not open his eyes, they wanted him to know who they were. The nightmares were not letting him get away this time.

Tristan crouched beneath the edge of the balcony. He had heard chants and voices from the refectory garden disturb the stillness of the night as he wondered back from Dagnen's quarters. He shouldn't be out. He shouldn't be hearing any of this. His mark burnt like fire but he tried to keep his pain hidden as he listened. He didn't want to risk peering over, he sensed too many bodies.

One thing was distinct; a clear direct voice of a leader perhaps was heading this rabble. He felt like he knew it, but there was no way he was risking confirming his suspicion.

A Keeper may only be seen if he wishes to be seen – echoed the voice of First Keeper Felix in his head as he dared to look over. He had only been a Scribe a matter of months, he had yet to master the most basic glyphs, let alone invisibility. So instead he listened, being sure to watch for guards who may pass him on patrol. Everyone had been on alert since Xavier's death a few weeks ago.

"My brothers," the leader addressed. "Our time is now! With Xavier dead we are presented with a perfect opportunity to finally make our stand. We have worked hard to infiltrate

ourselves back into the fold these past few years. My brothers, we should all be proud and welcome our new disciples together."

A low applause rumbled through the open space. Tristan had no idea how many Keepers were down there but it sounded like Dharsi had gathered quite the following.

"We must also welcome one of our brothers back into the fold. Brothers, please join me in welcoming back Borci!"

Something about that name struck him with an electricity that made the hairs on his neck stand up on his head and he dared to look over the edge of the balcony.

Before now whenever he peered over in his dreams, the face of Borci was not visible. It was blurred out and sometimes, he was nothing more than a shadow. But now, he was in full colour and Tristan could not believe his eyes.

It puzzled him; the face. He could never remember the suspicion before – perhaps back then he didn't peer over. But now...it was like someone was showing what something in the back of his mind knew. Maybe he had known it all along; but just like the Brothers of Unity cannot speak outside of their brotherhood, perhaps the same was true here. The moment he peered over the edge wiped from his memory the moment it happened. This disbelief shook him, but this was not the end.

The rest of Tristan's months as a Scribe flashed before him. Nothing was clear enough for him to focus on. It was still very much a blur, but perhaps his entire memory wasn't what was being shown to him here. He saw Sarisus' takeover and his death at the hands of he and his brothers. It occurred to him then the absence of some of the Keepers. Boris was a known traitor from that point, but Charles and Hagen had kept to the shadows, their cool and calm looks of silent fear ringing in him now. Sarisus must've gone against the plan surely, but perhaps there was more to it then even that.

When he first became an Acolyte came too. His love for Dagnen flew past; their marriage and Borci's eyes on them both like he was jealous of their union. Had there been a love there? No...impossible! But maybe it was more, perhaps he was jealous of what Tristan had and there was no love there for Dagnen at all.

Tristan and his brothers came back into the Compound secretly, the collapsing of the clocktower still raging in their minds. The screams from the Hammerites and townsfolk still ringing in their ears. They had intended on sneaking in, but the Keeper Council had other ideas. As much as the Reading had been for all the Keepers to hear, it was the Elders job to act on the prophecies and deal with them where necessary.

When time stops, The Interpreter had said, the Wretched One shall be pointed to. The Hammerite cathedral had to have been the clue; stop the hands and the traitor will come to light. Something had gone wrong though and brought the clocktower to its knees. As much as it was not their intention, it was clear the boys would face the blame for this.

"Please tell me you didn't!" Nielson stepped forward as the brothers entered the lobby, his eyes on his own sons more than the others. Ramien and Zhaine said nothing in return, they all just avoided his gaze. "This is out of my hands boys...I am sorry." Nielson was grave, his face pale and powerless.

Tristan's eyes flashed up at the members of the council, most of them looking equally as powerless. The brothers place as Unity had been known to them since Sarisus' defeat. They understood what had been done and how it looked. It was clear they did not want the outcome that was inevitably happening. His gaze loomed over Charles, Basso and Percy who stood together; crazed smiles flashing in the red glare of their eyes. Basso – why would he look thrilled? And why was Percy stood here now – perhaps he had been the one to rat them out. He shared a room with Cedric, he would know if they snuck out and from there it would be easy to guess where they had gone. But Basso – why was he smiling like he was? It was subtle but Tristan could see it there. But was he imagining it, simply because he stood with Percy and Charles?

"You boys disobeyed a direct order," Charles boasted. "You were asked to stay out of the matter and you went out of your way to cause destruction..."

"The clocktower was not meant to fall..." Ramien tried to defend he and his brothers, his father holding him back as he jumped forward.

"That is beside the point! Lives have been lost and you boys must be held accountable. Take them and hold them!"

Guards approached the brothers, but with a look from Felix they vanished, leaving even Nielson shocked.

He remembered how they had snuck back to the Compound that night to listen in on their own trial. Somehow, there was a majority vote that the brothers had swayed from our paths and committed a traitorous act just as they were always fated to do. The Enforcers were called upon to bring them in and an order was given to hold Dagnen in the hope it would lure Tristan back.

As they discussed other matters, they searched Charles' quarters only to find the fallen clocktower spire pointed straight to his veranda, even the hands of the clockface symbolising his own treachery. When they returned to the inn they were staying at; Myrina had been there with a heavily pregnant Dagnen. Felix had bought her in for her own safety having snuck out of the meeting once it was revealed the Council wanted to hold her captive.

Tristan had snuck back to the Shrine plenty more times. He was trying to keep tabs on Dharsi, not to mention Charles and whatever plan he might want to try next. Whispers had pointed to a meeting being held at midnight in the walled garden at the back of the Compound and Tristan intended on being a part of it.

"Welcome my brothers," Charles beckoned.

From where Tristan perched, he could peer through the gap in the balcony that overlooked the courtyard and the tower that was Death's Toll. Funny how many times he seemed to find himself in this exact position, his marked hand burning as usual. And as per usual he ignored the pain, listening intently.

"I thank you all for your patience." Charles continued. In the crowd, Tristan made out many a Scribe he recognised. He also spotted Boris and Hagen as expected. "But finally, our time has come. We have the Brotherhood of Union right where want them. Our time is now!"

The followers repeated the phrase, sending a shiver down Tristan's spine. He looked around, there were a fair few Keepers down in the Courtyard; it was a miracle it hadn't caught unwanted attention. But seeing as Charles was acting First Keeper now...

His thoughts were interrupted by raised voices and he scurried into the corner out of sight of the refectory which the balcony lead out of. His head thudded but he stayed silent.

"I don't understand why they are shutting me out," the voice yelled. It was weasel like and familiar. Biting his lip, he peered round the doorway where he caught a glimpse of Percy – no shock there. "It's because of me we've come this far."

"Without trying to take sides," the other voice said, just out of sight. Again, it was a voice Tristan recognised but didn't want to risk moving any closer. As much as they probably weren't aware enough to notice him, he was outnumbered here in more ways than one. "This war started long before you developed your own agenda."

"But you they have accepted as their own. You they follow...me; I'm still an outcast."

"Fret not brother. Our time is now and as much as they might not be giving you the thanks you are still a part of this.

"My followers," Charles beckoned now. This would definitely have to attract attention; if there was any attention to be had that is. "Please help me in thanking the man who has made all this possible." He could just about make out Charles holding up a hand towards the balcony. Tristan froze.

"You have got to be kidding me!" Percy exclaimed. "How do you get the thanks for this?"

"Not now Percy!" a shadow took a step forward and Tristan's heart began to race.

"If you don't see him, you will never remember..." an echoey voice found him in the shadows. It was a voice he remembered and it paralysed him. The voice belonged to something he thought destroyed. "I can help you there. You forgot before but this time can be different." Tristan shut his eyes, desperately trying to shut the voice out. "Let us help each other Keeper of Secrets. Let us bare the same burden. Come and find me and they will never see you. Come and find me and they will be immortalised in your mind. No more secrets...isn't that what you want?"

It was what he wanted, more than anything he wanted no more secrets. Secrets he kept from himself, secrets he kept from his own brothers because of stupid charms and rules which meant he couldn't speak about them. Yes, the Eye was supposed to be gone, and yes it was not to be trusted but perhaps on this occasion they could help each other. 'The enemy of my enemy is also my friend', he thought.

Before he even had chance to think of an answer to the Eye's proposition, the shadows stepped into the light and he was floored, just as though it were the first time he was witnessing this man...this brother betray.

"My followers," Charles called. "Our brother Borci!"

Tristan was crippled, he couldn't believe what he was seeing – who he was seeing.

That scene would come back to him in his dreams just like the others. In the nightmares the man that approached the balcony was a shadow, a void. But now, the man was in colour...the man had a face he very much knew.

Picking up a fallen hammer from where he knelt over Dagnen's lifeless body, Tristan struck the cackling diamond. It screeched in retort in his ears, deafening – this wasn't part of the deal. But then the Eye was supposed to release Trevor once it was united with the central fountain. But nothing was stopping, Trevor was unsavable.

With the Eye destroyed, Tristan collapsed to his knees, the rain beating down harder than before. He watched in remorse as Jacques caught Trevor in his arms. Even if the Eye had released him like he promised, he would never have been able to live with what he had done.

"Tristan..." Dagnen's weak voice called to him and suddenly he remembered she was there. None of it felt real.

He clambered over to her, taking her in his arms. What was she even doing out here? "I have to tell you…I had to…"

"Don't talk my love," Tristan begged. "Save your strength!"

"I have to tell you…the Wretched One…it's…"

In some of his nightmares she passed without saying a name and in others her lips moved but no words came out.

He had to pay, Tristan thought. He knew who was behind this all now and he had been their friend, their teacher and all this time he had been betraying them. The world may be crashing around him but he did not care. The fading Keepers were second to what needed to be down. He didn't even care to knock, he just barged right into the dormitory door that formed in front of him now.

"I wondered when you would come and find me!" The voice of a shadow echoed. It was like the man the voice belonged to was smoky, colours slowly coming into view as the memory became clearer.

"You have some explaining to do!" Tristan's voice broke. Dagnen's death was still raw in his mind – he saw it with every blink.

"Oh I have more than explaining to do." The face swam into view now and it smiled menacingly.

"Why? You are our teacher…our friend…why would you betray us?"

"You deserved way more than my betrayal…and now…you feel my pain."

"I don't understand. What did we do that was so wrong?"

"Technically it wasn't you but what you resemble." He got up from his chair, the smile still goading him. Tristan was rooted to the spot, unable to move as his teacher approached him. "It's who you are…and if you think I am finished with you…you have no idea."

He reached up his hands and pushed Tristan and suddenly they were in the sky. Or so Tristan thought. The wind whipped past him and he looked down to a stone floor. It was then he realised they were atop a tower with no apparent exit except over the edge. He was trapped.

"I have sat on the side lines waiting for my revenge long enough!"

Tristan looked up from where he crouched. He was stuck as his predator stalked him hungrily.

"You finally feel the pain I have felt for centuries. You want to know why I did all this...look around you Tristan. Look at what I am capable of. No one will ever doubt me again...no one will ever leave me alone again."

Tristan couldn't even speak. He was utterly paralysed and afraid.

"You will feel my pain Delhail!"

Who was Delhail – Tristan wondered. He thought he knew it as a circle of names entered his head.

In that moment he heard his brother yell his name, a blast shooting straight for him. Romeo took it instead and suddenly Tristan was on his feet, grabbing his brother by the arm as he tumbled over the edge of the tower, the waves ravishing below. All he could hear was the cackle of his enemy and the screams from his brother as he slipped from his grasp.

Romeo was swallowed by the waves below and Tristan launched himself at his teacher.

"You will pay for this!" Tristan stammered. "You will pay for it all!" He gripped Basso's collar tightly, but he just sneered like he was satisfied and vanished from sight, leaving Tristan all alone.

It was clear now. The shadows were no longer shadows but clear pictures. They were actually a person – someone he admired and looked up to. Basso took place of all those shadows now. The shadows were John Basso, and John Basso was Borci. Basso had killed Romeo, Basso had been the reason he lost everything, and as his dreams bought him back to that shattered glass ceiling in the Reading Room of the Compound where Charles stood over him, he realised how much of a fool he had been. The shadowed man, the one who took his memories was Basso. How could he have been so foolish to willingly take him along his journey of rediscovery?

CHAPTER 32 – ALL THESE THINGS I HAVE DONE

When Tristan woke up it was almost dark outside and the stars twinkled in the sky outside his balcony doors. His heart was racing as he started to process everything he had seen in his dreams. His hand started to burn and he looked down on it to see the scarred surface raised and sore looking. He knew who Basso was – he had all along. He felt sick from the discovery. How had he let him travel with him? Was this why he was so adamant he wasn't coming along? But then why did he change his mind? But then, were his actions more sincere – he had after all gone all the way to Az Lagní to apologise for what he had done.

He got up from the bed as a knock sounded at the door. Opening it revealed a guard who inclined his head in respect to Tristan.

"Dinner is served lord," The guard turned to leave.

"Wait, who is down there?" Tristan asked abruptly.

"Everyone within the royal palace lord. Just as usual. Is something a matter?"

"No nothing...thank you."

The guard bowed his head again and left the room. Wasting no time, Tristan followed him out and headed down to the dining hall where the room was bustling around a buffet table. He looked around at the faces of his brothers, his father, his uncles and cousins, his niece alongside Evelyn, the faces of his teachers...the face of a traitor.

Cedric was assisting Basso get himself a plate of food, Isolde watching over him carefully. He was clearly getting his strength back, but should still be cautious. Rage built up within him as he watched his old rune master favour his ribs. These last few months this man had helped him and guided him. Heck, most of his life he had. Was it all an act? Back in his forgotten past it clearly was, but now?

The sincere thoughts took a step back for hot rage and he took a breath, stepping towards where Basso and Cedric were sat. Both of them looked up at him, the red in his teachers eyes clearer now than it ever had been.

"You alright there Tristan," Cedric questioned concerned, his eyes looking his brother up and down. His complexion was pale and his eyes wide.

"It was you," He couldn't stop himself. It wasn't the time nor the place but he didn't care. "You were the traitor all along."

The room silenced and Basso's eyes floated up to meet Tristan's, was there a touch of remorse there? He hadn't realised how loud he had spoken, and suddenly Nielson was at his side cautioning him.

"Tristan, what's going on?" Cedric asked, confused as he rose from his seat.

"It was him Ced! He is the Ultimate Betrayer...The Wretched One!"

"Tristan perhaps you should get some rest, you aren't yourself." Nielson said in an undertone as he stood close to his traumatised Acolyte.

"I don't need rest I am fine!" Tristan shirked him off, his eyes not leaving Basso. "I see it clearer now than I ever did and I remember you!" He couldn't bring himself to say his name. "You did it...you did it all. You're the traitor!" his voice broke.

"Tristan this is..." Cedric started to say.

"No Ced!" Basso rose from his seat and winced as he grabbed his son's arm. "He's right! I am who he says I am."

Tristan stood aghast, surprised at his foe's confession. Why was he making this so easy?

Basso's voice was pointed and croaked like it pained him to say it. Pulling away, Cedric looked scornfully at his adopted father, begging it all to be some cruel joke. All eyes were on Basso now, each of them as confused as the next.

"What is this?" Cedric scorned.

"Basso...do you mean to say..." Nielson started.

"Tristan is right," He held up his right hand and a mark crawled out of his palm marking him as a traitor. "I am a Brethren Betrayer!"

"Guards!" Jensen called having risen from his throne.

Guards were upon Basso within moments.

"Wait!" Isolde called out. "The man is still injured."

The guards stopped around him, perhaps afraid.

"It's okay, I'll go quietly." Basso nodded to the guards and they escorted him away to the dungeons.

In his absence, Nielson looked to Tristan; shaken. The whole room clearly wanted answers but Tristan could only manage a few words.

"I remember! I remember him so clearly now. How could I have been so blind."

"Cedric, are you okay?"

Cedric looked grief stricken at his First Keeper, before shaking his head and storming out of the room. His whole life had been built on lies – first his own brother and now his father...he was distraught.

"Explain!" He turned to Tristan now.

"There's nothing to explain," Tristan's voice was ghostly – like he couldn't believe what he had just done. "I remembered what he did, that's all there is to it."

Nielson took hold of Tristan's scared palm and scanned the mark there. The Bearer of Secrets did not resist. "I knew all along what he did...I just couldn't remember. He killed Dagnen, he killed Romeo. He helped Dharsi gain control again...what else is there to tell Nielson. Fill in the gaps yourself...I'm sick of it being my job."

Deciding he wasn't hungry; Tristan took off for a walk. He could do with some time to clear his head.

His stroll eventually bought him down to the dungeons. The guard count was heavy, Jensen clearly didn't trust Basso as easy as he made it. He was right not to, especially after how easy Percy made it seem. They let Tristan pass without question, almost as though they hadn't seen him. He stopped down the corridor to see Nielson leaving the cell that belonged to Basso with Linford by his side. Both of them were ashen, but they said nothing to Tristan as they passed him.

In his cell, Basso was facing the window, staring out at the stars that twinkled. He didn't seem to notice Tristan walk in, he just continued to stare from his leaning position on the wall opposite the cot.

"Don't worry, I know you're there." He said crestfallen. Something about the tone in his voice was acceptant of how things had happened. "I did wonder how long it would take you to face me though after your little outburst." Tristan said nothing. "But I suppose I had always intended to come clean so I should thank you really. I feel kind of...relieved if I'm honest."

There was a silence and in that silence; Tristan was confused – like a lost child without its parents. So many questions came to him, this man held all the answers and he was owed that much. He had been left in the dark for too long.

"Why?" Tristan said simply, folding his arms where he stood on the other side of the bars.

"You wouldn't understand," he answered, turning and locking eyes with his once student. "But I suppose there's no harm in trying." He took a seat on the cot, wincing as he clutched his side where Percy had stabbed him. He looked awful, his eyes bloodshot from lack of sleep, his face pale and taunt, his composure weakened by his wound. But still he tried to make it look like nothing bothered him - he had always been a proud man. "Where would you like me to start?"

Tristan didn't answer.

"If I come clean – tell you everything and why...will you make me a promise?"

"If it's to forgive you then..."

"I don't want your forgiveness, Tristan. I mean, it would be nice but...it's unrealistic. What I would like is for you to understand why I have done all that I have done."

"I can't promise that..."

"Then maybe I will ask again after I explain my case."

He was silent for a while; their shared gaze at each other unbroken.

"Sometimes I wonder if I would have turned out different had there been a few differences. I wonder what I would have been like if my father hadn't shunned everything I ever wanted or became. If he had been prouder of the sons he had and not done everything he could to disdain us. It was like he knew what we would turn out to be – traitors! His golden legacy let down by us. Perhaps he felt helpless to even try to change that. I'm going to just treat you like its unknown to you so forgive me if I gloss on stuff you already know."

Tristan was silent – he was still in shock over Basso going so easy. But after everything good Basso had done for him, the least he could do was hear him out. He took a knife for him after all.

"As you know my father wasn't exactly a loving man. He was a cold man who held his duty above all else. We had no mother to guide us and back then children of the Keeperhood were seen but not heard – left to raise themselves among the shelves of books. My brother Murdoch kept us in check – he was my idol. One day, he and his friends took us to a rally. This was back in the time where the Keepers began living among the townsfolk as opposed to above. They wanted to integrate into the cities and become a part of it as opposed to separate. But there was those of us who wanted to remain above...keep the power for themselves like overlords I suppose. I remember standing in the crowd and being inspired by what the Herasin had to say. I remember how after we went to a nearby inn to talk about how much Murdoch and his friends wanted to join. But there was a test...to join Dharsi you had to prove yourself worthy – offer the Herasin something in order to be accepted as loyal."

Basso chose his words wisely. Tristan wondered if he was even able to speak out of turn about his own brothers. He looked pained after all but then that could be from the wound in his ribs.

"Gervais came up with a plan to assume some power. Above all else; those who sought to join Dharsi were those lacking in fathers...those seeking acceptance...a figure to lead them out of the darkness. You see Gervais wasn't just my brother's friend, he is my cousin and he has a brother – Gerard. Gerard was the golden child...couldn't put a foot wrong in my uncles' eyes, heck even my father's. I assume you can relate to that. Anyway, Gerard became a member of Unity and back then well it was a great achievement. The Third Generation is one you don't hear much about. They're known as the Brotherhood who sent Dharsi underground yes, but in truth it was the Elders who did that. The Third Generation was just rubbish they had to clean up in the process.

"You see Gerard was a gloating sort...we felt about him much like you boys did of Percy. His own brother's disdain for him verged on toxic...so much so he killed him and assumed his space – faking his own death in the process."

"Wait so Gervais became Gerard?" Tristan asked, confused. This part of the history was unknown to him. As much as Linford had told them as much, he didn't realise it was as gory as this. Basso thought for a moment before standing up from the cot and pulling up the sleeve on his right arm. The skin there was marked by the glyph of Unbinding – just as Cedric's was, a green glare emitting from it.

"My family share a mark...Unbinding. We got it from my mother's side! We hold power that not even we can fully control...I presume you know the properties of the glyph." Tristan nodded in response. "There was an argument of explosive circumstances and in the rubble, Gervais' body was discovered. We had no idea what he was planning, but he assumed the identity of his brother, twinning the glyph of Unity he possessed. I remember the look in Murdoch's eye when he came to them as Gerard to reveal who he really was. He was gleeful, this was their way in. He elected my brother and a few others to mimic the power of the rest of Unity, creating a mirror generation - a generation of opposites. I was not a part of that, as much as I followed my brother everywhere I was considered too young to be part of all the dealings. I guess even to my brother sometimes I was nothing more than a shadow."

"So Murdoch...he was part of this shadow generation of Unity?"

"Aye...just like Sarisus and Hagen...Boris! I always find it funny that you and Romeo were the ones who named them and yet they were your opposites. They were, in a way, just like you..."

"How are you even able to speak like this?"

"Remember what I said; no one ever sees me. I am nothing more than a shadow to most. To each of us Unbinding gives a different gift – mine I guess is this...that I am invisible.

"I remember the look on the Herasin's face when Gervais told him what they had to offer him. There was this like procession and all of Dharsi had heard what he had done and not a single face was not impressed. However, there was also fear there. This was insane power they had unlocked...the possibilities were endless. Of course in the coming months, the Elders moved against Dharsi and it became heresy to join them. Their numbers dwindled and the Herasin moved us underground.

"It was at this point that I sparked his interest and he began to notice me presence. By this time my brother had spoken in favour of Dharsi openly and removed himself from the Keeperhood. I would sneak out to join him in their rallies and Herasin saw this. He knew that I could be useful, and finally – I felt like I had a place in this world...a purpose. I was seen!"

Basso went quiet, pacing his cell like he was choosing what to say next.

"Do you know why every Brotherhood of Union was fated to betray after the fifth?" Tristan shook his head; he had his suspicions yes but they had never been confirmed. "It was revenge. You see Gervais as Gerard had its disadvantages and it left him open. The Elders found out where Dharsi was hiding and the Enforcers were sent after them. As far as the Keeperhood knew we were all sent to the Land of the Faded. There were one hundred of us including Gervais and only nine of us survived. But even the Elders never knew that. What remained of Dharsi wanted revenge against the Keeperhood for the loss of their brothers.

"But that wasn't where it ended. The Keeperhood continued with their mission to become part of the citizenship, but after what happened it seemed Unity had become the pinnacle of Dharsi's mission. After all they were the very image that held the Keepers together. But then given the Herasin's link to Unity I imagine you don't find that surprising.

"Sarisus found a way to use Sorren and Storm to curse Unity – use what we had become to corrupt an entire movement. So we gathered in the Maw, armed with The Ruby of Sorrow and The Eye of the Storm. By uniting them once more, we were able to command them to have their own revenge, to corrupt a legacy...and it did. The fifth betrayed eventually, the *sixth* betrayed...and so did every generation to come, even those that didn't peruse within the Keeperhood after their fate had been revealed - they became criminals and murderers, unacceptable people in society. They were fated to betray...forever..."

"You mention the sixth with such disgust yet you were them!" Tristan cut him off, a look of disdain and disgust screwed across his face. Basso looked somber.

"You see I told you!" He scorned, sneering in the young Keeper's direction. "I told you you wouldn't understand. But maybe that's because you do not want to understand. You don't want to open your mind to the prospect that maybe I really didn't have a choice in the matter, maybe I am no better than you...cursed to always betray in the end. I've lived long enough now and every time I try to make it right...I cast myself further and further into the abyss.

"They were my friends! When everybody else left me in the Maw, when Dangur was the only one to check in on me every now and then while I was welcomed back into the Keeperhood with open arms. They had no idea what I had done and in their abandonment of me I found true brotherhood. I didn't know what they were to begin with, to me they were my friends. Life could not have picked better brothers for me. And then one day Ercol tells me who they are and that they want me to be their ally. There was no question, I held no hatred for them and I was also a little compelled to see if Dharsi's curse had worked. Brotherhood and curiosity got the better of me.

"I came out with my own secret, telling them who I was and the power I held. Ercol was elated as were his brothers when I accepted their offer. What do you know about the power of Unbinding?"

"Probably more than I remember."

"Fair point. Unbinding is bound to the realm of Unbinding – otherwise known as the Land of the Faded – the Land of the Unbound. Ercol was curious of my link to the Faded Lands and thought that with their help we could unlock it...visit it. Ercol was an orphan...his father a member of Dharsi. I was the only one who knew that. He wanted to confront his father, ask him why he would abandon his own son for such a treacherous cause and as you can imagine I was all too happy to oblige. Before you say anything, it had nothing to do with my loyalty to Dharsi...I could relate to him for I too would give anything to know why my father shunned us the way he did.

"In taking them to the Land of the Faded I left myself open and Delhail stumbled across my secrets. I don't know how, but I suppose he was the one who was always of suspicious of me. He didn't trust me the way my other brothers did and sometimes I wonder if he somehow knew who I was all along."

"Delhail was Nobility wasn't he?" Basso's eyes widened and Tristan showed him his mark as the Bearer of Secrets in response. "Nobility are cursed with this mark. It is Nobility that gets the traitorous thoughts...the corrupter of the Brotherhood if you like. The mark is known as the Bearer of Secrets and we are those who kept secrets from our own brotherhood."

"Ironic that...Murdoch was the opposite of Nobility. Perhaps his death in the ritual is what fucked that up. I guess it didn't work as well as we thought."

Silence passed over them and each watched the other for a moment.

"All this history...I still don't understand why?"

"So you admit you want to understand...interesting. I always wonder if I was fated to betray...whether I had a choice in the matter at all. You remind me so much of him...if not for Delhail I might have had a chance at redemption a lot sooner. That's how the crack formed in the Land of the Faded – Boris followed us through and tried to find the spirits of Dharsi. He tried to free them and in doing so let Delhail see that I was a part of that. They thought I was a distraction...that I was trying to help what remained of Dharsi. They tried to overpower me, but their naivety left Unbinding open – even I am not its master. I suppose my creed kept a close eye on me, perhaps I was not abandoned after all."

Basso went silent again, his face grave. Tristan didn't push for more.

"They wronged me! They defeated me! Even Ercol was swayed into trying to rip me apart. Yes, it was ultimately an accident but that didn't stop what they wanted to do to me. Like I said...you were so like Delhail and when Dharsi came back into the fold they gave me a chance to finally have my revenge for what they did to me...how weak they made me feel.

"I never felt anything for what I did. I believed they deserved it for what they did to me. But my dreams...They aren't as empty as my conscience. I spent my life forever alone; my love of vengeance is what set me free. But it trapped me too, it trapped to a life of deceit and betrayal. I doomed myself! But you and your brothers...the taste of revenge that eeked from every single one of you was too great to resist. After all, Ramien and Zhaine were the sons of the brother of the man who killed my brother; Dante's nephews. It all sounded so easy...so promising. You all held my freedom in your hands."

"Then why did you save me from Percy?"

Basso frowned momentarily.

"In case you haven't noticed, over the past few months I've been trying to do right by you. I've been trying to redeem myself. The Basso you have known as your helper has been the genuine article. I honestly did want to help."

"But Dante…"

"Dante can go fuck himself!"

On his stroll through the palace, Tristan had crossed paths with Dante who had told him what he saw of Basso in Dilu. Keep your friends close but your enemies closer was his justification for why he never said anything. That and Tristan's lack of memory meant he wouldn't really understand.

"So you didn't follow me to Dilu because you made a deal with Boris?"

"No! I never wanted to go back to them, Dangur was the only one who ever looked out for me, the rest left me alone, even after they promised Murdoch they wouldn't. I followed you to Dilu to protect you!"

"Protect me?"

"I really did think that by doing all that I had done I would give myself peace. And I suppose for a time I did. After Hasaghar I retreated to Ragnur and although I convinced myself I was fine…ultimately I was once again alone. And in that loneliness curiosity got the better of me and I was compelled to see you…to revel in what I had done to you once again. But what I saw when I found you in that Smithy…it sickened me to think I had sunk so low. You were a shell of the man you were. I had no idea you were without Evie…as much as I intended to take Dagnen and Romeo from you I would never have wished a child alone in the world. I was ashamed of what I had done and when you asked me to join you in Ragnur I saw an opportunity to do right."

"But you said no at first…is Boris why you changed your mind?"

"I would be lying if I said no. Yes, their offer made me change my mind but not because of my loyalty to them…but because I felt compelled to put right what I had done wrong. I was afraid, and that is why I said no at first."

"You think that by saving me from Percy that I would forgive you for all that you did? That a few short months makes up for the lifetime you deprived me of?"

"You forget, I am not asking for your forgiveness - but your understanding."

Tristan thought for a moment. The man he had in his circle the past few months truly was genuine – him taking that blade from Percy was proof of that.

"You are, as you say; a man of circumstance." Tristan said finally, unable to think of anything else.

"Then you do understand my boy. And because of that, tomorrow when I assume my fate I will do so with a free heart a clear mind. I may not have righted *all* my wrongs, but at least the man I had wronged most understands why. Thank you, my boy...Thank you."

A single tear slipped from Basso's eyes and for a moment, Tristan let himself pity his teacher. He truly was a traitor of consequence and everything that had happened to him in his life lead him to where he was now, lead him to do what he did. He was of a legacy of failed fathers and for that Tristan related to him. He would never forgive him, but he would accept it and try to move on now. As he walked away, he dared to look back at the man Basso had become in the time they'd spent talking, a man wronged by all of those around him...a traitor by circumstance. But he was the Ultimate Betrayer all the same and that; no Keeper would ever forgive.

CHAPTER 33 – FINAL SACRIFICE

In Tristan's leave, Basso turned his back; overcome with emotion. Tears escaped his tired eyes. He was so tired. He watched the stars, wishing himself among them and imagining his brother by blood among them, waiting for him. He looked down on his mark still exposed on his forearm. Out of the corner of his eye a shadow flickered. He had an inkling who it might be.

"How long have you been stood there?" His voice broke as he asked the question, letting the fear slip off his tongue as though it were all too easy.

"Long enough!" The voice belonged to Cedric, his tearstained face coming into view. His green eyes were hot with anger.

Basso simply stared at his son, unable to say anything to him to soften the blow.

"Do you have nothing to say for yourself?" Cedric said aghast, the silence becoming unbearable.

"There is plenty to say, I just don't know where to start," Basso sighed, unable to make eye contact with his adopted son. "Sorry just doesn't seem like enough...not this time my son..."

"You have no right to call me that – not anymore! You're just the man who raised me.

"You still haven't figured it out have you?" Cedric looked puzzled, his eyes flicking past the mark on Basso's arm. "This mark is a blood rite Ced...not a sect like the Bearer of Secrets. You are my blood...you *are* my son." The confused look did not fade from his face but those eyes widened as though he half knew what Basso was about to say.

"Your mother, her name was Angelica...or Angel as I liked to call her in my time. She was the daughter of a baron who wasn't my biggest fan. We were courting for several months but her father never believed I was good enough for her. He must've suspected my past and perhaps he was right about me. Perhaps he thought me too old?" He chuckled then. "Bad timing Bass! Anyway, me and Angel, we tried to run away together one day, but it was no good. His men still found us and brought us back. I've spent my whole life running, I guess I was a fool to believe it would actually amount to me being happy for once. I didn't see her for a while and the next thing I knew he'd married her off to some rich landlord. I never saw or heard from her again!

"And then, seven years later you turn up at the Compound and I felt a connection, I knew...in your eyes I saw her, in you I sensed my kin. As much as I was who they left the orphans with anyway, I stepped forward all too freely to raise you, especially when I tried to find her the next day only to discover she had passed away. In that moment at her grave, I made a promise that no matter what I would do right by you - and I'd like to think I kept it."

Tears fell uncontrollable down Cedric's face. He could hardly believe what he was hearing, but the proof was there. It all made sense.

"You are my son Cedric...by blood and no matter what I knew when I first laid eyes on you, I could not let the legacy I had made for myself pass onto you. I tried to do right by you! Please tell me that it was enough. Please."

Cedric didn't answer him but he kept eye contact with his father. He was right – no matter what he had done to Tristan and his brothers, Cedric had always been left out of it; advised against being involved with them. Basso had always done right by raising him the way he did.

"You know when Tristan saw me in Ragnar I was afraid," Basso explained, breaking that contact and looking down at the floor. "So afraid he had suddenly realised. I was not ready then for all my secrets to come out. But he didn't remember me yet and I suppose that was a good thing considering all that I did, all that I wanted to repent for."

"So what do you want from me now...from Tristan you wanted acceptance...what do you want from me – father?"

"Forgiveness would be nice but even I can't forgive myself and if I cannot forgive, how on earth can others?"

"But you said..."

"What I said is perhaps unrealistic. In truth, there is one final act I must commit. One final sacrifice I must make."

"I don't understand."

"You will son...you will. The night I saw Tristan, when I turned down his original offer of helping him - I had a dream. I dreamt that I had gone missing and you were sick with worry. You were so scared. You ran around town and asked people if they'd seen me. You tried to get them to help you. But they wouldn't because they didn't care. To them, I was nothing more than a traitor. A worthless spine who didn't deserve anyone.

"When I woke up, I thought about what I was leaving you with. What kind of path had I been living down here? My legacy was so tarnished and if people found out the truth you would be tarnished too. I could not let that stain pass to you as well. That's why I followed Tristan."

Basso reached out for his son through the bars, but as he expected he remained where he stood. He was afraid, they both were.

"Don't ever be afraid of me my boy. I've taken my beating time and time again...I will gladly take it again."

"I'm not afraid of you...to be afraid of you would be to be afraid of me. I am afraid of what you are going to do."

"And I guess you should be. I am strong, but I am afraid; not enough for this." He paused, his breath caught in his lungs and he let a tear fall, almost as though it were a hint. "I need you to do something for me son, I need you to make me a promise. I know what I have to do now. But first, I want you to forget...forget all the pain I have caused, all the lies I have told and all the hurt. Forget the fear...God knows I need to. I need to stop pretending like I believe someone can save me...like I can be saved. Because the only person who can save me is me. I refuse to run any longer!"

Basso took a step back, finding himself in the centre of his cell and looking all around. His demeanour had changed and he was fearful now. But he didn't show it in his eyes. In his eyes all he could see was his son and that was just the way he wanted it.

"When my time comes son, I need you to forget...forget the wrongs I have done and help me leave behind a reason to be missed. Don't ever resent me for what I have done...please promise me that. When you feel empty think only of me. Keep me in your memory as your father and leave out all the rest. I beg you! Will you do this for me!"

Silence passed over the dungeon.

Cedric watched his father, tears still falling freely from his eyes. Could he really do it, of course he could. Basso was his father after all.

"I promise...father..."

Basso smiled.

"The key to Tristan remembering lies with me Cedric," Basso instructed. "For him to remember...I must undo what I did! He has to remember."

"You're rambling..."

"I am not rambling Cedric. I see clearly now, perhaps for the first time."

A glint flashed in Basso's hand and suddenly there was a knife there, striking fear into his son's soul. He wouldn't! His hands shook but he held the dagger strong, moving it across his mark of Unbinding and digging into the skin, piercing it through. Blood seeped out, pouring onto the floor as though it were creating a river and Basso winced as he chanted silently.

Cedric yelled out for him to stop but he knew he couldn't, Tristan had to remember or they would all be lost. He tried desperately to dull out the cries of his son begging him to stop, grabbing hold of the bars attempting to rip them apart as his cries fell silent to all those around him.

"Father!" He yelled. "Please stop!" Over and over again.

But he couldn't, one final act of sacrifice, one final act of redemption. The traitor fell to the floor, the sky outside lighting up in his wake as the bars were ripped free from their fixtures and he fell into the arms of his son. As Cedric held his dying father in his arms he screamed louder and louder in remorse, in helplessness. Basso took his last breath and looked at the sky through the window on the wall opposite. Falling stars was all he saw, falling stars in a blue night sky.

Outside in the courtyard, Tristan took a breath of fresh air, noting his brothers' presence over by a fountain talking quietly among themselves. But their attention was diverted as the sky lit up, the stars beginning to fall from their place in the night. As they fell Tristan was struck to the floor and his brothers raced to his side. Before they could make it though, a figure lit up before them, blinding them all.

CHAPTER 33 – FINAL SACRIFICE

In Tristan's leave, Basso turned his back; overcome with emotion. Tears escaped his tired eyes. He was so tired. He watched the stars, wishing himself among them and imagining his brother by blood among them, waiting for him. He looked down on his mark still exposed on his forearm. Out of the corner of his eye a shadow flickered. He had an inkling who it might be.

"How long have you been stood there?" His voice broke as he asked the question, letting the fear slip off his tongue as though it were all too easy.

"Long enough!" The voice belonged to Cedric, his tearstained face coming into view. His green eyes were hot with anger.

Basso simply stared at his son, unable to say anything to him to soften the blow.

"Do you have nothing to say for yourself?" Cedric said aghast, the silence becoming unbearable.

"There is plenty to say, I just don't know where to start," Basso sighed, unable to make eye contact with his adopted son. "Sorry just doesn't seem like enough...not this time my son..."

"You have no right to call me that – not anymore! You're just the man who raised me.

"You still haven't figured it out have you?" Cedric looked puzzled, his eyes flicking past the mark on Basso's arm. "This mark is a blood rite Ced...not a sect like the Bearer of Secrets. You are my blood...you *are* my son." The confused look did not fade from his face but those eyes widened as though he half knew what Basso was about to say.

"Your mother, her name was Angelica...or Angel as I liked to call her in my time. She was the daughter of a baron who wasn't my biggest fan. We were courting for several months but her father never believed I was good enough for her. He must've suspected my past and perhaps he was right about me. Perhaps he thought me too old?" He chuckled then. "Bad timing Bass! Anyway, me and Angel, we tried to run away together one day, but it was no good. His men still found us and brought us back. I've spent my whole life running, I guess I was a fool to believe it would actually amount to me being happy for once. I didn't see her for a while and the next thing I knew he'd married her off to some rich landlord. I never saw or heard from her again!

"And then, seven years later you turn up at the Compound and I felt a connection, I knew...in your eyes I saw her, in you I sensed my kin. As much as I was who they left the orphans with anyway, I stepped forward all too freely to raise you, especially when I tried to find her the next day only to discover she had passed away. In that moment at her grave, I made a promise that no matter what I would do right by you - and I'd like to think I kept it."

Tears fell uncontrollable down Cedric's face. He could hardly believe what he was hearing, but the proof was there. It all made sense.

"You are my son Cedric...by blood and no matter what I knew when I first laid eyes on you, I could not let the legacy I had made for myself pass onto you. I tried to do right by you! Please tell me that it was enough. Please."

Cedric didn't answer him but he kept eye contact with his father. He was right – no matter what he had done to Tristan and his brothers, Cedric had always been left out of it; advised against being involved with them. Basso had always done right by raising him the way he did.

"You know when Tristan saw me in Ragnar I was afraid," Basso explained, breaking that contact and looking down at the floor. "So afraid he had suddenly realised. I was not ready then for all my secrets to come out. But he didn't remember me yet and I suppose that was a good thing considering all that I did, all that I wanted to repent for."

"So what do you want from me now...from Tristan you wanted acceptance...what do you want from me – father?"

"Forgiveness would be nice but even I can't forgive myself and if I cannot forgive, how on earth can others?"

"But you said..."

"What I said is perhaps unrealistic. In truth, there is one final act I must commit. One final sacrifice I must make."

"I don't understand."

"You will son...you will. The night I saw Tristan, when I turned down his original offer of helping him - I had a dream. I dreamt that I had gone missing and you were sick with worry. You were so scared. You ran around town and asked people if they'd seen me. You tried to get them to help you. But they wouldn't because they didn't care. To them, I was nothing more than a traitor. A worthless spine who didn't deserve anyone.

"When I woke up, I thought about what I was leaving you with. What kind of path had I been living down here? My legacy was so tarnished and if people found out the truth you would be tarnished too. I could not let that stain pass to you as well. That's why I followed Tristan."

Basso reached out for his son through the bars, but as he expected he remained where he stood. He was afraid, they both were.

"Don't ever be afraid of me my boy. I've taken my beating time and time again...I will gladly take it again."

"I'm not afraid of you...to be afraid of you would be to be afraid of me. I am afraid of what you are going to do."

"And I guess you should be. I am strong, but I am afraid; not enough for this." He paused, his breath caught in his lungs and he let a tear fall, almost as though it were a hint. "I need you to do something for me son, I need you to make me a promise. I know what I have to do now. But first, I want you to forget...forget all the pain I have caused, all the lies I have told and all the hurt. Forget the fear...God knows I need to. I need to stop pretending like I believe someone can save me...like I can be saved. Because the only person who can save me is me. I refuse to run any longer!"

Basso took a step back, finding himself in the centre of his cell and looking all around. His demeanour had changed and he was fearful now. But he didn't show it in his eyes. In his eyes all he could see was his son and that was just the way he wanted it.

"When my time comes son, I need you to forget...forget the wrongs I have done and help me leave behind a reason to be missed. Don't ever resent me for what I have done...please promise me that. When you feel empty think only of me. Keep me in your memory as your father and leave out all the rest. I beg you! Will you do this for me!"

Silence passed over the dungeon.

Cedric watched his father, tears still falling freely from his eyes. Could he really do it, of course he could. Basso was his father after all.

"I promise...father..."

Basso smiled.

"The key to Tristan remembering lies with me Cedric," Basso instructed. "For him to remember...I must undo what I did! He has to remember."

"You're rambling..."

"I am not rambling Cedric. I see clearly now, perhaps for the first time."

A glint flashed in Basso's hand and suddenly there was a knife there, striking fear into his son's soul. He wouldn't! His hands shook but he held the dagger strong, moving it across his mark of Unbinding and digging into the skin, piercing it through. Blood seeped out, pouring onto the floor as though it were creating a river and Basso winced as he chanted silently.

Cedric yelled out for him to stop but he knew he couldn't, Tristan had to remember or they would all be lost. He tried desperately to dull out the cries of his son begging him to stop, grabbing hold of the bars attempting to rip them apart as his cries fell silent to all those around him.

"Father!" He yelled. "Please stop!" Over and over again.

But he couldn't, one final act of sacrifice, one final act of redemption. The traitor fell to the floor, the sky outside lighting up in his wake as the bars were ripped free from their fixtures and he fell into the arms of his son. As Cedric held his dying father in his arms he screamed louder and louder in remorse, in helplessness. Basso took his last breath and looked at the sky through the window on the wall opposite. Falling stars was all he saw, falling stars in a blue night sky.

Outside in the courtyard, Tristan took a breath of fresh air, noting his brothers' presence over by a fountain talking quietly among themselves. But their attention was diverted as the sky lit up, the stars beginning to fall from their place in the night. As they fell Tristan was struck to the floor and his brothers raced to his side. Before they could make it though, a figure lit up before them, blinding them all.

CHAPTER 35 – MEMORY

It starts with a memory, words that stick in your head for a life time even if the memory does not. Destiny has a habit of getting in the way of life. It straps down your dreams, it controls you, makes you feel like you had no choice. What they say will come to pass; it will eventually be a part of a memory long lost. He had tried so hard to convince himself that he had a choice and in the end he did good by it. John Basso had sacrificed himself so Tristan could remember. The repercussions were currently unclear but perhaps, either way, it was for the best.

Suddenly, the eyes of the man below spring open, darting all around in terrified circles. His breathing quickens and he notices how alone he is, here on this mountainside. Gulping, he pushes himself onto his knees, looking all around. There is a river below and a mirror lies beyond it. Four blue porticos lie in the distance, appearing as mere glints in his eye now.

A loud screeching sounds like a siren somewhere. It startles him, as though he had been asleep. It sounds loud and clear, as explosions are dropped from the sky and crash on the rocks below, not disturbing the scene around it. He watches now, marvelled by the sight of it as he sees them fall and leave nothing scathed, a pool of dust rising into the air by some invisible force. The young Keeper takes this time to reflect on all he remembered and begins to wonder whether who he is now his unknown past lies before him. Someone had once told him that the eyes were the windows to our souls. He could remember thinking about those who had lost their souls for whatever reason. What are their souls if not imaginative figures of our past selves? If we don't have a past to remember, does that mean we don't have a soul?

As the dust settles, he sits and stares at the rocks beneath him. Again, he is battling with himself, realising more and more that perhaps life is more planned than it seems. Something tiny and black moves below a rock, resembling an ant or some other form of bug. It scatters out of its hiding place and almost looks up at him, shaking its tiny feelers as it goes about its way. It weaves in and out of the tiny rocks in its path and he watches it as it heads for the river. Squinting, he tries to keep track of its movement, fascinated at the speed of which it is travelling. But he loses sight of it as a tear leaks from his clear blue eyes. His memories begin to consume him, hurting him. Like the opening of a wound he begins to pick himself apart and try to discover why it is that he screams at night at scenes he does not recognise and why it is that he loves faces he has never seen before. All those promises he made to break were just figments of his imagination because in truth, he had made those promises to keep his love alive and the passion deep.

His head jerked to the side and he sees the river again, the figure of a man standing on the other side. Rising to his feet – his pain suddenly gone, he sets off towards it, keeping his eyes firmly on the figure by the river's edge so as to make sure that he too did not disappear like the bug. He tried to call out to him, asking at once what this place is and why he was here. No voice comes in response, even though he thinks he hears the figure reply to him. Speeding up, he stumbles, toppling over and turning into a ball of flailing limbs and scattered fingers that roll down the mountainside and stop by the edge of the river.

Catching his breath, he sits up and looks around; panicked at the fact that once again he was alone – the figure nowhere to be seen. His head flopped backwards as he looked up at the sky, blank and starless - just like his mind; empty and soulless. Sitting up and crossing his legs, he sat awhile, resting his feet and watching the sky above, willing something to twinkle back at him. Suddenly, as if by magic, a God named Hope hears him and a shooting star streams across the sky. His eyes widen and he is amazed at the clarity of its form. Closing his eyes, he makes a wish, not telling it to a single soul for fear that it won't come true. He opens his eyes once more and it is almost as if his wish has come true. A bridge forms across the river, brick by brick becoming longer, stronger.

Getting to his feet, he makes for the bridge, treading carefully as he fears it will disappear at any moment. When he reached the centre, he placed tentative hands upon the barrier that stopped him falling over the edge, and looked at the river below. The ripples form faces the longer he stares. He squints, trying desperately to pinpoint them - how naïve was he to think it was that easy.

Slowly, his eyes fall upon the mirror on the other side of the river. He gulps and his grip tightens on the barrier as he realises that he does not wish to go any further. How naïve was he to think he had a choice in the matter? Suddenly, as if the scene around him could hear his fears, the wooden planks of the bridge started to fade, the barrier falling away and landing in the river below. Panicking, he starts to run, the end of the bridge never getting any closer. It was almost like he was running on the spot. His breathing gets faster and he falls, landing in the river in a sprawled and tangled mess of fear and panic. He was going to drown; he was sure this was the end. Flailing his arms around in the air and splashing water all over the place, he tried to reach for the river bank which slipped further and further away the harder he stretched. His legs kicked at the gravel beneath him, becoming wedged in the seaweed as he was pulled under again and again. He gasped for air, shutting his eyes as he was pulled down one final time.

Through the eyes of the river, he saw his life flash before him. Through the eyes of the river, he saw his life for what it was...a lie! Thoughts and visions consumed his mind, wiping away the confusion and replacing them with once lost memories. It was almost as if the water was purifying him, making him clean so that he could be reborn anew; opening the wounds and picking them apart until the infection was gone, then stitching them back up again to leave a scar which in time would fade. He gasps and the water ebbs, carrying him back to land once more.

Pulling himself up, he spews water onto the hard ground as he pulls himself from the net of water. He grabs at the grass stacks, snatching them from the ground in his struggle until finally, the water surrenders and becomes calm once more. Tristan breathes a little, catching up with himself and beginning to feel normal once more. He sits for a while, slowly drying off, smoothing his feet through his boots and resting awhile. Leaning back slightly he breathes; feeling at peace with the strange world around him. He opens his eyes, catching sight of as shooting star in the sky - restoring hope within him. It was brighter than the midday sun and fast as the speed of light, barely traceable against the empty sky. Shutting his eyes quickly tight, he made another wish, wishing himself to wake up from this terrible dream.

"Tristan!" speaks a voice suddenly. He jumps, his eyes snapping open as he looked around, shaken. He saw nothing, but he couldn't help but realise how alone he was. Suddenly, he is scared and he began to shiver, getting to his feet and looking all around. "Tristan!" called the voice again, this time louder and more shrill, like someone was screaming because of a sudden darkness.

He began to tremble, his eyes darting all around. They lingered on the blue lights in the distance. They called to him, willing him to come closer. They blink, they shine, they speak with an enchanting sound, one that he cannot ignore. Yet he tries, he wills himself to ignore it, not wanting to move from the spot where he is stood by the river. He gulps, staring into the distance at the ever-growing blue lights. As frightful as they are, he can't help but wonder at the entirety of them, the sheer mystical splendour of what they truly are.

"Tristan!" This time, the voice resembled a scream. His eyes panic stricken like a frightened rabbit as it scrambles out of sight finding them again now. The scream is hysterical and it brings back horrible memories of a time he thought he had forgotten.

"Tristan!" The scream is louder now and he crashes to the ground once more, his pale face tearful and grief-stricken. He looks up, seeing a black figure looming before him. The figure holds out a hand, just as the light had done six months ago when he first set off on his quest. He squints, the ringing fading from his ears. He smiles slightly, hardly believing that he is able to take the hand that is offered to him. The hands embrace – like a brotherhood, uniting as one in a common cause.

"Tristan!" The voice is calm once more, calm and contented – she is happy. He takes the hand of the figure and gets to his feet, smiling again as he does so. The figure fades, probably smiling too. Now he looks to the blue lights, the shining blue lights of hope. He stands tall and braces himself for the woes and the sorrow he will see in his past, the happy times of course, will be a breeze.

Now he stands within the mountains, surrounded by the four porticos; memories playing back and forth in each one. He looks from one to the other, thinking he can pick which comes first and which comes last. In his head, he goes over the different sequences in which he could experience them all again. Perhaps first he could see the broken hearts and the shattered dreams so that the pain is quickly erased by then facing the happy times that bought him love. Then perhaps he could watch back the promises that kept his love alive and his passion deep, but then, when would he remember all the bits in between, like The Brotherhood, The Union. He never had a choice in the first place – the order was always going to be pre-planned, just as life is.

Suddenly the porticos disappear, sinking into the ground and making him jump. The mirror appears before him and he can see himself within it. He stares at his bizarre reflection, unable to recognise himself amongst all the hidden scars. The siren sounded again but not like an alarm this time. This time it is like the distant singing of a beautiful maiden. He cannot see her, no-one can, they just hear her. She draws him closer, calling out to him above the mountains and the river and making him turn.

Then, the mirror cracks, causing his eyes to dart back at his reflection. His memories begin to seep through the cracks with blood, changing his appearance and revealing a scarred image scarcely similar to himself – an image of a past self, the self he had seen scared and helpless back in Az Lagní. He touched his face in the glass, unable to believe the transformation, almost feeling it change under his fingers. It bubbles and ripples like a river bursting at its banks. He backs away, not wanting to face it anymore, coming to a halt as he feels his back hit something hard. He turned to see a statue tower above him. Backing up even more, he felt as though he recognised the bearded stone face and the tall hat that sat on his head. The robes that drape down his body to reveal a pair of strapped sandals on his rocky feet. The book that he holds close to him in his left hand and his right hand pointing out the way, towards the porticos. He had no choice, he had to remember!

Could he really do it? Could he really relive it all in the hope that he would wake up and his memories intact? Perhaps it really was that easy, perhaps it really was that hard. He smiled, he wept, he screamed out inside, ready to embrace everything that was waiting him in the porticos of his memory.

...to be continued in Freedom

Printed in Great Britain
by Amazon